3-2022

CITY

of

SHADOWS

Center Point
Large Print

Also by Victoria Thompson and available from Center Point Large Print:

Murder in the Bowery
City of Lies
Murder on Union Square
City of Secrets
Murder on Trinity Place
City of Scoundrels
Murder on Pleasant Avenue
City of Schemes
Murder on Wall Street

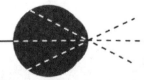

CITY

 of

SHADOWS

A Counterfeit Lady Novel

Victoria Thompson

CENTER POINT LARGE PRINT
THORNDIKE, MAINE

To all my loved ones who have passed over.
I'm looking forward to seeing you again,
but not at a séance.

CHAPTER ONE

Elizabeth looked up from the letter she'd been writing when the maid announced the unexpected arrival of her best friend, Anna Vanderslice. Before she could rise to greet Anna or even open her mouth to ask the maid to show Anna in, Anna brushed unceremoniously past the startled maid and cried, "Elizabeth, you've got to help me!"

Being a gently reared young lady, Anna wasn't given to outbursts like this, especially in front of the servants. "Of course, I'll help you," Elizabeth said, rising quickly from the small lady's desk where she'd been sitting and moving to where Anna stood, anxiously wringing her hands, just inside the library doorway. "Lucy, would you bring us something cool to drink?" Elizabeth asked the still-flustered maid.

Lucy scurried out, obviously glad to escape what promised to be a strange situation.

"What's the matter?" Elizabeth asked, taking Anna's hands in hers. They were like ice in spite of the warm day. "What kind of help do you need?"

The despair that clouded Anna's face truly

frightened Elizabeth. She hadn't seen her friend so upset since Anna's brother, David, had died of influenza last fall. "Oh, Elizabeth, I . . ." She glanced at the still-open library door, obviously just realizing that she shouldn't be discussing anything upsetting where the servants could hear.

"Sit down," Elizabeth said, hurrying to close the door and give Anna the privacy she needed.

Anna took one of the comfortable chairs placed in front of the now-cold fireplace, sighing wearily as she sank down into it. Elizabeth took the other chair when she had shut the door securely. The chairs had been chosen for comfort so two gentlemen could sit and smoke and converse in the quiet of this cozy book-lined room at the end of a long day, but they would serve just as well for women to share a bit of bad news.

"Now what is it?" Elizabeth demanded almost desperately.

"It's Mother."

"*Your* mother?" Elizabeth echoed in alarm. "Is she ill?"

"Oddly, no," Anna said with a frown. "You knew she took to her bed after David died. I think her heart was truly broken."

"She came to my wedding," Elizabeth reminded her.

"And she would sometimes go to church, but until recently, she rarely left her bedroom."

8

"But recently?"

Anna sighed. "Recently, she has discovered a medium."

Elizabeth blinked in surprise. "You mean, a fortune-teller?"

"Oh, she's far more than a fortune-teller. She conducts séances."

Elizabeth knew a little about séances and what she knew wasn't good. "Does she make the table move and do the spirits knock in coded raps to convey messages?"

"I have no idea, but Mother is convinced this woman, this *Madame Ophelia*," Anna added in disgust, "can contact David."

"Oh dear."

"Yes, oh dear," Anna agreed.

For a long moment, the two friends silently considered this very disturbing situation.

Then Elizabeth found something comforting to say. "I know it must be upsetting to you, but if it gives her some peace to think that—"

"You don't think this woman can really talk to David, do you?" Anna asked in outrage.

"Of course not. It's all a con."

Anna brightened at once. "Then you know all about it?"

"Not much. I may have been raised by a con artist, but even he had standards. Bilking little old ladies out of their last pennies is beneath him. But I do know it's a con."

9

"It's also more than just a few pennies," Anna said gravely.

"What do you mean?" Elizabeth asked, newly alarmed.

Before Anna could answer, Lucy knocked at the door and brought in a tray bearing two glasses of lemonade and a plate of cookies. Elizabeth insisted Anna drink some of the lemonade before continuing. "You must be parched after walking over here."

That made Anna smile at last. "Hardly. One of the best parts of you finally marrying Gideon is that now you only live a few blocks away."

Elizabeth could think of other wonderful reasons to be glad she and Gideon were married, but she knew Anna didn't want to hear about that part of married life. "It is nice being so close to you. Now tell me what you meant about it being more than pennies."

Anna's smile vanished again. "Madame Ophelia charges twenty dollars for each session."

Elizabeth winced. "That does seem expensive."

"And Mother has been going to see her three times a week." Three visits a week would cost as much as an average man would earn in a week, but Madame Ophelia most certainly catered only to the wealthy members of society. Her high prices would keep the riffraff away.

"Good heavens."

"Yes, good heavens. You do know that we aren't really rich, don't you?"

Elizabeth did know that. Many of the old New York families had seen their early fortunes dwindle with the generations. Gideon's family was one of them, but she certainly hadn't married him for his money. "Is it causing you a hardship?"

"More than a hardship. Father left us some money that provides a modest income, but we relied on David's salary, too. With David gone . . ." Anna's voice caught, and she needed a moment to compose herself. His loss was still fresh enough to cause tears.

"You don't have to explain," Elizabeth assured her as Anna dabbed at her tears with a handkerchief.

"But I do. I had to let some of the servants go, but if we're careful, we should be fine. Or at least we would have been, but now . . ."

"Have you explained this to your mother? I'm sure if she understood—"

"Of course, I explained it to her, but she refuses to understand. Father and David always took care of everything. She has no idea how much things cost or how much our income is. She thinks Father left us wealthy and the money will never run out and I'm just being mean because I don't believe in Madame Ophelia's powers. On top of that, this Madame Ophelia has bewitched her. Mother becomes furious if I even suggest she

11

stop attending these séances, and this morning she told me she's going to start seeing the woman every day. We can't afford that! I won't even be able to go back to college in the fall." Her tears were falling freely now, but at least Elizabeth could offer a bit of comfort.

"You don't have to worry about college, my darling girl. Your fees will be paid no matter what."

But this news was far from comforting, if Anna's scowl was any indication. "What do you mean?"

"Just what I said. The fees will be paid."

Anna's scowl deepened. "I can't take charity from you, Elizabeth."

Oh dear, now she'd hurt Anna's pride. "It's not charity and it's not from me."

"Who is it from, then? I won't take anything from Gideon, either."

Elizabeth sighed in defeat. "Not Gideon. Jake."

"Jake? Your brother, Jake?"

"The very same."

Anna's shock was almost comic, but Elizabeth knew better than to laugh. "Why would Jake pay my college fees?"

"Because you helped him with a con. Do you have any idea how much he made on that?"

Anna stiffened her spine. "No, I don't."

"Well, it was a lot, and he hardly had any expenses. By rights, you should have had a share,

12

but we didn't think you would take it, so Jake set up to pay your school fees instead, and there will be a nice little sum to get you started when you graduate."

"But . . . what about you? You helped, too, and a lot more than I did. Shouldn't you get that money?"

"Some of it, yes, but I couldn't possibly take it since I promised Gideon I had given all that up."

"But Gideon knows you helped with that con."

"Yes, and he did, too, in his own way, but we didn't do it for the money. That makes a difference, at least to Gideon."

"I didn't do it for the money, either."

"I know, dear one. You did it for the excitement, but there's no reason you shouldn't benefit. You don't have to answer to a painfully honest husband, after all."

"And I never will," Anna said with some satisfaction. "But why would Jake go to so much trouble for me?"

"Because you're his friend. I think you may be the only friend he's ever had."

"But I'm a female."

"That's what he likes best about you, I think. Men are always competing with one another and women want to get married. You don't compete and you don't want to marry him. You're also smart and clever, and I think he feels smart and clever when he's with you."

"And that makes him want to give me money?" Anna asked doubtfully.

"It's his way of showing his respect for the way you performed."

"He can be very aggravating," Anna reminded her.

"He's a man. Try not to hold that against him."

That finally brought a small smile to Anna's lips. It lasted only a moment, though, before she remembered her other problems. "I may need that money to support us if Mother ruins us, though."

"Nonsense. You're going to college so you can have a profession and support yourself for the rest of your life. Your whole future depends on it. You can't give that up."

"But what about Madame Ophelia?"

Elizabeth pretended to consider this very seriously. "Hmmm, Madame Ophelia. She's surely a con artist. I've never tried to con another con artist, but I think it could be a lot of fun."

Elizabeth wore a veil when she went to Dan the Dude's Saloon on Twenty-eighth Street. She wasn't ashamed of her connection to the place, but she didn't want Gideon to be embarrassed if someone saw her and reported it in a gossip column. Why anyone should care where she went was a mystery, but Gideon's family was one of the oldest society families in New York, and people did care.

She didn't actually enter the saloon, of course. She slipped down the alley, found a nondescript door and knocked a coded knock. This put her in mind of her question to Anna about spirits knocking out messages, but then the sliding panel in the door opened, distracting her from her musings. A curious eye peered out, and then the door opened at once.

"Contessa!" the elderly man said with obvious pleasure, using the title of respect she had earned. "Come in, come in."

"How are you, Spuds?" she asked.

Spuds, so called because his face resembled a dried-up potato, grinned. "I'm better for seeing you. I am guessing you're here for the Old Man."

"Good guess!"

"He's out, but I expect him soon. Come in and say hello to the fellas."

Spuds led her back to a large room where several men of various ages sat playing cards or reading the *Daily Racing Form* and arguing over upcoming races. Dan the Dude's back room was where New York City con men gathered to tell one another lies and hopefully meet up with someone who had a job for them. She knew every man there, and they enjoyed a few minutes of conversation where they teased her about marrying a Mr. Bates, which was her new husband's name but also what con artists called their marks.

After a while, Spuds went to answer another knock, and a silver-haired gentleman wearing a tailor-made suit came in. The Old Man was already smiling because Spuds had told him Elizabeth was waiting for him.

"Lizzie," he said with mock consternation, "what are you doing talking to all these old reprobates?"

"You mean, when I could be talking to just one old reprobate?" she asked, making everyone laugh.

"Exactly. Come into my office before you are completely corrupted."

Elizabeth followed him into his spartan office and waited while he dusted off the visitor's chair with his snowy white handkerchief. When she was seated beside his desk and he was comfortably ensconced in his own chair, he said, "Does Gideon know you're here?"

"Do you think I need my husband's permission to visit my own father?"

He didn't exactly roll his eyes, but he might as well have. "If you want to visit me, you invite me to dinner. If you want to see me on business, you come here. So, does Gideon know you're planning another con?"

"Not yet," she said shamelessly.

The Old Man groaned with feigned dismay.

"He'll be only too happy about it when he finds out, though," she said.

He didn't seem so sure. "Who are you helping this time?"

"Anna Vanderslice."

He blinked in surprise. "How has the lovely Miss Vanderslice gotten herself into a situation that requires her to be rescued?"

"She hasn't. It's her mother. She's been going to séances."

"Séances? I thought they'd fallen out of fashion after those famous women admitted they were frauds and that the spirit tapping was just them cracking their toe joints or something."

"I don't know about that, but Mrs. Vanderslice found this medium named Madame Ophelia and—"

"Why are they always *madame* something or other?"

"I'm sure they have their reasons. At any rate, Mrs. Vanderslice wants to contact her son, David. I imagine a lot of people want to contact loved ones they lost in the war or to the flu."

The Old Man didn't look like he thought that was a good idea, but he said, "Why should Anna care, though? If it gives her mother some comfort, I mean."

"Because the medium is charging her twenty dollars a session, and Mrs. Vanderslice wants to go see the woman every day. Anna and her mother are already in reduced circumstances because of David's death, and they can't afford it. And yes, Anna explained that to her mother, but her mother doesn't want to believe it."

"Or give up seeing the medium, I expect. I don't suppose it would help to reveal the woman as a fraud."

Elizabeth gave him a pitying look. "You know people never want to admit they've been bamboozled. That's the basis of every con ever devised."

The Old Man shrugged apologetically. "Then what did you have in mind?"

"I don't know yet. I thought I should find out more about mediums and how they work first. Do you know anything about them?"

"Besides what I read in the newspapers, you mean? Let me think."

She gave him a minute to do so, and after a few seconds, a slow smile spread across his handsome face.

"I just remembered old Barney. He had a slick little racket out in Chicago about ten years ago. Set himself up as a fortune-teller. He followed the market and was pretty savvy about guessing which stocks were going to do well. People would come to him, and he'd advise them which stocks to buy. When they increased in value, the marks thought he really could foretell the future."

"And when he was wrong?" Elizabeth asked.

The Old Man shrugged again. "You know how people are. They forgot about it."

"If he was so good, why not just set himself up in a legitimate business?"

"What fun would that be? Besides, he had an interesting little sideline going. That's how I know about all this. He put me onto a mark one time. Took the woman for almost a hundred thousand."

"Good heavens. So how did it work?"

He sat back in his chair as he tried to recall the details. "He had set himself up as a swami or something. Heavy draperies and I think he even had a crystal ball. He'd ask the mark to write his question on a piece of paper and fold it up. Then Barney would lay down on this couch he had. It was all fixed up with connections at the bottom and he had matching ones on the heels of his shoes. He'd put his heels into the connections, and that would hook up some kind of telephone with his assistant."

"A telephone?"

"Yes, because Barney would pass the paper with the question on it to his assistant through the curtain. Then Barney would put an identical piece of paper on his forehead and pretend to read the question through some kind of mental process. The assistant would tell him over the telephone what the question was."

"How did he hear the assistant, though?"

"He was wearing some kind of headset, like telephone operators do."

"Didn't the mark notice the headset?" Elizabeth asked, totally confused now.

"Oh, I forgot to mention, he had on this big turban that covered his ears. Also added to the effect. So, the assistant would tell him the question over the telephone. Then Barney would get up and burn the paper without unfolding it and tell the mark what his question was and give him an answer. It was all very impressive."

"I'm sure it was," Elizabeth said uncertainly. "How did all this lead to the big score you mentioned, though?"

"Well, sometimes people just wanted general advice on things like matters of the heart, and Barney would give commonsense advice that usually worked, but sometimes people wanted advice on things like what to do with a big inheritance or whatever. This wealthy woman came to him and asked what she should do with some extra money she had, so he told her she would soon meet a tall man with white hair who would offer her an investment opportunity, and she should do just as he advised."

"How devilishly simple," Elizabeth cried.

"Yes, it was. No need for a lot of fancy setup. I just had to figure out how to encounter this lady in a way that wasn't too suspicious and come up with a reasonable-sounding investment opportunity. Once she saw me, she was willing to do whatever I suggested with her money."

"I guess it's a good thing Mrs. Vanderslice doesn't manage their finances."

"Maybe this woman she's been seeing is satisfied with just bilking her marks out of the cost of the séances."

"Even that is outrageous, but if people can afford it and it makes them feel better, I guess there's no reason to wish her ill. But we can't let her keep draining Mrs. Vanderslice."

"What are you going to do?"

"I don't know yet. I have to give it some thought."

"While you're thinking, don't think of me."

"What?"

"Don't think of me. Or Jake. We can't help you with this."

Elizabeth sighed. She hadn't really thought it through. "No, of course you can't."

Because con artists didn't interfere with other con artists, even if they didn't particularly like them or approve of their methods. If she set out to help Mrs. Vanderslice, she was on her own.

Gideon was already smiling when he unlocked his front door and stepped inside because he knew Elizabeth would be there to greet him. When she heard him come in, she always rushed out to give him a kiss and let him know how much she'd missed him. And here she was, smiling at him like he'd hung the moon. She was so beautiful and bright and special, and how amazing that she loved an ordinary and unexciting estate attorney as much as he loved her. Even more amazing that they'd found each other in such an extraordinary way.

When she kissed him, he knew a moment's nostalgia for their monthlong honeymoon cruise, when they could sneak off to be alone in their stateroom whenever they liked. As much as he wanted to take Elizabeth by the hand and lead her upstairs to their bedroom right this moment, he couldn't possibly do that with his mother waiting in the parlor. He adored his mother but living with her did have its drawbacks.

Elizabeth took his hand and led him into the parlor.

"How was your day, dear?" his mother asked, looking up from her mending.

"Mercifully dull and routine," he said. Many of his days had been much too exciting since he'd met Elizabeth, and he was enjoying the peace that had followed her vow to give up her old profession.

He sat down beside Elizabeth on the love seat facing his mother's chair, prepared to hear about his mother's latest efforts in getting the United States Congress to pass the Woman Suffrage bill. But then he glanced at Elizabeth and saw the glitter in her lovely blue eyes.

"Uh-oh," he said. "What have you been up to?"

She feigned astonishment, which was success-ful, and innocence, which was not. "What makes you say that?"

"The look in your eyes. What did you do today?"

She sighed in defeat. She was an excellent actress, but she couldn't fool him. "Anna came to see me today." Elizabeth turned to his mother. "Did you know Mrs. Vanderslice has been visiting a medium?"

His mother frowned. "She did say something about it. I'll admit, I was a little surprised, but she seemed so happy that I didn't . . . Is some-thing wrong?"

Elizabeth briefly explained the situation.

"How awful," his mother said when Elizabeth had finished. "Poor Anna, but I can't believe Clarissa would be so reckless if she understood they really can't afford this."

"That's just it," Elizabeth said. "She doesn't want to understand it. She wants to keep seeing the medium and hearing messages from David." She gave Gideon a sympathetic glance.

David hadn't been the sharpest fellow, but he'd been Gideon's best friend since childhood. Gideon still missed him every day, and he could under-stand Mrs. Vanderslice's desperation. Still . . . "But she isn't getting messages from David. This woman is a charlatan. Nobody can speak to dead people."

Elizabeth took his hand in both of hers. "Of

course not, darling, but when someone chooses to believe it's possible, no one can convince them otherwise."

Gideon narrowed his eyes as he suddenly realized the truth about this medium. "It's a con, isn't it?"

She sighed. "Yes, it is."

"What does your father say about it?"

If she was surprised that he'd guessed she would consult her father, she didn't show it. "He didn't know much about it. Séances went out of style a while ago."

"Oh my, yes," his mother confirmed. "They were very popular when I was young, though. We used to have them for fun, my friends and I. We'd sit around a table with a Ouija board, trying to get messages from beyond. We could never get the table to move, though."

"That's because you didn't have a medium there to move it," Elizabeth said with a small smile.

This was all so sadly ridiculous. "Can't we just explain to Mrs. Vanderslice that it's all fake?" he said.

"If she doesn't want to believe she can't afford the séances, she certainly won't want to believe they're fake."

"People do become unreasonable about these things," his mother confirmed. "I remember when the Fox sisters admitted they were phonies."

"Who are the Fox sisters?" Elizabeth asked.

"They were famous mediums back in the day. Two sisters, or maybe it was three. I can't remember. One of them finally wrote a book telling all their secrets. They would get messages from the spirits by having them make knocking sounds. The one sister admitted they were using their feet to make the sounds somehow. I can't remember exactly . . ."

"Then we should get a copy of this book for Mrs. Vanderslice," Gideon said, happy to have found a logical solution.

But his mother was shaking her head. "Even after that, the sisters went back to holding séances, claiming they had lied when they said it was all fake."

"And people still believed in them?" Gideon marveled.

Elizabeth gave him a pitying look. "Of course, they did, darling, because they wanted to."

"Then what does Anna expect you to do?"

"She doesn't expect anything. She merely hopes I can help."

"And can you?"

"I have no idea. The Old Man doesn't have any ideas, either, and he won't help at all."

"Why not, dear?" his mother asked in amazement. Mr. Miles wasn't the best father in the world, but he had always helped Elizabeth when she needed it.

"Because there is honor among thieves, or at

25

least among con men. They don't interfere with one another."

"Not even when they're cheating someone?" Gideon asked without thinking.

"They're always cheating someone, darling," she gently reminded him.

Of course, they were. He was an idiot. "Well, we certainly can't let Mrs. Vanderslice's obsession bankrupt her and Anna."

"No, we can't," Elizabeth said. "I have been wondering if there is something you can do to protect their money, darling. You do help manage David's estate, don't you?"

"David named me his executor, but everything is settled now, so there isn't much I can do."

"But Clarissa won't know that, will she?" his mother said archly.

Gideon couldn't help smiling. "Are you suggesting that I lie to her, Mother?" Gideon's aversion to lying was legendary, and both women smiled at the very suggestion.

"No," Elizabeth said, "but Anna could. She can blame you for holding up their funds or something. I'm sure you won't mind bearing the brunt of Mrs. Vanderslice's wrath until we figure out what to do, will you?"

"Not at all. But how are you going to figure something out if your father won't help you?"

"I'm not sure, but the first step will be attending a séance with Mrs. Vanderslice."

"Do you think that's a good idea?" Gideon asked.

"Absolutely not, but I don't know any other way to get to know this woman."

Then to his dismay, his mother said wistfully, "I've always wanted to attend a real séance myself."

"I can't believe Gideon didn't forbid us to attend this séance," Mother Bates said as she and Elizabeth left the house the next morning.

"Can Gideon forbid you to do things?" Elizabeth asked with great interest.

Mother Bates, who was usually the most independent woman Elizabeth had ever known, had to give this a moment's thought. "Well, I suppose he can't, not really. He is the head of our household, though."

"And your *child*," Elizabeth reminded her. "Isn't *he* supposed to obey *you?*"

"It's been a long time since I had to tell him what to do and not to do, so I haven't really put it to the test lately."

"And if Gideon did forbid you to do something, would that stop you?"

Mother Bates sighed. "I suppose not, if it was something I really wanted to do."

"Did you ask his permission before you went to Washington City to demonstrate for Woman Suffrage?"

"Not exactly. I simply told him I was going. He was worried, of course."

"As he had every right to be," Elizabeth agreed. She and Mrs. Bates had ended up sentenced to three months in a workhouse from that adventure. "But you didn't need his permission to go in the first place."

"He does support my work—or *our* work, I should say—so there was no question of his disapproving."

"Do you know what the Old Man told Gideon before we got married?"

"I can't imagine," Mother Bates said with amused anticipation.

"He warned Gideon not to forbid me from doing anything, because that was the best way to ensure I would do it."

That made her laugh, and Elizabeth joined her. "Then I guess it was good advice," Mother Bates said.

"It was, and it saved me the trouble of telling Gideon myself."

They'd reached the corner, and Mother Bates flagged down a cab. When the vehicle was carrying them uptown to Madame Ophelia's, Mother Bates said, "Do you have any idea what will happen at this séance?"

"From what Anna told me, it's pretty simple. This woman doesn't go in for a lot of fancy stuff, like moving tables and floating ghosts."

"Ghosts?" Mother Bates echoed in alarm.

"All tricks, you understand. But Madame Ophelia just lets the spirits speak through her. I'm kind of disappointed. I was hoping for some ectoplasm, at least."

"What's that?"

"I'm not really sure, but I remembered reading something about it once. We'll just have to see. Do you have anyone in the afterlife you'd like to contact?"

Mother Bates frowned as she considered the question. "I suppose I should say my husband or perhaps my parents, but I'm not sure what I would even ask them. I've always felt confident they were at peace in heaven, and what if the medium told me something different?"

"Mother Bates, have I ever told you how much I appreciate your wisdom and good sense?"

"Not nearly often enough, my dear," she replied graciously. "What about you? Would you like to speak to your mother?"

"Oh my, what a prospect. I had no idea my father was a con man until after she died. I just knew he traveled a lot and was rarely home. I've always wondered if she knew how he made the money he used to support us, and if she knew about Jake and Jake's mother." The Old Man had never married Jake's mother.

"Surely not," Mother Bates said. "No woman would tolerate that."

"Women tolerate an awful lot in exchange for a comfortable home."

"I suppose you're right. But if you really want to know those things, can't you just ask your father?"

"I don't want to know them that much." Indeed, Elizabeth couldn't imagine broaching the subject of his infidelities with the Old Man. She'd needed years to forgive him for foisting her off on Jake's alcoholic mother to raise after her own mother died. In some ways, she was even still angry at her own mother for dying and leaving her in the first place, although the more sensible part of her realized her mother wouldn't have done such a thing on purpose.

"I can understand, dear. One doesn't like to discuss such things with one's parents," Mother Bates said.

"Here we are, ladies," the driver said, pulling the motorcar over to the curb.

Elizabeth insisted on paying, since this was her project, and the two women hesitated for a long moment when they stood in front of the storefront bearing a discreet sign that read, MADAME OPHELIA, READINGS.

The front window was covered by heavy bloodred draperies blocking any view of what might have been inside. Elizabeth checked the watch pinned to her lapel and saw they were a few minutes early. "Let's try not to chat about anything personal while we wait."

Mother Bates's eyes widened. "Do you suppose she eavesdrops on her clients?"

"I can't imagine that she would miss an opportunity to pick up useful information."

Having made that decision, they entered the shop. With the draperies blocking the spring sunshine, the interior was dim, and they needed a moment for their eyes to adjust. The front room was obviously a waiting area with an Oriental carpet on the floor and the dark red walls lined with a variety of wooden chairs, none of which matched one another. Four people appeared to be waiting. Two of them were a couple Elizabeth didn't know. She was surprised to see a man here, but perhaps his wife had brought him. If his expression was any indication, he was here against his will.

Elizabeth did recognize the other two people.

"Elizabeth, I'm so glad you could come," Anna said, leaving her mother's side to greet them. "And, Mrs. Bates, what a surprise."

"I hope I'll be welcome. I told Elizabeth how much I've always wanted to attend a séance, so she invited me to join her. Clarissa," she added to Anna's mother, who had remained seated, "how nice to see you."

Mother Bates wandered over to greet her friend, and Anna whispered, "I can't believe she came with you."

"When I told her the story, nothing would keep her away," Elizabeth whispered back.

Anna started to respond, but someone in the next room screamed before she could.

CHAPTER TWO

Gideon looked up from the file he had been reviewing when his clerk tapped on his office door to tell him Mrs. Darlington had arrived for her appointment. Smith was a firm believer in appointments, as his satisfied expression revealed. Gideon rose and walked around his desk to greet the lady, whom he knew very well. Her husband had been a longtime client of the firm and had left them in charge of his estate when he passed several years earlier.

Mrs. Darlington looked much as Gideon remembered her. She was a tiny birdlike woman with a helpless air who must have always inspired people to look out for her. Her blond hair had given way to silver now, and her face had settled into a web of wrinkles that only increased her air of fragility. Her eyes, however, no longer held that expression of vague confusion he had always known.

Gideon got her seated in one of the comfortable client chairs and exchanged the usual pleasantries about the state of her health and the weather. By then, he could see Mrs. Darlington was fairly bursting to tell him something.

"Now what can I do for you today, Mrs. Darlington?" he finally asked, thinking perhaps she was expecting a new grandchild or some other happy event and wished to make some financial arrangement for it.

She actually squirmed a little in her chair, as a child might when trying to contain her excitement, and then she glanced over her shoulder, as if checking to make sure Smith had closed the door behind himself. "I have come into some important information," she confided with a sly little smile.

"Information about what?" Gideon asked.

"It's confidential, you understand."

"Of course. Anything you say to me is confidential, Mrs. Darlington."

"That's just it. I can't share it with anyone at all, not even you."

Gideon frowned and reminded himself that Mrs. Darlington was elderly and might well have been losing her faculties. Patience was key here, and he would be as patient as he needed to be. "If you can't tell me about it, then I don't think I can be of much help to you."

"Oh, but you can. All I need for you to do is release some funds to me from my trust."

Since Gideon had just been reviewing the Darlington file, he knew exactly what she meant. "As I'm sure you know, you receive an allowance from the trust your husband established for you,

34

and if you require a larger sum for something, you need only ask and any reasonable request will be granted."

Mrs. Darlington was nodding vigorously even before he had finished his explanation. "That is why I've come, you see. I need a larger sum for something."

For something she obviously didn't want to explain to Gideon. Perhaps she was afraid he would consider it frivolous or even silly, but Gideon's job wasn't to decide if new furnishings for her house or a new wardrobe for herself or gifts to children or grandchildren were silly or frivolous. Her husband had been a generous man, and he had created the trust to protect his wife from being taken advantage of, not to keep her from indulging the occasional whim.

"How much did you have in mind?" Gideon asked with an encouraging smile.

"A hundred thousand dollars," she said blithely.

For a long moment, Gideon couldn't even speak. "That's a . . . a rather large sum," he finally managed.

"Is it enough, do you think?" she asked with a tiny frown.

Gideon was now confused. "Enough for what?"

"Enough for . . . Oh, I almost forgot. I can't tell you. But perhaps . . . Let me ask you something, Mr. Bates. If you had an opportunity to invest in a . . . a project that would result in doubling your initial investment, how much would you put into it?"

This time it was Gideon who shifted in his chair and not from excitement. Every nerve in his body had tensed in alarm. This was not at all what he had expected to hear from sweet Mrs. Darlington. He made himself smile politely. "I'm afraid I can't think of any kind of investment that would earn a return of one hundred percent."

"Is that how much it is? I thought it might be two percent since it was twice as much. One hundred percent is rather impressive, isn't it?"

"Yes, it is." Gideon swallowed, hoping to keep his voice even. "Without divulging anything secret, can you confirm that this is what you have been promised?"

"Oh yes. Perhaps more, in fact, so you see how important it is to invest as much as possible."

Gideon's mind was racing. Even if he hadn't married a con artist, he would have known something was very suspicious about Mrs. Darlington's request. In the first place, who on earth would have approached an elderly widow with no understanding of finance to invest in anything reputable? Even if they had, no one reputable would have promised any sort of return and certainly not such an outlandish one. And finally, why had Mrs. Darlington been instructed not to tell anyone about it? "Have you discussed this with your children, Mrs. Darlington?"

"Certainly not! It's none of their business what I do with my money, is it?"

Gideon's smile was beginning to feel stiff. "Perhaps it is, since it will be their inheritance."

Mrs. Darlington waved away any such thought with her gloved hand. "My husband left them very well fixed, and if they're worried about their inheritance, this will make them even richer."

But not if Mrs. Darlington lost the entire one hundred thousand dollars, which Gideon felt sure would be the outcome of this scheme. How to explain that to Mrs. Darlington, though?

"I can understand your desire to leave an even greater legacy to your children," Gideon said in an effort to flatter her and perhaps win her confidence. "It shows how generous and loving you are. The terms of your husband's will are very strict, however, and I will have to discuss this request with my partners before making a decision."

She frowned at this. "But you always just give me whatever I ask for."

"When you ask for a few hundred dollars for a specific purpose, I am free to use my judgment. This situation is entirely different since it is such a large sum and you haven't even told me why you want the money or what you plan to do with it."

"I did tell you. I want to invest it." She was annoyed now, but that couldn't be helped. "I understand that you already have it invested for me, in fact."

She had him there. "Yes, we do, but—"

"And are any of those investments earning a return of one hundred percent?"

"No, they aren't—"

"And yet when I give you the opportunity to make an investment like that, you rebuff me." She was as outraged as a tiny old lady could be.

Gideon drew a calming breath. One of them should be calm. "I am not rebuffing you. Your husband trusted us to protect your interests, so naturally, we are going to be careful about advising you."

"I don't need advice from you. I just need my money."

Gideon nodded sagely, or at least he hoped he looked sage. "As I said, I will have to discuss this with my partners, but the first thing they are going to ask me is what you will be investing in, and if I can't tell them that, I'm afraid they will never approve."

Mrs. Darlington rolled her eyes in disgust. "Well, you can tell them they don't have to worry. This is something of which Mr. Darlington himself would approve."

"How can you be sure of that?" he asked kindly.

"Because he told me so himself just the other day."

38

The scream was followed by a loud thump from another room, and for a moment everyone in the waiting room was frozen in place. Then everyone who was still seated jumped to their feet, and Mrs. Vanderslice cried, "Madame Ophelia!"

Elizabeth and Anna exchanged a look and then turned to where the scream had come from. A door marked the entrance to the other room, and she and Anna hurried toward it.

Anna got there first and threw it open. This room was also rather dark, having no visible windows at all and being illuminated only by a small lamp sitting on a table near the door. A groan drew their attention to a large shadow on the other side of a round table sitting in the center of the room. They cautiously made their way toward it.

Another groan encouraged them to come closer, and now they could see a rather buxom woman dressed in some sort of brightly patterned robe lying on the floor.

"Madame Ophelia?" Anna asked uncertainly.

The woman groaned again, raising a hand to her head.

"Are you injured?" Elizabeth said, deciding that was the best question to ask under the circumstances.

The woman opened her eyes and peered up at them. "You!" she cried. "You have done this."

Before they could decide which one of them she was accusing, Elizabeth and Anna were unceremoniously shoved aside by Mrs. Vanderslice, who instantly fell to her knees beside the prone medium.

"Are you all right, Madame Ophelia? What happened?"

"I was overcome," Madame Ophelia declared, allowing Mrs. Vanderslice to help her sit up. "So much doubt! So much disbelief. I cannot think with all of this swirling around me."

"No one doubts you, Madame," the lady from the waiting room insisted. She had obviously followed Mrs. Vanderslice into the room, along with everyone else. "How can you even think that?"

"Not you, Mrs. Lindhurst. It is these new ones, I fear." Madame Ophelia glared at Elizabeth and Anna, which Elizabeth felt was patently unfair. They hadn't even had a chance to express their disbelief yet.

"They're my guests. Should I send them away?" Mrs. Vanderslice asked humbly, earning a black look from her daughter and an exasperated one from Elizabeth.

But Mrs. Bates knew exactly how to handle the situation because society women always did, even if they'd never actually had a medium faint at the very sight of them before. "Madame Ophelia, I assure you we only came because Clarissa told us you can put us in contact with

40

our loved ones, and we wanted that above all else. We certainly didn't come to question your powers or to doubt you. How silly would we be to waste our time like that?"

Gideon might have been a terrible liar, but his mother was among the best. Elizabeth wanted to weep with joy, but of course she couldn't indulge herself right now. Instead, she concentrated on looking suitably sincere.

"That makes perfect sense," Mrs. Lindhurst said with genuine sincerity. "Norman, help Madame Ophelia up."

Norman, the man from the waiting room, did so with a minimum of enthusiasm.

When Madame Ophelia was seated at one of the chairs clustered around the central table, she nodded her thanks to him and gave the girls a suspicious glance. "I will trust you this once, but do not blame me if your lack of faith makes it impossible for me to contact the spirits."

Mrs. Vanderslice was on her feet again, and she gave both Elizabeth and Anna a warning glare.

"If you have trouble, it won't be because of us," Elizabeth said as sweetly as she could manage. "I'm very anxious to hear from the spirits."

"So am I," Anna insisted.

"And so am I," said Norman Lindhurst, "if they can tell me what horse to bet on at Belmont."

That earned him a swat from his wife and a frown from Madame Ophelia.

"Maybe it's Mr. Lindhurst's skepticism you were feeling," Elizabeth couldn't resist saying.

"He is always making the jokes," Madame Ophelia said. "Do not believe him."

"Are you feeling all right now?" Mrs. Lindhurst asked her. "Do you think you are up to doing a sitting?"

Madame Ophelia heaved a great, weary sigh, but she said, "I cannot disappoint so many of you. I will try my best."

They heard the front door opening and someone called, "Madame Ophelia?" in a rather urgent tone. Then a young woman appeared in the doorway, stopping short when she saw everyone standing around. "What's going on?"

"Madame Ophelia fainted," Mrs. Lindhurst said.

Now that her eyes were accustomed to the dimness, Elizabeth could see that Mrs. Lindhurst was a woman of about fifty, dressed in a conservative but expensive outfit. She had never been a beauty, and life had obviously caused her to scowl far too often, if the lines on her face were any indication.

"Fainted?" the young woman echoed in alarm. "Madame, are you all right?"

"I am fine," she snapped. "Everyone must leave here while I prepare. Persephone, take care of everyone."

"Of course, Madame," the young woman who

apparently bore the unlikely name of Persephone said. She looked to be no older than twenty, and her fashionable gown complemented her lithe figure. She was also apparently Madame's assistant.

Persephone proceeded to escort everyone back into the front room, where she managed to collect their fees without the slightest awkwardness. "I'll just go check to see if Madame is ready for you yet," she said when she had finished.

When Persephone had closed the door behind her, Mrs. Lindhurst said to Mrs. Vanderslice, "You never should have brought so many new people all at once. You know how she is."

"I only invited my daughter," Mrs. Vanderslice said in dismay.

"It's my fault," Anna confessed. "I knew how excited Elizabeth would be to attend a séance."

"And I insisted on coming along when Elizabeth told me about it," Mother Bates said. "I hope we didn't ruin everything."

Elizabeth knew that wasn't a lie. Mother Bates really, really wanted to see what a séance was like. Somehow Elizabeth didn't think they'd ruined anything, though. A professional like Madame Ophelia would know the show must go on, especially after she'd set the stage herself so dramatically.

In fact, although Elizabeth knew gambling was

a fool's game, she would have bet real money that Madame Ophelia was going to put on a better show than usual.

She did, however, make them wait for it. Almost fifteen minutes passed before Persephone came out and invited them to enter. Madame Ophelia was already seated at the table. In the interim she had donned a large turban that matched the vibrant print of her robes. Elizabeth wondered if she was wearing an operator's headset underneath it.

Persephone directed them where to sit at the table. To Elizabeth's surprise, she was seated to Madame Ophelia's right and Anna was on her left. Perhaps Madame Ophelia wanted to keep a close eye on them. Mrs. Bates was beside Anna, then Mr. Lindhurst. Beside him was Mrs. Vanderslice, and then Mrs. Lindhurst was next to Elizabeth. If she'd expected a crystal ball, she was disappointed. A silver tray sat in the center of the table. On it were a stack of papers about three inches square and a collection of pencils.

"If you have a question for the spirits, take a paper and pencil and write it down," Madame Ophelia said.

Everyone took a pencil and a piece of paper. There were just enough to go around. Elizabeth tried to think of something she'd like to ask a spirit, but since she thought this was all hooey, she had a difficult time of it. Finally, she came up with something she thought would be harmless and scribbled it down.

Madame Ophelia, she noticed, kept her eyes closed through the whole exercise. Elizabeth supposed she didn't want to be accused of peeking.

"When you have finished," Madame said suddenly, startling everyone, "fold the paper in half and then in half again. Persephone will collect them."

Everyone folded their papers as instructed, and Persephone came around with an odd brocade bag mounted on a handle. She held it out to each person so they could drop their questions into it. When she had them all, she reached into the bag, pulled them all out and dropped them on the now-empty silver tray. She produced a small bottle from her pocket and sprinkled its contents over the papers. The scent indicated it was alcohol, and then she struck a match and dropped it on top of the pile. The papers with their secret questions burst into flame and in seconds had been reduced to ash. Elizabeth managed a surprised gasp along with everyone else so she couldn't be accused of a lack of belief.

Madame waved her hand over the spiraling smoke, as if sending it heavenward. "The spirits will see your questions, and if they choose, they will answer them."

Persephone slipped out of the room, taking her funny little bag with her. Madame then instructed everyone to lay their hands on the table. No need to hold hands since the small lamp still burned, so everyone could see that no funny business was going on.

"You will tell me who you are," Madame said. "Just your name. I do not need to know more. The spirits know you already."

She turned her piercing gaze to Elizabeth, who was so startled, she almost gave her maiden name. "Uh, Elizabeth, um, Bates. Mrs. Gideon Bates," she added for accuracy.

Everyone introduced themselves, even though Madame presumably knew at least half of them. When they were finished, Madame said, "Now I will try to contact the spirits, although as I said, it will not be easy. My spirit guide is named Peter. He was a monk in sixteenth-century Germany. If he chooses to communicate with you, he will speak through me. He may answer your question or he may have something else to communicate to you. When he does speak, I will be unable to hear or respond to you as myself, and I will have no memory of what he said. Peter will quite take over my body. Try to remain calm. The spirits do not like to be disturbed. Am I clear?"

Everyone nodded. The excitement in the room was almost palpable. Even Elizabeth could feel it, the sense that something momentous was about to happen. No wonder poor Mrs. Vanderslice was so determined to continue this. Her life had been

46

incredibly boring even before David's death had sent her into seclusion. Something as fascinating as this would be irresistible.

For a long moment, no one spoke or moved, and then Madame closed her eyes and began to hum. The Lindhursts and Mrs. Vanderslice closed their eyes as well, and after a while, Mother Bates did, too. Anna and Elizabeth exchanged a glance. Anna's eyes were enormous, silently telling Elizabeth she didn't intend to miss a thing.

The humming seemed to go on for a long time, but then Madame stiffened visibly, as if she had sustained a slight shock. "Peter, are you there? Can you hear me?"

Madame shuddered slightly, and when she spoke again, the voice was deep and resonant, like a man's voice. "I am here. I sense the presence of new beings. Anna, are you there?"

Elizabeth thought Anna's eyes were as wide as they could possibly go, but she had been wrong. "Yes," Anna replied uncertainly.

"David is here. He wishes to speak to you."

Anna didn't look like she wanted to speak to him, but she said, "All right."

"He says to tell you he is in a better place, and he is quite happy."

Mrs. Vanderslice made a sound that might have been a sob, and Anna shivered slightly.

"I'm very glad to know that," Anna said. She probably was.

Madame frowned and shook her head slightly. "David is confused," she said in Peter's deep voice. "He says someone is there who could not possibly want to hear from him."

Even if Anna, Mrs. Vanderslice and Mother Bates hadn't all turned to her with their eyes open now, Elizabeth could have guessed she was the one. "But I do want to hear from him," she said, glad to hear she sounded appropriately earnest.

"And do you really care if he forgives you or not?" Which proved someone had seen her question.

Luckily, Elizabeth was a very good liar. "Of course I do. I always thought we would have time to become friends again, but then you were taken so suddenly. . . ." Sadly, that last part was true. She had expected to become great friends with David once he got over being disgruntled about their broken engagement. David had been Gideon's best friend and Elizabeth's best friend's brother. How could she and David not become friends as well?

"Even after you broke his heart?" Peter asked with haughty disapproval.

"Come now, David," Elizabeth said, feeling a little silly because she knew none of this was real. "You were the one who broke our engagement, so if anyone's heart was broken, it was mine."

This time Mrs. Vanderslice gasped. No one

had ever told her the truth about that unfortunate turn of events. Elizabeth didn't dare give her
mother-in-law so much as a glance, either.

But Peter was not gasping on David's behalf.
"Do you even have a heart to break?"

Elizabeth managed not to laugh. "Now I know
you forgive me, David. You would never insult
anyone you didn't love dearly."

To everyone's surprise, Madame/Peter/David
(which one was it really?) chuckled in response.

"David?" Mrs. Vanderslice said in a tremulous
voice. "Do you have a message for me?"

"Have you done as he asked?" Peter inquired.

"I . . . I'm trying."

Elizabeth glanced at Mrs. Vanderslice, and her
heart ached to see how desperate she looked. Was
it David's spirit who had insisted she increase her
visits to Madame Ophelia? No wonder she had
been so adamant about it.

"David is fading," Peter reported brusquely.
"He's very tired."

"No, wait," Mrs. Vanderslice begged.

"Annabel is here," Peter reported, and Mrs.
Lindhurst jolted to attention. From the conversation between her and Peter, Elizabeth surmised
that Annabel was a child Mrs. Lindhurst had lost
almost thirty years ago. Mr. Lindhurst looked
pained through the discussion of Annabel's care-
free life, and he received no message from the
child himself.

When they had finished with Annabel, Madame Ophelia slumped a bit and then shuddered. When she finally raised her head, she glanced around the room, checking everyone's expressions. Some were happy, some sad, and Mother Bates looked disappointed. How unfortunate that she had not received any attention. But then neither had Mr. Lindhurst.

"The spirits never tell me what horses to bet on," he reminded Madame Ophelia. "Can you tell me why that is?"

Elizabeth studied him while Madame simply glared at him, and suddenly, Elizabeth gave a little cry and straightened in her chair, throwing her head back and gasping.

"Elizabeth, what is it?" Anna cried, and Mother Bates echoed her concern, but Elizabeth hardly heard them. She shuddered and gasped again, and then she said, in a voice no one had heard before, "Don't bet on Mill Due in the fifth. He's going to scratch so Cupid's Arrow can win."

Then she sighed and sagged in her chair until Mrs. Lindhurst was forced to catch her and set her upright again. After a moment, she shuddered again and opened her eyes. "Why is everyone staring at me?" she asked in alarm.

"You had a little fit of some kind," Anna said, her lovely face full of worry.

"A fit? Did I . . . ? What did I do?"

"You gave me a tip about a horse in the fifth

race at Belmont," Mr. Lindhurst said, obviously delighted.

"I did?" Elizabeth asked in surprise. "Did I say he would win?"

"No, you said he would scratch." Mr. Lindhurst shook his head in wonder. "He's the favorite, too."

"He would *scratch?* Do you mean, scratch himself? I didn't know horses did that, like dogs and cats do."

"No, it doesn't mean that," Lindhurst explained, still amused. "It just means he'll be pulled from the race."

"Oh. Would that information help you in some way?" Elizabeth asked. "To know he's going to . . . to *scratch?*"

"Not really, although it might increase the odds on the other horses if he doesn't scratch until the last minute. And you did say another horse would win instead."

"But no one knows who will win a horse race, do they?" Elizabeth asked, still confused. "That wouldn't be fair."

"You're right. It wouldn't be fair," Lindhurst said, "which is why people bet on them. But it would sure be interesting if it happens."

"I can't imagine that it will. I hardly know anything about horse racing." That was a lie, of course, but no one would ever have guessed it from looking at her. "I can't imagine why I'd say something about a racehorse. I don't even remember doing it."

"Was a spirit speaking through her, do you think, Madame Ophelia?" Mother Bates asked.

Really, Mother Bates was a treasure.

"I . . . I cannot say," Madame said, eyeing Elizabeth speculatively. "Sometimes the spirits play little jokes on us. Perhaps this was one of them."

"I do feel a little funny," Elizabeth said with a smile. "Did I say anything else?"

"No, dear," Mother Bates assured her. "Just that advice about the horse. Perhaps the spirits felt sorry for Mr. Lindhurst and decided to send him a special message."

Elizabeth laughed and Lindhurst chuckled, but no one else saw any humor in it. The door to the waiting room opened and Persephone came in. She had been smiling, but she stopped dead and her smile vanished, as if she sensed something amiss.

"Did the séance go well?" she asked with a worried frown.

No one spoke for a long moment, and then Madame said, "Mrs. Bates had a special message from the spirits." She did not look happy about it.

"I'm sure it was just a fluke, if that's even what it was," Elizabeth said. "I certainly don't have any supernatural powers."

52

"One never knows," Madame said, her razor-sharp gaze still fixed on Elizabeth as if searching for evidence of something. Elizabeth revealed nothing, however, simply staring back innocently.

Mr. Lindhurst was the first to move, shoving back his chair and rising to his feet. "I'm sure you'll excuse me. I want to get out to the track."

"Honestly, Norman," his wife said, but he didn't even pause, brushing past Persephone on his way out.

Everyone else rose more sedately and began to take their leave. Elizabeth turned to Madame Ophelia. "I'm sorry if I disturbed anything. I have no idea what happened."

"You disturbed nothing. Will I see you again?"

"I . . . Well, I'll have to see if my husband allows me to return," Elizabeth managed to say with a straight face. How convenient to be able to blame Gideon for things. Marriage had all sorts of advantages she'd never understood before.

"You may have the gift," Madame said, although Elizabeth was sure she was being sarcastic. Madame couldn't possibly believe that, especially when she knew perfectly well there was no "gift" to have.

"Are you sure you're feeling all right?" Anna said with genuine concern, having come to her side. Or at least her concern *appeared* to be genuine.

"I feel a bit strange, but not like I'm going to

have another fit or anything," Elizabeth said with an attempt at a reassuring smile.

"I should hope not," Mother Bates said, slipping an arm around her waist. "You frightened me there for a minute."

"I'm so sorry," Elizabeth said quite sincerely. She wouldn't cause Mother Bates a bit of worry if she could help it.

"Just don't do it again," Mother Bates teased.

Mrs. Vanderslice cleared her throat to remind everyone that she was there.

"Allow me to escort you out," Persephone said quickly with an apprehensive glance at Madame Ophelia, who was still sitting in her chair and had made no attempt to rise.

They allowed it, and Persephone closed the door to the séance room behind them.

"That was quite a display you put on," Mrs. Vanderslice said with just the slightest touch of disapproval.

Elizabeth pretended not to notice. "Was it? I hope I didn't make a fool of myself."

"I think you made more of a fool of Mr. Lindhurst," Anna said. "He couldn't get to the racetrack fast enough."

"I hope Mrs. Lindhurst isn't angry with me. I couldn't help it, really. I have no idea what happened."

"Whatever happened, we need to get you home," Mrs. Bates said. "Why don't we share a cab, if you're going straight home, too?" she added to Anna.

"That would be fine," Anna said, and led the way outside, ignoring her mother's frown.

"I'm sorry you didn't get your question answered, Mother Bates," Elizabeth said as the four of them strolled to the corner in search of a cab.

"That's all right. It wasn't much of a question. I think I just said I'd like to hear from my mother."

"That would be a difficult one to answer," Elizabeth remarked.

"*Your* question seemed to upset David, Elizabeth," Mrs. Vanderslice said, still disapproving.

"I certainly didn't mean for it to," Elizabeth said quite honestly. She didn't think anything she did could upset David now.

"But she made him laugh," Anna said. "Or at least the monk laughed. What was his name again?"

"Peter," Mother Bates said. "I was wondering if they had monks in Germany in the sixteenth century. Or if there was even an actual Germany then. I've been trying to remember my history and—"

"Really, Hazel," Mrs. Vanderslice said, "what does it matter? If Peter says he was a monk, who are we to argue?"

Who indeed? Elizabeth purposely didn't glance at Anna, for fear they might both laugh.

They found a cab, and they all managed to squeeze into the backseat with room to spare. Mrs. Vanderslice's presence made it difficult to speak of anything that had happened at the séance, so they did their best to find some safe topics until the cab pulled up outside the Vanderslice home.

Anna helped her mother out, and then leaned in to get her purse from where she'd left it on the seat. "I'll try to come over after I get Mother settled," she whispered before following her mother into the house.

As soon as Elizabeth and Mother Bates were safely inside their own house, Mrs. Bates said, "What on earth was that all about?"

"My fit, you mean?" Elizabeth asked with a grin as she removed her hat.

"Yes, your fit where you gave poor Mr. Lind-hurst racing tips."

"What do you know about racing tips?" Elizabeth asked in amusement.

"I know what they are even if I don't understand them. Was that a real tip?"

"It was a true tip."

"And where on earth did you get it?"

Elizabeth strolled into the parlor and seated herself on a sofa, enjoying the slightly cooler temperature in the darkened room. Mother Bates followed her and took her usual chair after ringing for the maid.

"I went to see the Old Man yesterday, and while I was waiting for him, I was visiting with some of the men I know who happened to be at Dan's. They were talking about a race being held this afternoon. The favorite is going to be scratched at the last minute so another horse has a chance to win."

"Cupid's Arrow," Mother Bates confirmed.

"Is that the horse's name?" Elizabeth asked with feigned confusion. "I really don't remember."

Mother Bates gave a contemptuous huff. "Is that what a fixed race is?"

"Oh, Mother Bates, you never cease to amaze me!"

"Stop teasing me and answer my question."

Elizabeth sighed. "There really isn't any good way to fix a horse race. It would be too complicated, and too many people would have to be bribed and would know and might talk later. And even if you managed to bribe everyone else to lose, there's always a chance the horse that is supposed to win will pull up lame or throw his jockey or get injured in the gate or . . . Well, so many things can go wrong, not to mention all the other horses want to win and one of them might just decide to in spite of its jockey trying to hold it back."

"So Cupid's Arrow isn't going to win?"

"I have no idea. Scratching Mill Due will give Cupid's Arrow a much better chance, though. The fellows in Dan's back room were arguing about that very thing, which is how I knew about it."

"I see. So why did you pretend to go into a trance and deliver this information to Mr. Lindhurst?"

"Because I knew that Mill Due was going to be scratched, and Cupid's Arrow might win— although you will recall I didn't say for sure that he would, only that he'd have a better chance."

"Which means you made a fairly accurate prediction, or something that sounded like one anyway."

"Yes, and it will sound even better if Cupid's Arrow wins."

"But why? Did you just want to embarrass Madame Ophelia?"

"Oh no. I just happened to think that if I could convince her I really could tell the future, I might be able to figure out a way to con her."

CHAPTER THREE

Gideon wasn't nearly as good at hiding his emotions as Elizabeth was, so his grim expression gave him away the moment she came to welcome him home.

"Are you all right?" she asked, her beautiful face creasing into a worried frown.

"I'm fine. Just something at work. Is Mother here?"

"Yes, we've been anxious to tell you all about our trip to see the medium."

He nodded and allowed her to lead him into the parlor. His mother greeted him, and he sank down onto the sofa with a weary sigh. His mother frowned but didn't ask any questions. She knew he couldn't discuss his work with them. He forced a smile. "Now tell me how your séance went."

"It was quite enlightening," his mother said. She was embroidering something and didn't even look up, although he noticed she was grinning.

"Was it what you expected?" he asked Elizabeth.

"Yes, exactly. Madame Ophelia was wearing a turban, so I'm guessing she had an operator's headset under it. She must have been hooked up to a telephone system somehow. She was already in her chair when we came in, and she never got up until after we left, so it must involve wires or something. Anyway, that would be how she was told . . . Well, I'm getting ahead of myself. First, she had us write down the questions we had for the spirits."

"Tell him about the bag," his mother prodded, still grinning over her embroidery.

"We wrote our questions down and folded the papers up. Then we dropped them into a cloth bag her assistant passed around."

"And then the assistant pulled them out and burned them all up right in front of us," his mother couldn't resist explaining. She finally looked up, and her eyes were fairly glittering with delight.

"Then how did the medium know what the questions were?" Gideon asked.

"Tell him," his mother said to Elizabeth.

"The bag we put the questions into was a magician's bag. It has two sections and a lever in the handle that allows you to switch the opening back and forth between them. We dropped the questions into one side, the assistant switched the opening to the other side, and she pulled out blank papers identical to the ones we dropped in."

"How do you know all this?" Gideon asked in amazement.

"Simple magic tricks can come in handy when you're conning someone," she explained. Gideon decided he didn't want to know any more.

"Except the papers she burned were blank," his mother added, in case he hadn't figured that out. "She burned the blank ones and took the real ones away with her."

"And then she read them to the medium over the telephone thing," Gideon guessed. "But how does the medium know what to tell people? Obviously, she's not getting messages from real spirits."

"She collects information," Elizabeth said. "She probably makes her clients sit in the waiting room for a long time so she can eavesdrop on what they talk about."

"It's only natural to talk about who you are hoping to contact and what you hope to find out while you're waiting," his mother said.

"I suspect she might also have confederates who pose as clients and sit in the waiting area to ask questions and get people talking," Elizabeth said.

"Do you think the Lindhursts were confederates?" his mother asked in dismay.

"Maybe, but Mrs. Vanderslice has been seeing Madame Ophelia for a while now, and I suspect Mrs. Vanderslice has already told her everything she knows about me and all there is to know about David."

"Did you hear from David?" Gideon asked with a pang. How odd to be speaking of his friend as if he could still communicate with them.

"The monk claimed to be speaking for him, yes," his mother said.

Gideon frowned in confusion. "The monk?"

"Her spirit guide is a German monk named Peter," Elizabeth said.

"I see," Gideon said, not seeing at all. "And what did David have to say through him?"

"That David still hasn't forgiven me for breaking our engagement," Elizabeth said.

"But David was the one who broke it," Gideon said.

"Yes, he was," his mother chimed in, "which is how we knew this Peter couldn't really be talking to David."

"Well," Elizabeth allowed, "that was one of the reasons, at least. But Mrs. Vanderslice thought I had broken it, so we know that's who told Madame Ophelia all about it."

Gideon nodded, beginning to understand. "And did you get a message from the spirits, Mother?"

"Sadly, no," she said, plainly disappointed.

"I'm sure that's only because Madame Ophelia didn't know anything about her, though," Elizabeth said.

"And my question was too vague," his mother added. "Next time, I'll do better."

"Next time?" Gideon echoed in alarm.

"Oh yes," his mother said. "Tell him what you did, Elizabeth."

Gideon managed not to groan. "What did you do?"

"She had a visit from the spirits, too," his mother told him with great delight before Elizabeth could even open her mouth.

"I just happened to have a racing tip that I picked up when I went to see the Old Man yesterday," Elizabeth added, "so I passed it along to a gentleman there as if it had come from the spirits."

"Because no one would ever suspect you of knowing anything about horse racing," Gideon guessed.

"That was my hope."

"And what did you mean to accomplish with this bit of playacting?"

"I'm not sure, but I couldn't help thinking that if I could convince Madame Ophelia I really can tell the future, I might be able to . . . Well, I'm not sure exactly what just yet, but I might be able to do something to save people like Mrs. Vanderslice from being impoverished by this woman."

Gideon couldn't help flinching, but not for the reason Elizabeth obviously thought.

"Oh, darling, I know you can't possibly approve, but if there's any way to help Anna's poor mother—"

"It's not that," he hastily assured her. He rubbed a hand over his face, wishing he didn't know what he knew, but there was no help for it now. He did know, and he had to do whatever he could to make things right, no matter the consequences. "You see, I had a disturbing visit with a client today."

"I knew something was wrong the minute you walked in," his mother murmured.

"So did I, but I thought you were just annoyed with us about the séance," Elizabeth said.

He shook his head. "Well, normally, I might mention that I had a visit from a client who sent their regards to Mother, but of course I would never mention the purpose of that client's visit with me."

"Because it's all confidential," Elizabeth said, nodding her understanding.

"But today I had a visit from a client, and I feel I must share with you the purpose of her visit, so I can't tell you who it was."

"And of course, we'll never mention it to anyone," Elizabeth promised, raising her hand as if to swear an oath of silence.

He couldn't help smiling at that and somehow resisted the urge to kiss her for being so earnest. "This client came to ask me to release a very large sum of money to her so she could invest it." He quickly explained what Mrs. Darlington had told him about the investment. "But the most astonishing thing she said was that she knew this was a sound investment opportunity because her dead husband had told her so himself."

Both women understood the implications immediately. "Did she tell you she had consulted a medium?" Elizabeth asked.

"I naturally questioned her about that amazing claim, especially after our conversation last night, and she admitted that she had. She refused to tell me the medium's name, but when I suggested Madame Ophelia might be the one, I could tell from her reaction that I had guessed correctly."

"Oh dear," his mother said. "Obviously, Madame Ophelia is not content with cheating little old ladies out of their last pennies."

"And who knows how many other people she has already cheated?" Elizabeth mused. "Did you give this lady the money she asked for?"

"No. Fortunately, her husband named our law firm as executor of his estate and we manage the trust, so we can refuse her request if we think it is ill-advised. I already spoke with the other partners, and they agreed with me not to release the funds. But we discovered while discussing it that another client had asked for and received a somewhat smaller amount because it didn't raise much of an alarm at the time. The partner involved hadn't been concerned, but now he thinks he might not have gotten all the information."

"So we really need to do something to stop this woman," his mother said.

Gideon turned to her in amazement. "Mother, you really don't need to worry about this."

"But I am worried about this. Someone who is probably one of my oldest friends is being cheated and probably others whom I know as well, since I know almost everyone who is a client at your firm."

That was true, although Gideon didn't want to confirm it. Mrs. Darlington was certainly one of his mother's oldest friends. He turned to Elizabeth. "What can we do, though? I'm guessing the police won't be too interested."

Elizabeth sighed and shook her head. "They might be, if we could convince the victims to file charges, but in cases like this, people usually refuse to even believe they've been cheated. Without that, the police are helpless, which is why my entire family isn't locked up in prison."

"So our only hope is to con the con artist," his mother said.

"But Elizabeth said she didn't have any idea how to do that," Gideon protested.

"Not yet, but maybe . . . Well, we'll just have to see if Cupid's Arrow won today in the fifth at Belmont."

"Did you see?" Anna demanded when she barged into the Bateses' parlor the next morning.

Elizabeth and Mrs. Bates had been perusing the newspapers, reading accounts of the Paris Peace Conference being held in France to hammer out the terms of settlement between Germany and the Allies. "Cupid's Arrow won the race!"

"We saw," Mother Bates informed her happily. "Or rather Gideon saw it. He got the newspaper first this morning."

"Now what do we do?" Anna asked, plopping down on the love seat beside Elizabeth.

"We?" Elizabeth asked with a teasing grin.

"Yes, we. You don't think you can leave me out of this, do you? It's my mother you're trying to save."

"And we'll need her," Mother Bates reminded Elizabeth, "since your family can't be involved."

Because Elizabeth had only the vaguest idea of what she might do, she had no idea if she needed either of them, but she certainly wasn't going to say so at this point in time. "I think the best thing we can do right now is wait."

"Wait for what?" Anna cried, obviously outraged at the very thought.

"Wait for Mr. Lindhurst to tell Madame Ophelia my tip was correct."

"Oh, I see," Mother Bates said. "That is your proof that you really can speak to the spirits."

"I doubt Madame Ophelia will think so. She'll probably think I'm another con artist trying to horn in on her scam, which is why I have to just wait for her to come to me."

"Do you think she will?" Anna asked in amazement.

"I'm thinking Mr. Lindhurst will nag her until she does. She certainly never gives him racing tips."

"Will you give him more?" Mother Bates asked.

"Heavens no, for the simple reason that I'm not likely to know any, unless something just falls into my lap. But I intend to make some other, completely different but equally accurate predictions."

"You mean, the way that fortune-teller that your father told you about did?" Anna asked.

"No, not at first anyway. I just need to predict something that actually happens."

"How can you possibly do that?" Mother Bates asked.

Before Elizabeth could answer—which was just as well because she hadn't quite figured it out herself yet—the maid stepped in to announce that Mr. Jake Miles had come to call.

When she showed him in a moment later, he stopped dead just inside the doorway. "I didn't expect a hen party."

"What kind of a greeting is that?" Elizabeth scolded him.

Her brother sighed. "Good morning, Mrs. Bates. Good morning, Anna. And nuts to you,

Lizzie." He was gratified when both Mrs. Bates and Anna both laughed at his nonsense.

"It's a good thing *I've* learned good manners or I'd clock you one for that," Elizabeth said. "Come and sit down and tell us to what we owe the honor of your company."

Jake took a chair and grinned. "The Old Man told me you were asking about some medium."

"Yes, and he already warned me that you and he would be no help to me."

"Oh, Lizzie, how can you think that just because you deserted your loving family to make a fancy society marriage that we would fail to help you in your time of need?"

"Now I really am going to clock you one."

Anna was laughing but she managed to say, "Have pity on him, Elizabeth. I think he's here to help."

"I don't need his help," she huffed, feigning a confidence she did not feel.

"Not even if I can tell you a thing or two about your Madame Ophelia?"

"Oh, do tell," Anna said, having no pride at all. This was the last time Elizabeth let her brother get to know her friends.

Jake glanced at Mrs. Bates, who was smiling appreciatively, and gave his sister a smug grin. "This Ophelia is from St. Louis. She arrived a few months ago with this medium thing already figured out. She's got a girl working for her."

"Persephone," Elizabeth confirmed.

"Per-what?" Jake asked with a frown.

"Persephone."

"Persephone is a Greek goddess, the queen of the underworld," Anna added.

Jake nodded his head in approval. "I'm glad to see I'm not wasting my money sending you to college."

"You have my permission to clock him," Elizabeth told Anna, who was frowning now.

"About sending me to college . . ." Anna said ominously.

Jake held up his hands in a sign of surrender. "I'm joking," he claimed. "It's really your money."

"What on earth is he talking about?" Mother Bates asked.

"What he's always talking about," Elizabeth said, "nothing of importance. So Madame Ophelia has a young woman working for her."

"Yes, but as far as I could find out, she hired the rest of her crew right here."

"What kind of a *crew* does she need?" Mrs. Bates asked.

"Probably those confederates I mentioned to pose as clients to find out things about the real clients while they're chatting in the waiting area," Elizabeth guessed.

"Yes, but she also convinces clients to recruit their friends and relations," Jake said.

"I guess they tell everyone what a wonderful experience they had, talking to their dead loved ones," Anna said, making it clear that she had not had a wonderful experience.

"It's a little more than that," Jake said. "When she's milked a mark for as much as she can get, she offers them free sittings if they bring someone new, preferably someone with money, and of course they have to tell her everything they know about the person first."

Mrs. Bates gasped at the perfidy. "Anna, do you think she offered your mother a free sitting for bringing you?"

"I hope so," Anna said. "If not, I'll demand it, and she should get two more for bringing the two of you as well."

Jake sighed dramatically. "I'm so proud of you, Anna."

"You are really trying my patience today, Jake," Elizabeth said.

Jake ignored her.

"What else does she need a crew for?" Mother Bates prodded, getting them back on the subject.

"I gather she tells some of her clients that they will meet a tall, dark stranger or something like that, and when they do, they should take his advice."

"That's the con the Old Man told me about," Elizabeth said. "I guess that's how they make their big scores."

"Yeah," Jake agreed. "The séances pay the rent, but she'd have her eye on the big money."

"Mother hasn't said anything about meeting a tall, dark stranger," Anna said.

"Probably because Madame Ophelia knows she doesn't have a lot of money, but she still has friends who do," Elizabeth said. "Gideon had a client come in yesterday and ask him to give her a large sum from her late husband's estate so she could invest it. Apparently, the dead husband had advised her to do it."

"Through Madame Ophelia, I presume," Anna said.

"That's what Gideon surmised. He didn't give her the money, but I'm guessing Madame Ophelia won't take no for an answer, so she'll put some pressure on the widow."

"How awful," Mother Bates said. "Taking advantage of poor widows like that."

"I think they're rich widows, Mrs. Bates," Jake said with a twinkle. "Poor widows wouldn't be worth the trouble."

Elizabeth gave him a glare, but Mother Bates just smiled benignly at him. She wasn't helping a bit.

"Now, what kind of a plan did you come up with, Lizzie?" Jake asked.

"A very clever one," Anna said. "She's going to pretend she can really talk to the spirits."

The look Jake gave her was insultingly skeptical.

"It won't be that hard. I already started."

"Yes, she predicted that Cupid's Arrow would win his horse race yesterday," Mother Bates said.

"She did, did she?" Jake said, mystified. "Just because Mill Due scratched?" Jake was apparently using his spare time to follow the horses.

"I heard some of the boys discussing it when I went to see the Old Man the other day. I didn't really predict Cupid's Arrow would win, just that Mill Due would scratch so he'd have a better chance."

Jake was impressed, although she knew he'd die before admitting it. "Are you going to keep on predicting horse races?"

"Of course not. I need to make *accurate* predictions."

"How are you going to do that?"

"I'll need some help."

"I figured. Have you thought about who can help you?"

"I've thought about a lot of people, but they're all con men, so they won't."

Jake nodded sagely. "I guess that just leaves Cybil."

"Cybil?" Mother Bates echoed in amazement. "Your aunt, Cybil?"

"The very same," Jake said.

"But she's a college professor," Anna said.

"She is now," Jake said.

"Did she used to be a . . . a . . ." Plainly,

73

Mother Bates couldn't bring herself to say it.

"Not willingly," Elizabeth said. "She grew up in that family, so she learned a lot, but she was determined not to do what they did. She convinced her father to send her to college instead so she could make her way in the world."

"What a wonderful story," Mother Bates said.

Elizabeth supposed it was. For the first time she realized she should have done what Cybil had, except then she would probably never have met Gideon Bates. Maybe things worked out the way they should sometimes.

"Do you think Miss Miles would help?" Anna asked. Cybil Miles was a professor at Hunter College, where Anna was a student.

"If we explain everything to her, she might," Elizabeth said, having not had time to really decide if this was a good idea or not.

"And if Cybil says yes, Zelda would help, too," Jake said.

"I can't imagine Miss Goodnight participating in a con," Anna said.

Elizabeth couldn't either, but she also knew Zelda would support Cybil in anything. "Well, it won't hurt to ask them."

"They'll be thrilled," Jake predicted.

They were not thrilled.

"I can't believe you'd ask me to do something like that," Cybil said.

Elizabeth had waited until evening to go see her aunt at her ramshackle home in Greenwich Village. She'd had to wait until Cybil and Zelda had returned home after a day of teaching and Anna had finished her classes. Now the four of them were sitting in Cybil's parlor, a room stuffed with as many seating options as possible to accommodate the literary salons they held every Monday evening.

"I told Elizabeth I couldn't imagine either one of you being willing to do something like this," Anna said, "but Jake seemed to think you'd be delighted."

Cybil and Zelda exchanged a look that spoke volumes about Jake and how they had both indulged him far too much. They really were an odd couple. Cybil was tall and imposing, like her brother. Her thick dark hair was threaded with silver but her blue eyes sparkled with life. She dressed like a respectable college professor during the day, but at home she preferred colorful flowing robes or loose-fitting trousers. Zelda was exactly the opposite, blond and tiny and always dressed as conservatively as any mother could wish. They had been in love for over twenty-five years and happier together than any of the married couples Elizabeth knew except her and Gideon.

"Jake," Zelda said affectionately. "I should have known this was his idea."

"But why would he involve us?" Cybil asked, obviously annoyed.

"Because he and the Old Man can't help," Elizabeth said. "You know that."

"Oh yes," Cybil said sarcastically. "They can't possibly offend a fellow con man, no matter how low he has sunk."

"Or in this case, how low *she* has sunk," Zelda added. "But ethically speaking, are there really degrees of evil when cheating someone out of their money?"

Cybil reached over to where Zelda sat next to her on the sofa and patted her hand. "If we're going to consider ethics, we'll never get anywhere with this, dear."

Zelda sighed in defeat. "I suppose you're right."

"I just want to somehow remove Madame Ophelia's influence over my mother before she bankrupts us and forces Mother to lure her friends into this woman's web," Anna said, sounding as desperate as she must have been feeling.

"And you say that Mrs. Vanderslice isn't the only one this Madame Whatever is cheating?" Zelda asked.

"No. We know of one and possibly two others, but that is just by chance, because they use Gideon's law firm and he happened to find out. I'm sure there are more, and if not, there certainly will be if she isn't stopped," Elizabeth said.

"But what do you hope to accomplish?" Cybil said. "You know her clients aren't going to believe she's a fake."

"Driving her from the city for a start," Elizabeth said.

"And taking back the money she has stolen," Anna added.

"Or at least what's left of it," Elizabeth said. "She would only get half, at most. She'll have to split it with whoever is helping her. She must have at least one accomplice to approach the victims about investing their money."

"But if you chase her out of the city, won't she just go somewhere else and do the same thing?" Cybil asked.

The four of them sat in awkward silence for a moment as they considered the magnitude of the problem.

Then Zelda said, "She wouldn't do it again if you could frighten her, though."

Everyone turned to her in amazement. Zelda's lovely face was the picture of innocence, and Elizabeth could hardly believe she had come up with such a fiendishly clever idea.

"Frighten her?" Anna echoed. "What do you mean?"

"Yes," Elizabeth said knowingly, "what do you mean?"

Zelda blinked in surprise at the intensity of their questions. "I . . . I'm not exactly sure, except that she probably frightens her victims to get them to do what she wants them to do, so why not try to frighten her into seeing the error of her ways?"

"Zelda is an idealist," Cybil said by way of apology.

"Because she wasn't raised by con men," Elizabeth said, "but she may have something. In fact, she may have something very important."

"And so, darling, I'm going to have to return to Madame Ophelia's at least a few more times," Elizabeth concluded after bringing Gideon and his mother up-to-date. At least she had waited until after dinner to do so. She probably hadn't wanted to spoil his appetite.

They were seated in the parlor, enjoying an after-dinner drink of sherry for the ladies and whiskey for Gideon, who was going to need a second glass now that he understood the situation.

"I told Elizabeth I would help," his mother said, "but she said I can't really because we're related and my testimony that Elizabeth's predictions were accurate would be suspect."

Plainly, his mother found this exceedingly disappointing, but Gideon's relief that she wouldn't be involved was short-lived.

"I told her she could attend a séance or two," Elizabeth said. "It would probably look odd if she didn't."

"We certainly wouldn't want anything about this to look odd," Gideon said, defeated.

"Oh, darling, I know how much you hate this, but it isn't the least bit dangerous," Elizabeth said.

"You always say that," he reminded her.

"But this time it's true," she said, not even bothering to deny it. "I'm hardly likely to let Madame Ophelia con me out of any money, and she isn't really a medium, so she can't ask the spirits to haunt me or anything, so what can she do?"

"You said she has a crew," he reminded her.

"Of other con men. No one is less violent than a con man, darling. You know that. And Anna will be with me."

"Oh yes, Anna will make a perfectly adequate bodyguard." He drained his whiskey glass and got up for a refill.

"Which is fine because I won't need a bodyguard at all. You'll see."

When he had generously refilled his glass, he returned to sit beside Elizabeth on the love seat. "So how do you plan to convince this woman you're a real medium?"

"It seems simple enough. I'm just going to predict things that will then actually happen."

"But won't this Madame woman just think you're faking it the way she is?"

"At first she will, I'm sure. In fact, I'm counting

79

on it. I'm not even going to try to convince her I'm legitimate."

"Why not, dear?" his mother asked with a frown. "Isn't that the whole point?"

"Yes, but if I'm trying to convince her, she'll be suspicious. A real medium who is just discovering her powers would be skeptical herself, I imagine."

Gideon supposed he could see some sort of twisted logic in that. "And then what?"

She gave him what could only have been called a pitying smile. "And then we figure out what to do next."

Elizabeth was not at all surprised when Mrs. Vanderslice came to see Mrs. Bates the next afternoon. Mrs. Vanderslice had been visiting Madame Ophelia on Monday, Wednesday and Friday each week, so this morning would have been her next visit after the séance Elizabeth and Mrs. Bates had attended.

Although Mrs. Vanderslice was approximately the same age as Mother Bates, she now looked far older. David's sudden death had drawn thick streaks of gray in her fair hair and deepened the frown lines in her face. Elizabeth knew a moment of guilt for planning to ruin the one thing that had finally inspired her to leave her bed. If only that thing didn't threaten to ruin her in every other way.

After they had served her tea and discussed the weather and some gossip about mutual friends, Mrs. Vanderslice felt comfortable mentioning the real reason for her visit.

"Madame Ophelia was asking about you this morning," she told Elizabeth.

"Was she?" Elizabeth asked in feigned surprise. "I hope she wasn't offended that we didn't return, but I didn't want to try Gideon's patience by asking for another visit. He finds the whole idea rather silly."

"He wouldn't if he would attend one," Mrs. Vanderslice said. "I'm sure David would have a special message for him, too."

"Did he have a special message for you this morning?" Elizabeth asked with the utmost sincerity.

"He always does. He . . . Well, actually, he asked me to invite you back."

"He did?" Both Elizabeth and Mrs. Bates asked in unison.

Startled by their reaction, Mrs. Vanderslice nevertheless remained undaunted. "Yes, he did. He wants to . . . to speak with you about something important."

"Oh my, that's very disturbing," Elizabeth said. "What did Anna say about all this?"

"Anna? Why should she say anything at all?"

"Surely she had something to say about David's request, I mean," Elizabeth said.

Mrs. Vanderslice frowned. "Anna did not accompany me today. She is not a believer."

Elizabeth nodded, secretly approving Anna's reluctance. She had done just what they'd decided she should do.

"I can understand why she wouldn't want to go back," Mother Bates was saying. "I did think she found the whole experience rather upsetting."

"She doesn't believe we're really communicating with David," Mrs. Vanderslice said. "I don't know why she refuses to believe the evidence right in front of her."

"Well, I can't imagine what David would need to tell me," Elizabeth said. "So I can't imagine I'll go back, either."

"But you must!" Mrs. Vanderslice said. "Surely you know that the horse won."

"What horse?" Elizabeth asked in all innocence.

"I don't know. Cupid or something. Mr. Lindhurst was raving about it."

"You remember, Elizabeth," Mother Bates said helpfully, "that thing you said when you had that little, uh, fit or whatever it was."

"Don't remind me," Elizabeth said, covering her cheeks with both hands as if to conceal a blush. "I was hoping everyone forgot all about it."

"Hardly. Even Peter was talking about it," Mrs. Vanderslice said. "You were quite amazing."

"And quite embarrassed. To tell the truth, that is

the real reason I can't even think about returning. How can I face everyone after that?"

"It's nothing to be ashamed of," Mrs. Vanderslice said. "In fact, I should feel quite honored if the spirits chose to pass a message through me."

Indeed, she actually sounded a bit miffed that she hadn't been the chosen vessel.

"I'm afraid I can't feel anything but mortification," Elizabeth said. "So Madame Ophelia will never see me again."

"Then you can expect Mr. Lindhurst to show up on your doorstep. He won a lot of money, to hear him tell it, and he is anxious for another revelation."

"I hope Mr. Lindhurst does not actually know where her doorstep is," Mother Bates said with a frown.

"Oh no," Mrs. Vanderslice assured them. "Madame Ophelia informed him your prediction was certainly a result of having been in her presence, so he would have to encounter Elizabeth there."

"Please thank her for me," Elizabeth said, and she was truly grateful, because returning to Madame Ophelia's was the very next step in her plan.

CHAPTER FOUR

E lizabeth enjoyed a lovely weekend with Gideon. They went to see a play and had dinner afterward at Delmonico's with an old friend of Gideon's and the French war bride he had brought home with him after the war. On Sunday Mrs. Vanderslice sought her out after church and begged her once again to attend another séance at Madame Ophelia's, which she politely declined to do. Then she and Anna exchanged secret smiles.

Elizabeth and Mother Bates spent most of Monday writing letters to various elected officials in support of the Woman Suffrage Amendment, which had failed to pass in the last session of congress. This meant they would have to wait until the new congress convened in December, eight long months away.

"Do you think there is any chance President Wilson will call a special session of congress to vote on the amendment?" Elizabeth asked while the two of them were eating lunch.

"He's been surprisingly supportive of late, but he is still the most intractable man I've ever known," Mother Bates said in disgust.

"At least he finally came out in support of Woman Suffrage."

Mother Bates gave an unladylike snort. "But only when he saw which way the wind was blowing. After the Democrats lost control of congress in last year's election, he knew the Republicans would eventually pass the amendment and get all the credit. But he'd waited too long and let his own party get out of his control, so he still couldn't get it passed."

"It's so infuriating," Elizabeth said. "What good does it do us to have a new congress that will probably pass the amendment if they don't meet until December? Even if they pass the amendment right away, there won't be time to get it ratified by enough states before the 1920 election."

"I know, it's a horrible way to run a government, making the people wait almost thirteen months for the new congress to convene after they're elected. But maybe Wilson will surprise us and call a special session."

Elizabeth smiled. "Maybe I should predict that at my next séance."

Mother Bates sighed. "I thought you only wanted to predict things you knew were going to happen."

Elizabeth was still working the cramp out of her writing hand late that afternoon when the maid came into the parlor to announce a visitor. From the look on her face, Elizabeth could guess who it was.

"There's a . . . a lady here to see you, Mrs. Gideon."

Elizabeth took pity on her. "Is her name Madame Ophelia?"

The poor girl nearly sighed with relief. "Yes, ma'am. I didn't want to say it in case you didn't believe me."

"Please show her in and bring us some tea, will you?" Luckily, Mother Bates had gone upstairs to lie down, so Elizabeth could receive her visitor alone.

Madame Ophelia had dressed conservatively today, but she would still attract notice with her brightly patterned walking suit and a stylish turban adorned with a peacock feather. This one, Elizabeth noticed, didn't cover her ears since she wouldn't need to conceal a telephone headset today.

"Thank you for seeing me, Mrs. Bates," Madame Ophelia said as Elizabeth rose and moved to welcome her.

"How could I not? I'm dying of curiosity to know why you're here," Elizabeth said. "Please, sit down. I've ordered tea, unless you'd prefer something else."

"No, tea is fine," Madame said, taking a seat on the sofa.

Elizabeth chose a chair opposite her so she could watch her more easily. Madame took a moment to glance around the room. Elizabeth knew what she would conclude: an old family without a large fortune. The house had been in the Bates family for three generations and the furniture had been reupholstered instead of being replaced. The room was comfortable but not fashionable. Elizabeth could have used her substantial dowry to refurbish it, but she didn't want Mother Bates to think she was trying to usurp her. Besides, Elizabeth liked the tradition of the place, and it gave her a sense of permanence. Her own family had no home or traditions worth upholding.

"I hope you didn't go to any trouble to find where I live," Elizabeth said, sounding gracious instead of annoyed, which is what she should have been.

"No, I did not," Madame admitted without shame. "Mrs. Vanderslice urged me to come, and she was happy to give me your address."

Elizabeth was sure she was. "I'm concerned that Mrs. Vanderslice is becoming too . . . too emotional about the séances."

"How can one be too emotional over one's only son?"

Madame must have thought she'd have no answer for that. "Perhaps dwelling on David's death so much isn't good for her."

"Who is to say? But that is not why I have come."

"If you're going to try to convince me to come to another séance, I'm afraid you've wasted your time." Elizabeth managed an apologetic smile.

"Why are you so determined not to return?"

"How can you even ask?" Elizabeth could cry on demand, but she had never mastered blushing on demand. She still covered her cheeks, though. "I made an absolute fool of myself at the last one."

"Was that your first visit to a medium?"

"Couldn't you tell? Of course, it was."

"And yet you were able to speak to the spirits."

Elizabeth shook her head. "I'm not too sure about that."

"Mr. Lindhurst is sure."

Elizabeth couldn't help smiling at that. "Mrs. Vanderslice told me the horse I mentioned won, but I'm sure that's just a coincidence."

"Mr. Lindhurst said everything you predicted came true."

"Since I don't even remember what I supposedly predicted and I don't know anything about horse racing, I can't be sure, so you'll forgive me if I'm not impressed."

"Mrs. Bates, let me be frank with you. I have never had anyone besides myself receive a message from the spirits during one of my séances."

Elizabeth felt certain this was true, mainly because nobody could receive a message from the spirits. Before she could think of a suitable response, however, Lucy returned with the tea tray. She had added some tea cakes, Elizabeth was happy to see. Elizabeth served her guest and then herself, which allowed her plenty of time to formulate her reply.

"You said you have never had anyone else receive a message from the spirits, but how do you know that is what happened with me?"

Madame Ophelia smiled benignly. "I know these things, Mrs. Bates. I could see it even before I knew what you said would prove true."

Elizabeth didn't believe that for a minute, but she said, "I'm sure I should be flattered, but I'm still mortified."

"You should not be. The spirits, who know everything, spoke through you. I am the one who is flattered that they chose to do so under my eye. They knew I would take care of you and help you cherish your gift."

Elizabeth frowned. "My gift?"

"Yes, you have the gift, the second sight. I can see it."

"How very interesting. And just what does that mean?"

"It means you can speak to the spirits and they to you. It means you have an obligation to use your powers to help others."

"I can't imagine how it could help others. The only thing I've done so far is help someone win a racing bet, and let me assure you, that is not how I would like to serve mankind."

"You are new to this. I understand you are frightened."

"I'm not frightened, just puzzled."

"Then allow me to answer your questions. I am responsible for you now."

Elizabeth liked the sound of that, although she didn't let her guest see it. "How can you be responsible for me? I'm a married woman and I have a husband to look after me."

"I am responsible for teaching you to manage your talent. The spirits chose me, and I will not fail you."

Elizabeth allowed herself a skeptical frown. "And exactly how will you do that? By teaching me how to do séances? I assure you I would never do such a thing."

"You are free to use your power however you wish. My only task is to teach you to use it well."

"By attending your séances, I suppose," Elizabeth said. "Is this how you get people to keep coming back time after time?"

"Not at all. I have never before found anyone with the power, and do not think I will do this for profit. No, I will teach you out of the goodness of my heart, as others did to me."

Did Madame Ophelia actually have any goodness in her heart? It seemed unlikely. "I don't know about that. What if I don't want to be taught how to use this so-called power? What if I don't even believe in it?"

"If you have the power, it will not desert you now that it has been made manifest. You will not be able to ignore it no matter how hard you try."

This was disturbing news. "And what can you do? Can you teach me to control it?"

"I can teach you to manage it. It would be my great honor."

Elizabeth was sure this was true. She could hardly wait to see how this woman would try to con her once she agreed to Madame Ophelia's plan.

"I'll have to ask my husband's permission, of course," Elizabeth said.

But Madame Ophelia shook her head. "And if he refuses to allow it, how will you suffer the torture of dealing with this all alone?"

"Then what do you suggest?" Elizabeth asked in some distress.

"He will not know what you do during the day, will he?"

Elizabeth sighed her resignation. "He won't if I don't tell him."

"I think I would have been happier if you didn't tell me," Gideon said after Elizabeth had explained to him about Madame Ophelia's visit.

They were in a cab on their way to the weekly literary salon at Cybil and Zelda's house, and Anna was with them. He was wishing he had adopted the habit of carrying a flask since Cybil never served anything stronger than sherry at the salons. If this kept up, he was going to become a raging drunk.

"What kind of wife would I be if I snuck around, attending séances without your permission?" she asked with feigned outrage.

"A thoughtful one," Gideon said quite honestly.

"What do you think Madame Ophelia has in mind?" Anna asked. She was much too enthusiastic about all this. He should probably have been worried, but if he couldn't control his own wife, how could he hope to influence his best friend's sister?

"I'm sure she has some kind of plan to get money out of me. Why else would she offer to let me attend her séances for free?"

"Then not charging you for the séances doesn't even make any sense," Gideon said.

"Of course, it does. You give something away because you hope to get something more valuable in return. That's how I know she wants to con me."

"Do you think she really believes you have the sight or whatever you call it?" Anna asked.

"I can't imagine she even believes in the sight. She might think I'm just another con artist trying to horn in on her business, which is why I'm pretending to be so reluctant, but she might also be trying to convince me I'm really gifted. If I'm any good at all, she can probably use me to draw in more customers."

"Now that makes sense," Gideon said. "But it seems like a lot of trouble to go to for a few new clients."

"You didn't see how excited Mr. Lindhurst was when he thought he'd gotten a good tip," Anna said. "And Mother said he was even more ecstatic after the horse won."

"And he probably told everyone he knew about his good fortune," Elizabeth said. "You see, I'm good for her business."

"Do you think she'll try to use you in her other cons as well?" Anna asked.

"Maybe, but I would have to be completely naïve for that to work, so I have to convince her that I am. I can't use any of the usual tricks mediums use to read people, either. Everything I do must seem to be completely legitimate."

Gideon couldn't help shaking his head. "And just how do you fake legitimacy?"

"That, my darling, is a con artist's stock-in-trade," Elizabeth said as the cab pulled up to the curb outside Cybil's house.

Gideon paid the driver and escorted the ladies up the front walk. Welcoming lights glowed in the windows of the old house, and the door opened before they had even crossed the large wraparound porch.

"Where have you been?" Jake demanded.

"We're not even late," Anna informed him, "although I'm gratified to know you missed us."

"I didn't miss you. It's just that I didn't have anybody to talk to."

"Isn't Miss Adams here?" Gideon asked, trying to sound perfectly innocent.

Jake gave him a murderous glare. "She's a hundred years old, and she only talks about poetry."

"I'm sure she isn't a day over ninety," Elizabeth said, "and she obviously adores you."

"Just come in, will you?" Jake groused.

When they were all inside, crowded into the foyer, Jake asked, "What's happening with the medium?"

"She wants Elizabeth to become her partner," Anna reported gleefully.

Gideon almost laughed out loud at Jake's horrified expression.

"Don't be silly, Anna," Elizabeth scolded her. "She just wants to train me to use my powers."

"It's about time somebody did," Jake said, earning a black look from his sister. "I thought of something you could do to prove your powers, though."

"Good. I'd love to hear it," Elizabeth said.

"It'll cost you."

Elizabeth pressed her fingers to her temples and closed her eyes, as if communing with the spirits. "I could have foreseen that."

Jake rolled his eyes, but he took her by the arm. "Come upstairs where no one can hear and I'll explain." They headed up the stairs to the room that had been Elizabeth's when she lived here before her marriage.

Anna stared after them wistfully.

"She'll tell you all about it later," Gideon said.

"I hope so. Well, let's go inside. There's someone I want you to meet."

They made slow progress through the crowded parlor. Cybil and Zelda had furnished the room for entertaining many guests, and every seat was filled. Several lively conversations were going on, but they stopped in turn as the participants greeted Anna and Gideon. At last they reached the far side of the room where a young woman was sitting on a love seat next to the infamous Miss Adams, who was regaling her on the hidden meanings in Walt Whitman's poetry. Miss Adams was oblivious to their arrival, but the girl looked up politely.

What Gideon saw next startled him. The girl's expression changed from polite interest to absolute rapture in a matter of seconds as she gazed up at Anna. When he glanced at Anna, he saw the same expression on her face.

Good heavens, Anna was in love.

The girl was on her feet in another instant. "I'm so glad you came, Anna."

"I told you, I always come," Anna said gently, then remembering her manners, she added, "Miss Adams, of course you know Mr. Bates, and, Miss Quincy, this is Gideon Bates, one of my oldest friends. Gideon, Miss Quincy is also a student at Hunter."

As were most of the young women in attendance. Gideon knew they came to the salons because they admired their professors, Cybil and Zelda, and were honored to socialize with their literary friends. They also seemed to enjoy the discussions that went on at the salons, although perhaps not as much as the older attendees.

"It's a pleasure, Miss Quincy," Gideon said, taking the hand she offered. He always thought smart women were attractive, and Miss Quincy's eyes fairly glowed with intelligence. He found himself smiling in delight. "Are you a native New Yorker?"

She was from nearby Connecticut, and Gideon learned she was in her second year at Hunter, studying social work. She already knew all about Gideon and Elizabeth, it seemed, so he didn't have to answer many questions in return as they got to know each other the way strangers do in social situations. This was special, however, because Anna was obviously smitten with this girl, and Miss Quincy seemed smitten in return. Elizabeth would be thrilled.

"Is this your first visit to the salon?" he asked at last.

"Yes, I . . . Well, I'm a bit shy, you see, but Anna . . . Miss Vanderslice, I mean, insisted that I would enjoy myself."

"And I've been keeping her entertained until you arrived," Miss Adams said, reminding them of her presence.

"And we're very grateful for that," Anna said with a straight face. "But now I'll have to steal her away. I want her to meet some of the other guests."

As much as he wanted to see Jake's face when he realized Anna had fallen in love, Gideon knew good manners compelled him to sacrifice himself. "Then I'll take Miss Quincy's place, if you'll have me, Miss Adams."

Miss Adams was only too happy to accept his company, and he watched Anna and Miss Quincy stroll away, arm in arm.

"We're just friends," Anna insisted on the cab ride home in response to Elizabeth's questions.

"I'm still very happy for you," Elizabeth said, feeling more than happy. "She is lovely."

"How did Jake take the news?" Gideon asked.

"Remarkably well," Elizabeth reported. "At least he didn't challenge Miss Quincy to a duel or anything."

"Why should Jake care if I have a friend?" Anna protested.

"I told you, you're Jake's only friend," Elizabeth said. "I was afraid he might be jealous."

"Anna is Jake's only friend?" Gideon marveled.

"According to Elizabeth," Anna said. "At any rate, a person can have more than one friend, and there's absolutely no reason for him to be jealous. What a preposterous idea."

"As long as you maintain your position as an amateur con artist, I'm sure Jake will be happy," Gideon said.

"Why am I only an amateur?" Anna asked, affronted.

"Because you don't get paid."

Both women stared at him in the shadows of the cab.

"What?" he demanded.

Elizabeth patted his hand. He really was so sweet. "Nothing, darling."

"So did Jake have a good idea for one of your predictions?" Anna asked, obviously anxious to change the subject.

"Oh yes. I never would have thought of it myself, but it's brilliant. We have to wait, though, because it has to come later. It's the convincer."

"What's a convincer?" Gideon asked.

"Usually, it's the money you let the mark win to convince him the game is really fixed in his favor. That just gets him more excited and greedy, so he bets more and more. In this case, it means the final prediction that will make Madame Ophelia believe I really have the sight."

"Do I want to know what it is?" Gideon asked.

"No, darling, you don't."

"But I do," Anna insisted.

"And so do I," the driver called from the front seat.

Elizabeth didn't tell them, of course, but the driver wouldn't even let Gideon tip him.

"You folks were the most interesting passengers I've had all week," he said.

Elizabeth decided to take Mother Bates with her to her first training séance. If she were at all nervous about it, she would naturally want someone with her, and Mother Bates would provide whatever support was necessary. She could be unsure about the whole situation, and she wouldn't even have to pretend.

"Mrs. Bates and . . . Mrs. Bates," Persephone said by way of greeting when they arrived at the storefront.

"You can call me Mrs. Gideon to make it easier," Elizabeth said.

Persephone smiled her agreement. She was dressed conservatively but fashionably in a brown silk chiffon dress with stylishly large pockets and oversized buttons. No one would stare at her in the streets the way they did at Madame Ophelia.

Her fair hair was tucked into a chignon in what might have been an attempt to make her appear older. It was a wasted effort.

"Is anyone else coming this morning?" Elizabeth asked uneasily.

"Just two ladies who are longtime clients," Persephone said. "Is Mrs. Bates"—she nodded at Mother Bates—"going to sit in as well?"

Elizabeth slipped her hand into Mother Bates's. "I hope that's all right. I just . . . I wanted someone I knew I could trust to be with me since I have no idea what is going to happen."

Persephone gave her what was probably intended to be an encouraging smile, but she just looked worried and very uncertain. "I'll ask Madame to see what she thinks. Please have a seat while you're waiting. The other ladies should be here soon."

Elizabeth and Mother Bates claimed two of the chairs lining the walls of the waiting room.

"How are you feeling, dear?" Mother Bates asked. They'd discussed what could and could not be said in a place where they might be overheard.

"I'm a little nervous. I'm so glad you're with me."

"I'm glad I am, too, and don't worry. I won't let anything happen to you if . . . well, if you fall into a fit like you did before."

Elizabeth laid a hand over her heart and drew

a calming breath. She really was a bit excited. Starting a new con was thrilling, after all.

They waited in silence for a few more minutes, knowing that was the only way to ensure that they didn't give anything away. Then the shop door opened and two ladies came in. They were middle-aged and well-dressed in traveling suits with skirts and matching jackets in deference to the fickle spring weather. One wore heather green and the other's suit was tan and cut in the military style that had become so popular during the war.

They hesitated just inside the door, staring at Elizabeth and Mother Bates and whispering behind their hands. Elizabeth would have known this was the height of rudeness even if she hadn't read about it in an etiquette book, and she frowned her disapproval. Poor Mother Bates must have been fuming. Then they stopped whispering, smiled and came forward. The one wearing tan said, "You must be Mrs. Bates. Madame Ophelia told us you have the sight."

"And she told us you are longtime clients," Elizabeth retorted, making her smile a bit disdainful.

The women were not offended at all. "Oh yes, we've been seeing Madame Ophelia for . . . well, for months, I suppose. Forgive me. We should have introduced ourselves. I'm Mrs. Kirkwood and this is my friend, Mrs. Regis."

Elizabeth rose and shook their hands. "And this is my mother-in-law, Mrs. Bates."

"Two Mrs. Bateses," Mrs. Kirkwood said. "That might be confusing."

"You can call me Mrs. Gideon," Elizabeth said. "How did you discover Madame Ophelia?"

The two women exchanged a glance as if trying to decide something. Elizabeth was pretty sure she knew what it was, but she kept her expression only mildly curious.

"We heard about her through some friends," Mrs. Regis said. She looked to be about fifty, with mousy brown hair liberally streaked with gray. She looked a bit careworn, too.

"And did you know each other before coming here?" Mrs. Bates asked. This was exactly what one society matron would ask another in this situation, and it also happened to be what Elizabeth wanted to know. Or at least she wanted to hear their answer.

"Oh yes," Mrs. Kirkwood said. "We've been friends for ages." Mrs. Kirkwood seemed to be around the same age as her friend, although her dark blond hair did not have as much gray. Her face showed her years, though, and Elizabeth noticed she never quite met her gaze.

"I suppose you've had success in communicating with . . . well, with whoever it is you wanted to communicate," Elizabeth guessed.

"Great success," Mrs. Regis confirmed. "Madame Ophelia is truly gifted."

"She told us you heard from your fiancé, who died from the flu," Mrs. Kirkwood said.

Elizabeth chose to be surprised and a little offended that they knew this. "I can't believe Madame Ophelia would share such personal information about her clients."

Obviously, the ladies hadn't expected her reaction. "I'm sorry, but . . . you see, she was simply preparing us," Mrs. Kirkwood said. "We are here because Madame thought we could help you get in touch with your spirit guide."

"Because we're so experienced ourselves," Mrs. Regis added.

"I'm sure Madame Ophelia didn't mean any harm," Mother Bates said.

"Perhaps not," Elizabeth allowed. "I suppose I'm just a bit sensitive under the circumstances."

"Anyone would be," Mrs. Regis said, and her friend agreed.

"I'm sure discussing your fiancé is difficult as well," Mrs. Kirkwood added.

Elizabeth chose not to comment on that or any other subject the ladies raised. They didn't even wonder why she was talking to her dead fiancé when she was married to someone else now.

After an excruciating wait, during which the two clients grew increasingly frustrated trying to make conversation with Elizabeth, Persephone reappeared and escorted them into the séance room. It looked exactly as it had before, including the papers and pencils on the tray in the middle of the table.

Madame was already seated, wearing her enormous turban. Persephone had removed a few chairs, so only four remained. At Persephone's direction, Elizabeth sat beside Madame and Mother Bates sat beside her. Mrs. Kirkwood and Mrs. Regis took the remaining chairs, with Mrs. Regis beside Madame.

"Are we going to write questions?" Elizabeth asked.

The two ladies both glanced at Madame Ophelia for guidance.

"I think we will, to get us started," Madame said.

"Perhaps Mrs. Gideon will be able to answer them," Mrs. Regis said with more enthusiasm than was really warranted.

Elizabeth just gave her a weak smile and deliberately removed her gloves so she could write her question. Mrs. Bates removed her gloves as well, and after a moment of hesitation, the other two ladies did, too. They proceeded with the same ritual, folding the papers, dropping them into the bag, and Persephone burned them on the tray. Then she left them alone, closing the door quietly behind her.

"Do I need to do anything special?" Elizabeth asked uncertainly.

"Not at all," Madame Ophelia assured her. "We will put our hands on the table as we always do." The other ladies did so. Elizabeth stared at the hands for a long moment before laying hers down as well. Then she glanced at Madame as if seeking assurance. "Now try to relax. Take some deep breaths and make your mind blank. Do not think of anything in particular. If the spirits choose to visit you, that is fine. If not, that is fine, too. Do not trouble yourself."

Elizabeth nodded her understanding, and Mother Bates patted the hand nearest her. Elizabeth obediently drew some calming breaths and closed her eyes, ready for whatever would come.

Madame began to hum, as she had done before. After a while she cried out, "Peter, are you there? Can you hear me? Speak to me, Peter. We seek your help."

A little more humming and a little more waiting. Then Madame spoke again, this time in Peter's voice.

"Adele, are you there?"

"Yes, I'm here," Mrs. Regis confirmed, sitting up a little straighter. Her eyes were closed, too, as Elizabeth noticed when she peeked. "Who wants to speak to me?"

"Your husband is here. He says you have done very well."

"I did just what you said, Arthur."

"You found the man I described to you?" Peter asked.

"Yes, yes. He sat next to me at the theater. I couldn't believe it. He looked exactly like you said he would."

"And you did as he suggested?"

"He was quite surprised when I knew he had a business venture. I believe he was impressed."

"I am relieved, Adele. I could not leave you a fortune, but now you will have one."

"I'm so grateful, Arthur. Thank you so much." Was she weeping? She seemed to be. How effective.

Peter fell silent, and after a few minutes, Mrs. Regis said, "Arthur, are you still there?"

Apparently not. Peter did not answer, but after another moment, he said, "Mrs. Bates, are you there?"

Mother Bates perked up, although she glanced at Elizabeth in case he meant her. "Who's there?" Mother Bates asked.

"Your mother. She wants you to know she is very peaceful. The pain is gone."

"That's . . . good to know," Mother Bates said weakly.

Before she could say more, Mrs. Kirkwood said, "Do you have a message for me, Brother Peter?"

They all jumped when Peter let out a tortured moan.

"What is it?" Mrs. Kirkwood demanded desperately. "Who's there?"

"I cannot rest."

"Wesley, is that you, son?" she asked, her voice breaking.

"You must find me. You must bring me home."

"I want to, but they said you were lost," Mrs. Kirkwood said, and she was weeping, too. This was very sad. "They couldn't find you."

"I will tell you. You must find me and bring me home so I can rest."

Elizabeth wanted to squirm in her chair. How awful. Many people had lost young men in the war, and most of them were buried in France, so very far away, if they were lucky enough to have remains to bury at all. This was disgraceful. She wanted to scream.

"But how can I do that?" Mrs. Kirkwood asked brokenly. "How can I go to France?"

"I will send someone to you. They will help you find me."

"Who will you send? How will I know?"

"You will know. They will tell you."

"But how will I get to France? How will I—"

"Do not question me," Peter said in a voice that sent shivers up Elizabeth's spine.

"I'm so sorry," Mrs. Kirkwood said, nearly sobbing now. "I didn't mean to . . . I would never . . . Please forgive me!"

"Do not doubt. You must believe."

"I do!" she insisted. "I do believe. You'll see. I'll do whatever you ask."

Elizabeth drew a calming breath, keeping her eyes closed and waiting, ready for just about anything.

"Elizabeth?" Peter said, and this time his voice was gentle, as if speaking to a frightened child. "Are you there?"

"Yes," she said timidly.

"Someone here has a message for you."

Elizabeth opened her eyes and let out a bloodcurdling scream.

CHAPTER FIVE

E lizabeth couldn't see their reactions because she'd squinted her eyes as tightly shut as she possibly could, but she heard the gasps of shocked surprise.

"How dare you?" she demanded in her spirit voice. "Liars! All of you, liars!"

"Elizabeth?" Mother Bates whispered tentatively.

But Elizabeth couldn't hear her because the spirit had taken over. "I see you. I know you. You're all liars. Actors. Pretending to believe, but you're only trying to fool the fools. I know you for what you are, and I will expose you."

"What . . . ? Who are you?" Madame Ophelia asked in an obvious attempt to regain control of the situation.

"A spirit. A real spirit, not like your phony Peter. Not someone you made up to fool the fools and take their money."

"What do you want?" Madame Ophelia's voice had lost its air of authority.

"I told you. I want to expose you for the fake that you are and then I will *destroy you!*"

More gasps, and Elizabeth shuddered violently

and went limp, falling heavily onto Madame Ophelia, who tried to catch her but failed, being unable to move from where she was wired into her chair. Elizabeth landed on the floor in an untidy heap.

"Elizabeth!" Mother Bates cried in genuine distress.

"What happened?" Mrs. Kirkwood cried. "Is she dead?"

Mother Bates gently turned Elizabeth over. "Elizabeth, can you hear me?" She slapped Elizabeth's face lightly in an attempt to rouse her. "She's fainted. Does anyone have any smelling salts?"

"Persephone!" Madame shouted. "Smelling salts!"

"I . . . I think I have some," Mrs. Regis said frantically.

The door opened and someone came in. "What happened?" Persephone asked.

A moment later, the harsh odor of ammonia assailed her, and Elizabeth jerked awake. Mother Bates was leaning over her, her beloved face creased with worry. "Elizabeth, can you hear me?"

"I . . . Yes," Elizabeth said, lifting an unsteady hand to her head. "What happened?"

"You . . . you fainted," Mother Bates said.

Elizabeth moaned in despair.

"Can you sit up, dear?" Mother Bates asked anxiously.

"I . . . Yes. Help me up off the floor," she said desperately.

Persephone hurried over to assist, since Madame Ophelia could not get up, and they got Elizabeth back into her chair. She was pleased to note the way Mrs. Kirkwood and Mrs. Regis were still staring at her in stunned surprise. Madame Ophelia was much too professional to betray her true feelings, but even she looked nonplussed.

"Are you all right, dear?" Mother Bates was asking. "Can I get you anything?"

"Perhaps another dose of smelling salts," Mrs. Regis tentatively suggested.

"Heavens no," Elizabeth said, raising her hands to ward her off. "I'm much too awake now." She turned to Mother Bates. "Did I say anything?"

"Well, yes," she admitted reluctantly.

"Not something about another racehorse, I hope," Elizabeth moaned.

"Oh no, not at all."

Elizabeth hazarded another glance around the table. "But I said something shocking, didn't I? I can tell by your faces." When no one responded, she grew more desperate. "What was it? What did I say?"

Mother Bates cleared her throat when no one else responded. "You said we were all liars and that Peter was . . . was made up."

"Why would I say a thing like that?"

"It wasn't you, of course," Mother Bates

explained. "It was . . . well, it was another voice, like the way Peter sounds when he speaks through Madame Ophelia."

Elizabeth looked around the table again. "And this voice said you were all liars?"

Madame Ophelia merely glared at her, but Mrs. Regis and Mrs. Kirkwood both nodded stiffly.

"But why . . . ?" She considered her own question for a long moment. "But you are liars, aren't you?" she finally determined. She turned to Madame Ophelia. "You just pretend that a spirit speaks through you, and you . . . ." She scowled at the other two ladies. "You two are just pretending to receive messages from the spirits to trick me. Does she pay for that?"

Both ladies tried to deny it, speaking at once and babbling anxiously but making no sense at all.

"Is that true?" Mother Bates asked in outrage. "How despicable! But, Elizabeth, how could you have known such a thing?"

"I didn't," Elizabeth said. "Not until . . . But this is preposterous. There's no such thing as the sight and no one can speak to the spirits. Madame Ophelia is just pretending and you ladies are assisting her. I have no idea why you've gone to so much trouble for us, but you've wasted your time. We never should have come."

Elizabeth tried to rise, but almost fell, and Mother Bates and Persephone, who was still

114

hovering nearby, caught her and eased her back into her chair. She rubbed her temples and sighed in defeat.

"Just rest a moment, Mrs. Bates," Madame Ophelia said kindly. "You have had a shock. Communing with the spirits can be exhausting, especially when one is new to the experience."

Elizabeth frowned at her. "I told you—"

"Yes, yes, you do not believe, and yet the spirits spoke through you, did they not?"

"If you're talking about that silly thing with the horse race—"

"And today you knew these ladies were only pretending."

Mother Bates gasped, but Elizabeth merely stared at her in wonder. "You admit it, then? That this is all fake?"

"Certainly not, but today was a test for you. I asked these ladies to help me try your powers, to see if you would know they were pretending."

"That was . . ." Elizabeth caught herself. Would a society matron say "a dirty trick"? Probably not. ". . . outrageous."

"And very unkind," Mother Bates added with a disgruntled frown. "Elizabeth could have been injured."

Elizabeth rubbed her elbow meaningfully and gave Madame Ophelia an accusatory look.

"I'm sorry. I had no idea she would faint again," Madame said with apparent regret.

"And what did you hope to accomplish with this charade?" Elizabeth asked.

"Two things. I hoped to discover if your powers were real and then to convince you that they are."

"How can my so-called powers be real if I don't even believe in them myself?"

"And yet how do you explain what just happened?"

Elizabeth opened her mouth to protest, but no words came. She turned to Mother Bates, who was looking so distressed, Elizabeth wanted to hug her. "I . . . I can't."

Madame Ophelia turned to her two compatriots. "Ladies, are you convinced that Mrs. Bates has the sight?"

They both nodded solemnly.

"But I don't have it," Elizabeth insisted.

"Then test yourself some more," Madame Ophelia challenged.

"How can I?"

"Attend another séance with genuine clients who are strangers to you and see if the spirits speak through you again."

"And what if I refuse? What if I decide this is all a lot of nonsense and forget I ever even heard of you and your séances?"

"Then you will pay the price, I'm afraid," Madame Ophelia said rather ominously. "You may not want the gift, but once you have it, it will haunt your dreams and your waking hours. You will not be able to control it. Better by far to accept it and use it as the spirits intended."

Elizabeth frowned as if torn by indecision.

"This is so difficult," Mother Bates said. "How can she possibly make a decision like this?"

"As I said, she can test the spirits again," Madame Ophelia said. "Perhaps it will come to nothing, after all."

"You mean if I attend another séance and nothing happens, that will mean I'm free of all this?" Elizabeth asked.

Madame shrugged. "It will be a sign."

"And you'll have real clients there? Not people who are just *pretending?*" she added with a censoring glance at the other two ladies. At least they had the grace to look ashamed.

"I promise, although these ladies are genuine clients under ordinary circumstances."

Elizabeth highly doubted that, but she nodded. "And the clients can't be anyone I know, either."

"Of course. It would be too easy for you to guess at a prediction for someone you already know."

"I suppose that's true, but I won't be guessing at anything since I don't want any of this to be true. Actually, I was thinking that I didn't want anyone who knows me to see me when I'm, uh, doing whatever it is that I do when the spirits move me."

"I can understand your concern. No one you know will be there."

"Except for me," Mother Bates said a little plaintively.

Elizabeth gave her an apologetic smile. "In this case, I'm afraid not, dear. I don't want anything to taint this trial. I want to find out once and for all if I have the sight or whatever it is or if this is all someone's idea of a practical joke."

"It is not a joke," Madame Ophelia assured her. "Practical or otherwise."

"I don't know about this, Elizabeth." Gideon gave her his most concerned frown in hopes that she would take pity on him, because he knew that was his only hope of swaying her. Using whatever power he might possess as her husband to forbid her would have been a waste of time and effort, ordinary persuasion would have been worthless, and logical arguments would have just provided amusement.

"You mustn't listen to your mother," Elizabeth said, giving his mother a knowing little grin where she sat nearby doing her mending. "I couldn't possibly have hurt myself when I fainted."

He would happily make a point of checking her thoroughly for bruises later, after they retired for the night, but he knew she wouldn't have a single one. "I'm not worried about that and you know

118

it. What do you think is going to happen when Madame Ophelia finds out you aren't really a medium?"

"Not a thing. First of all, she's not going to find out, and even if she suspects, she's going to see that I'm very good at faking it. In fact, I'll be much better at it than she is, and she's either going to want to learn my secrets or—if I can convince her I really have powers—she is going to want to manage my career."

"Do you think you could have a career doing this?" Mother Bates asked, looking up from her sewing. They were in the parlor, waiting for dinner to be served while Elizabeth and his mother told him all about the séance this morning.

"Oh yes. I'm very good at reading people and lying, too. I could probably make a fortune."

Gideon managed not to wince.

"Tell Gideon how you knew those ladies were just pretending," his mother urged.

"Yes, how did you know?" he asked with great interest.

Elizabeth frowned. "I've been trying very hard not to use any of the tricks mediums usually use, like eavesdropping on the clients or getting them to reveal things in normal conversation. I actually made a point of not conversing with those two women, so no one would think I figured it out from talking to them."

"And yet you did figure it out," his mother said.

"So how did you do it?" Gideon asked.

"Their clothes, for one thing. They were stylishly dressed, but their clothes came from a department store, not a modiste. They didn't look wealthy enough to be longtime clients of Madame Ophelia if they had to pay for the séances themselves. But it was their hands that really gave it away."

"Is that why you took off your gloves, dear?" his mother asked.

"Yes. I hoped they would follow suit, and they did. Their hands had done far more work than yours or mine, Mother Bates."

"But Mrs. Regis's husband said he hadn't left her a fortune, and Mrs. Kirkwood might well have had a son who died in France. They were both weeping by the end of their readings."

"So it seemed, but people who are really weeping cry real tears. Neither one of them even pulled out a handkerchief."

His mother blinked in surprise while she thought this over. "I believe you are right, dear. How strange."

"Strange indeed. And I already knew Madame Ophelia was a phony, so it wasn't hard to guess she would have her cohorts there to assist her today."

"I still don't understand how you expect to

convince Madame Ophelia's clients that she's a fraud," Gideon said.

"I don't, of course. I just hope to put her out of business."

Gideon couldn't help his grin. "By becoming her biggest competitor?"

"What a wonderful idea, darling," she laughed. "Why didn't I think of it myself?"

Mother Bates frowned. "But seriously, dear, how can you do that?"

"I haven't quite worked it all out yet, but it will come to me, I'm sure."

"And you can do this without any help from Jake or your father?" Gideon asked.

"I have Anna and Aunt Cybil and Mother Bates," she said.

For some reason, that did not comfort him.

"And Jake already gave her a good idea," Mother Bates reminded him.

Gideon was unimpressed. "Has she told you what it is?"

"Well, no, but I'm sure it's wonderful."

Gideon wasn't sure at all. "I discovered today that another of our clients has been investing in a scheme Madame Ophelia led her to."

"Oh dear," his mother said. "Anyone I know?"

"I can't tell you, but . . ."

"But I know most of your clients," she finished for him. "I hope it isn't a ruinous amount."

"Too much to lose, which I assume is what is going to happen."

"I hope you've warned all your partners," Elizabeth said.

"I have, but this happened before I found out what was going on. Besides, not all the estates we manage are as well protected as Mrs. . . . as the one I originally discovered. Not every widow needs our permission to withdraw funds, so all we can do is advise them."

"And of course they aren't going to take your advice over Madame Ophelia's," Elizabeth said in disgust. "We need to find out who she has employed to fulfill her prophecies."

"Do you think it's someone you know?" Mother Bates asked. "Could you convince them to stop?"

"Con men don't usually operate in their home city, although I still might know them, but even if I did, they'd hardly give up such an easy con just because I asked them to."

"And going to the police is a waste of time," Gideon recalled.

"Yes, so the only solution is to cut the head off the snake," Elizabeth said.

"What a horrible expression, my dear," Mother Bates scolded her.

"I know, but it fits, doesn't it?"

"Freddie wants to help," Anna informed Elizabeth the next morning. She had no classes on

122

Wednesday morning and had stopped by to give Elizabeth this amazing information while her mother was attending another séance. They were sitting in the library so they wouldn't disturb Mother Bates, who was discussing constitutional amendments with some friends in the parlor.

"Who is Freddie?"

"Frederica," Anna said impatiently. When Elizabeth still did not respond, she added, "Miss Quincy."

"Oh. Did you tell her about all this?" Elizabeth asked in surprise.

"It's not a secret, is it? I mean, the part about Mother wasting all our money on a medium. She knew there was something wrong. Freddie did, I mean. She saw how worried I was, so I told her about Mother's obsession, and . . . well, I had to tell her you were going to help so she wouldn't be concerned."

Elizabeth nodded. "I see." And she did. Freddie was indeed more than a friend.

"So of course, she wants to help."

"Is Freddie an experienced con artist?"

"Don't be silly. You know she isn't."

"Then how can she help?"

"I wasn't an experienced con artist when you asked me to help the first time."

"Yes, but—"

"And don't tell me it's dangerous because I know you've sworn to Gideon that it's not."

123

Elizabeth sighed. "It's not dangerous, but we can't have inexperienced people making mistakes and giving the game away."

"Freddie won't give anything away."

"Perhaps the best thing she can do is provide moral support for you, since you won't be participating in this much, either."

"I don't need moral support, and I don't expect you to give her anything important to do. She's still very innocent."

And so was Anna, although Elizabeth knew better than to suggest it. "Then I wouldn't want to be the one to corrupt her."

"I'm being serious here, Elizabeth. I don't want to hurt her feelings."

"Neither do I. Perhaps you could bring her to luncheon someday soon, so I can get to know her."

"That would be perfect. I'll find out when she's free. So, when are you going back to Madame Ophelia's?"

"I'm waiting to hear from her. She's organizing an evening séance during a time when she usually doesn't hold one. That way she can invite only the people she wants to attend."

"People you don't know."

"Supposedly."

"And what is going to happen at this séance?" Anna asked with a gleam in her eye.

"I will go into a trance, and my spirit guide will

give some kind of prophecy that will then come true."

"All right, but you still haven't said how Freddie can help."

"Tell her to think up a prophecy. That should keep her busy."

"It's not quite as exciting as actually helping with a con," Anna said.

"No, but it's a start."

Gideon insisted on escorting Elizabeth to the séance on Friday evening, even though he wouldn't be attending.

"You don't need to worry about me," Elizabeth said as they snuggled in the backseat of the cab. "Cybil will be there."

"I still don't know how she managed that."

"She's quite clever. She's a college professor, you know," Elizabeth teased him.

He tried to frown at her, but she looked so beautiful that he couldn't manage it. She was very different when she was involved with a con, as if someone had lit something inside her. Everything about her seemed brighter somehow. It worried him, but he would never admit it.

"What should I do when I see Cybil?"

"Absolutely nothing," she said sternly. "I'm planning to ignore everyone and you can nod politely, but don't make conversation or reveal any emotion whatsoever."

"That should be easy. I'm actually trained for it."

"For not showing emotion?" she marveled.

"It is an attorney's most important skill. Clients tend to get their backs up if they know you think their decisions are idiotic."

"I can imagine," she said with a smile.

"Are you planning to faint this evening?"

"I think not, although I'll be weak afterward. That's the only reason I allowed you to come. Madame Ophelia wasn't too happy about it, but I assured her that you would sit in the waiting area and wouldn't interfere in any way."

"I wouldn't dream of it. Will I have to carry you out?" he teased.

"Only if it amuses you."

"I'll decide when the time comes."

"Just try not to *look* amused when the time comes."

"Don't worry. I will be furious and alarmed."

"That should work nicely, if you think you can carry it off."

"I'm sure I can, since this whole thing makes me furious and alarmed."

"Oh, darling, I love you so much."

"And I love you, too." Which was the only reason he put up with all of this.

Madame Ophelia's domain was a bit of a disappointment. If she was robbing her clients blind, she wasn't spending any of her gains on decorating. Only a cheap wooden sign marked the entrance, and the storefront window was heavily draped. Somehow he had expected some sort of exotic theme inside, but the only mysterious thing about the room was why the walls had been painted such a dark color and how many trash heaps she had raided to collect such odd chairs.

A gentleman and a lady sat together against one wall. They were middle-aged and well-dressed and looked a bit nervous, if their anxious glances when Gideon and Elizabeth walked in were any indication. Gideon nodded to them but quickly looked away and escorted Elizabeth to the opposite side of the room.

Soon two women came in, obviously mother and daughter. The younger woman appeared to be in her twenties and had shingled her light brown hair. He thought it looked hideous, but he supposed Elizabeth would want to cut off her lovely hair eventually as so many other women were doing, and he would just have to get used to it. The girl looked around and said a tentative "Hello" to no one in particular. The greeting was not returned, and her mother took her arm and led her to chairs on the end of the row where Gideon and Elizabeth were sitting.

The two exchanged a series of whispered comments and then fell quiet. Everyone sat in awkward silence, avoiding eye contact. No wonder the séances were so emotionally fraught.

People were a nervous wreck by the time they started.

Finally, the front door opened and a tall, middle-aged woman came in. She was dressed in a dark blue walking suit but still managed to look eccentric because she had added a scarlet scarf and wore a man's fedora. Many of the suffragists had adopted that style of hat, but it was still a bit outrageous, so he could be excused for staring a little longer than was necessary. She quickly found a seat at the end of the older couple's row.

Then the woman's sharp gaze took in the other occupants and finally rested on the mother and daughter. "Are you the one?" she asked the girl.

The girl was startled. "I beg your pardon."

"Are you the one? The one we came to see tonight?"

The girl exchanged a questioning look with her mother, and the older woman frowned her disapproval.

"I . . . I don't know what you're talking about," the girl finally said.

The tall woman huffed her disappointment and gave up her attempt to engage her, leaving the mother and daughter scowling.

After a few moments of continued silence, a door on the side of the room opened and a young woman came out. She wore the kind of dress his mother and Elizabeth wore when they went out to lunch, fancy but not formal, although the brown color was a bit dull, in his opinion.

"Good evening," she said, her glance touching each person in turn and hesitating only a moment longer on Gideon. "We'll begin in a moment, but first I'll speak to each of you individually."

"That's Persephone," Elizabeth whispered, although Gideon had already guessed. He watched in admiration as the girl made the rounds, collecting money from each person without the slightest awkwardness. When she came to them, he had pulled out his wallet, but she made a gesture that indicated he need not pay and then moved on without batting an eye.

"Madame Ophelia will receive you now," Persephone announced, opening the door at the back of the room.

The others filed out, but Elizabeth lingered. They had both stood up, and she looked up at him with what appeared to be genuine apprehension. "I'll be fine," she assured him.

"And I'll be right here. If you need me, just call out."

"Mr. Bates," Persephone said, hurrying over to them, "you must not interrupt the séance under any circumstances. If Madame Ophelia or . . . or someone else is in a trance, the effects could be disastrous."

"You may also hear someone call out,"

Elizabeth said, "but don't be alarmed. If I really need you, I'll call your name."

"And what if you faint?" he asked,

"Then Madame will call for me," Persephone said. "Don't worry. Everything will be fine. It always is."

Gideon could have argued with her, but he nodded because that was what he was supposed to do.

Elizabeth gave him a reassuring smile and followed Persephone into the séance room, leaving him to wait.

Only one chair remained vacant when Elizabeth entered the room. This time she would be seated directly across from Madame Ophelia, who was ensconced in her chair as usual. Tonight, she was dressed all in purple and a jewel of some kind glittered in the center of her turban. Plainly, this was a special occasion. The mother-and-daughter pair was seated to Elizabeth's right, with the daughter beside her and the mother beside Madame Ophelia.

The other three were on her left, with the tall woman next to Madame and the woman in the remaining couple beside Elizabeth. The tall woman was already reaching for the papers and pencils on the tray in the middle of the table.

"Shall we write our questions down?" the woman beside Elizabeth asked.

"Yes, please do," Madame said, giving the tall woman a sharp look, which she ignored.

"I don't know why I bother," the tall woman said. "I always ask the same question and I never get an answer."

"The spirits answer in their own time," Madame Ophelia said, earning an impatient glance from the tall woman.

Elizabeth jotted down her question and folded the paper, then glanced around the table again. This time she noticed that Madame had a few sheets of paper and a pencil lying on the table in front of her as well. How curious. She wouldn't ask about it, though. Why ruin Madame Ophelia's surprise? Elizabeth had known Madame would need to upstage her if she did go into a trance, and this was probably part of it.

When everyone had dropped their questions into Persephone's bag and the girl had ceremoniously burned them on the tray, Persephone withdrew, leaving them in the eerie half-light from the single lamp by the door. Poor Gideon, he must have been in a state. He did so hate having no part in this. She would have to think of something important for him to do. It was the only kind thing.

Madame began her humming and called for Peter a few times. "Spirits, are you there? Can you hear us?"

They all jumped when Madame let out a

dramatic groan. Then she said in a completely new voice, "Mother, are you there?"

"Andy, is that you?" the woman who had come in with her daughter asked almost desperately.

"It hurts. It hurts."

"Oh, Andy, what's wrong?" the woman asked. "I thought you'd be at peace."

"How can I be at peace? I left you alone with no one to look after you."

"I'm fine, really. I have Tilly." She glanced at the girl beside her, who was watching her mother intently and not very happily.

"Tilly," he scoffed. "How can she take care of you? You are helpless, the both of you."

"We're not helpless," Tilly said, earning an astonished stare from her mother. "I can look after Mother."

"You need a man to take care of you," Andy insisted. "I cannot rest until you are safe."

"Oh, Andy," his mother said. "You shouldn't worry about us, not if it keeps you from resting in peace."

"You must listen to me," Andy said. "I will send someone. He will find you. Listen to him."

Tilly, bless her, frowned ferociously, but her mother's eyes lit up with hope. "How will he find us? How will we know him?"

"You'll see. I will tell you when the time comes. I must go now."

132

"No, not yet," his mother begged. "Please, I want to ask you something."

But Madame Ophelia's head drooped, her chin resting on her chest for a long moment while she ignored the mother's pleading. Then the humming started again.

"Mama," Madame said, this time in a childish voice.

The woman on Elizabeth's left straightened to attention. "Cindy? Is that you?"

"Yes, Mama. What's wrong? You sound so sad."

"I'm sad because I miss you."

Her husband made a sound in his throat, and Elizabeth couldn't tell if he shared her grief or if he was protesting this charade.

"Don't be sad, Mama," Cindy said in her singsong voice. "I have lots of friends here. I'm very happy."

"Are you, my darling? I'm so glad."

Elizabeth winced when she saw the tears streaming down the woman's face.

"Papa? Are you there?" Cindy asked uncertainly.

The man looked up as if he expected to see his daughter hovering over the table. His face was awful to behold, a terrible mixture of hope and despair. "Y-yes."

"Papa, you must believe. I'm really here. I will send you a sign. You will hear from someone and you will know I sent them."

His despair transformed into naked pain, but his wife said, "Yes, darling, yes. Send someone to Papa so he will believe."

"I will, I will," Cindy promised as her voice faded away.

A long moment of silence followed. Madame wasn't even humming.

"What about me?" the tall woman said sharply, shocking everyone. "Your spirits keep promising to tell me what I want to know, but no one ever does. When are they going to speak to *me?*"

Elizabeth waited, giving Madame her chance.

Madame raised her head, eyes closed tightly. "Spirits, can you hear me? Are you there?"

And Elizabeth moaned and hissed, the long sibilant sound finally forming into a word. "SSSSS . . . Cybil? Is that you?"

CHAPTER SIX

E lizabeth heard the gasps but did not open her eyes.

"Yes, I'm here," Cybil said in apparent surprise. "Who are you?"

"SSSSS . . . Cybil, why do you torment me?"

"Uncle, is that you?" Cybil demanded.

"You must let me rest."

"I will! I promise, but first you have to tell me where you hid the will. I've looked everywhere and can't find it."

"I'm so tired," Elizabeth complained.

"I'm sure you are," Cybil said quite reasonably under the circumstances. "But if you'll just tell me where you hid the will, I swear I will never bother you again."

"So greedy . . ." Elizabeth muttered.

"How dare you say such a thing!" Cybil cried in outrage. "You left me your money for a reason."

"So impatient . . ."

"Just give me a clue!" Cybil almost shouted.

"Miss Miles, please," Cindy's mother soothed her.

"He's a cantankerous old fool," Cybil muttered.

"Don't offend him," Andy's mother warned.

Cybil sighed with long-suffering patience. "Just one clue, Uncle," she said in a somewhat strained but noticeably calmer voice.

Elizabeth moaned, causing everyone to tense, but then she said, "Fire . . . place."

"Which one?" Cybil asked.

"Bed . . . room."

Cybil's voice took on a rather desperate edge. "*Your* bedroom?"

"Yesssss," Elizabeth slurred. "Looosssse brick."

"Where?"

"Bottom. Right." Elizabeth moaned again and rocked her head from side to side. "Bottom. Right."

"Is that all?" Cybil asked urgently.

Elizabeth froze for a long moment, and then her eyes flew open. She turned to Andy's sister, Tilly, who was watching her with mingled fascination and horror. *"You,"* she barked, making everyone jump but especially Tilly. *"You* can take care of your mother. Trust no one else." Then she shuddered and her head dropped forward, chin resting on her chest as Madame Ophelia had done at the end of her spirit visitation.

She sat that way for a long moment until Tilly said, "Miss, are you all right?"

Before Elizabeth could decide whether to answer or not, Madame Ophelia cried out, "I'm getting a message."

"What is it?" Cindy's mother asked anxiously. "Is it for me?"

"Is it Andy?" his mother demanded.

Elizabeth shook herself again and roused with a small moan. No use in trying to steal the attention back. Her work was done, and besides, she wanted to see what Madame Ophelia was up to. She raised both hands to her face and opened her eyes. Everyone else was watching Madame scribbling on the paper that had been lying on the table beside her with the pencil that had been with it. Oddly, she was writing with her left hand and not even looking at the paper. Her eyes were blank, staring at nothing, and she held the rest of her body perfectly still.

"What is it? What's happening?" Elizabeth asked, not even needing to pretend she was confused.

"Spirit writing," Tilly whispered with what might have been disdain.

Whatever it was, it was impressive if what she was writing ended up making any sense.

After another minute or two, Madame stopped. The pencil fell from her fingers and she sighed wearily, sagging back in her chair.

"What does it say?" Cindy's mother demanded.

Andy's mother snatched up the paper and peered at it in the dim light. "I can't . . ." she said, squinting at it.

"Here," Tilly said impatiently, grabbing it from

her mother. She looked over the paper and then smiled slightly. "It says, 'Trust the words she speaks. They are the truth.' "

"Trust whose words?" Cindy's mother asked.

"Madame Ophelia's," Andy's mother guessed.

"But you always trust her words," Tilly said, still smiling smugly. "Why would the spirits need to confirm them? They must mean this lady. What's your name? You never told us."

"Mrs. Bates," Madame Ophelia quickly supplied, reminding everyone she was in charge.

"Are you supposed to be a medium, too?" Cindy's father asked, his doubt apparent.

"I have no idea," Elizabeth said. "I just . . . Did I say something? Did it happen again?"

"Mrs. Bates is just learning about her abilities," Madame Ophelia said. "I invited her here tonight to see if the spirits would speak through her once more."

"Once more?" Andy's mother echoed. "Have you done this before?"

"I . . . I don't know. They say I did," Elizabeth admitted.

"What do you mean, you don't know?" Cindy's father scoffed. "How can you not know?"

"I don't remember. What did I say this time?" She glanced around the table, meeting everyone's eye with a silent plea.

Finally, Cybil said, "You told me where my uncle's will is hidden."

"That's ridiculous," Elizabeth said. "How could I know a thing like that? I don't know you and I certainly don't know your uncle."

"You can't know him now, either, because he's dead, but he spoke through you and told me where it's hidden."

"Even if I did, how could whatever I told you be right?"

"That's true," Cindy's father said with a bit too much satisfaction. "She could have just made something up."

Cybil was undeterred. "Shall we vow to meet in a few days, after I've searched for the will again, and I can tell you if she was correct or not?"

Plainly, everyone wanted to do that very thing, if their hopeful expressions were any indication. Even Cindy's doubting father looked eager. Elizabeth shrugged helplessly. "Why would you even believe me?"

"I don't suppose I can, not really, but I've been here twice before, asking that same question," Cybil said, "and this is the first time anyone tried to answer it. It's easy enough to check, too. I'll go to my uncle's house tomorrow and find out."

"When shall we meet again, then?" Tilly asked.

"Sunday?" Cybil asked.

"We can't hold a séance on a Sunday," Andy's mother declared, as if that were some well-known rule. Elizabeth wondered exactly what objection the woman could have. Did she consider a séance too pagan to conduct on the Sabbath? And if so, why was it acceptable to hold on another day? But there was no use trying to apply logic to this, as she well knew.

"I have a previous engagement on Monday evening," Cybil said. "I can join you on Tuesday evening, however."

After a few minutes of discussion, they set the date and time. Madame summoned Persephone and she began to escort everyone out. Before Elizabeth could rise, Tilly laid her hand on Elizabeth's arm to stop her.

"Did you really mean what you said about me?"

Elizabeth frowned. "I'm sorry. I have no idea what I said about you. I hope it wasn't hurtful."

"Not at all," Tilly said with another of her smug smiles. "You said—"

"Tilly," her mother said sharply. "We must go."

Tilly waved away her mother's concern with a flip of her hand, her gaze never leaving Elizabeth's face. "You said I could take care of my mother."

"Then it must be true, mustn't it? The spirits don't lie," Elizabeth lied.

Tilly seemed to grow taller, even though they were still sitting down. "No, they don't," she said, her eyes twinkling as if they shared a secret.

"Tilly," her mother snapped. "Leave Mrs. Bates alone."

Elizabeth and Tilly exchanged one more glance

140

of understanding before Tilly obeyed her mother and followed her out. Then only she and Madame Ophelia remained.

"Do you still doubt your powers?" Madame asked.

"I suppose we'll have to wait until next Tuesday to find out, won't we?"

"I suppose we will. But if you are right—"

"If I am right, then we'll talk. Until then, I just want to forget all about this." Elizabeth rose from her chair and hurried out to the waiting room. Poor Gideon was the center of attention as everyone tried to explain to him what had happened and how she had given Miss Miles the answer she had been seeking. Miss Miles was the most enthusiastic of all of them, babbling about her good fortune and how important it was to find her uncle's will because otherwise his fortune would be inherited by his no-good son, who would squander it while she intended to use it for good works.

When Gideon saw Elizabeth, he rudely turned his back on the others and pushed his way to her side. "Are you all right?"

"I'm very tired," she admitted. "Would you take me home?"

"Of course." He tucked her hand into the crook of his arm and escorted her past her admiring fans out to the quiet of the sidewalk.

"Well?" he whispered when they were far

enough away from the door not to be overheard.

"I think it went fine."

Jake had been waiting in the shadows for a while when he finally saw the girl come out the front door of the storefront and begin to lock it. He started down the deserted sidewalk at a reasonable pace, and then speeded up as if just catching sight of her, hurrying to reach her before she walked away.

"Wait!" he called.

She looked up startled as he skidded to a halt beside her.

"Am I too late? Are you closed?"

She smiled politely as she pulled the key from the lock. "I'm afraid we are. Did you want to schedule a sitting?"

"I . . . Yes, I, uh, I wanted to find out more about it, but I wasn't sure. . . . So I was thinking and trying to decide, but I guess I thought too long and missed my chance."

"We'll be here tomorrow morning, and you can come back then," the girl said helpfully.

"I can't come in the daytime. I have to work."

"I see. Well, you could—"

"Are you her? Are you the Madame?" he asked, and then clapped his hand over his mouth in embarrassment. "That didn't sound right, did it? I meant, are you this Madame O . . . How do you say that name?"

"Ophelia," she said, smiling a little at his awkwardness.

"Ophelia," he repeated, trying the name out for size. "Are you Madame Ophelia?"

"No, I'm merely her assistant," the girl said modestly.

Now that he'd had a chance to look her over, he realized she wasn't bad. Nice face, good figure. This shouldn't be too hard. "If you're her assistant, then maybe you can answer my questions."

She looked up and down the dark street meaningfully. "It's getting late."

"I guess this isn't the place for a chat, is it? But maybe I could walk with you. You shouldn't be out alone this time of night anyway."

"I don't have far to go," she said.

"And I don't have many questions. Would you mind? I'm a customer, after all. Well, maybe I am, depending on your answers."

"I suppose." She turned and started walking. He fell into step beside her. "What did you want to know?"

"I wondered what happens, at a séance I mean. How do the right spirits know you're looking for them?"

"No one knows how they do it. They just do."

Jake couldn't argue with that, and he didn't even want to. "How many times would I have to come? I mean, if I got the answers I'm looking for the first time, I wouldn't have to come back, would I?"

"Most people find comfort in contacting their loved ones, so they usually return. It can also take time to contact them in the first place."

Of course, it did. "I guess that's to be expected, but you see, I don't . . . I mean, how much does it cost?"

"Madame charges twenty dollars for a sitting if you attend with a group. Individual readings cost more, naturally."

Jake whistled. "Twenty dollars. That's a lot."

"Madame Ophelia has a rare talent. She must charge accordingly," she said primly.

"Oh, I'm sure she does," he hastily agreed. "It's just . . . Well, I don't know how many of these sittings I could afford."

"It would be worth every sacrifice."

He thought that over for a moment. "But wait. You said you're her assistant, didn't you?"

They had reached the corner and stopped to check for traffic. She looked up at him warily. "That's right."

"Then maybe you could do a séance for me. You know how to do it, don't you?"

"Yes, but—"

"I'd be very grateful. I just need to ask my mother one thing, something really important, but it's just one thing. Couldn't you do that,

Miss . . . ? I'm sorry. I didn't even introduce myself. I'm John Miller."

"I'm Pen . . . Persephone Highland."

"What a pretty name, Miss Highland. Persephone was a goddess, wasn't she?" He gave her his most winning smile.

She smiled back in the light of the corner streetlamp, obviously pleased that he knew this. He'd have to thank Anna. Persephone was almost pretty when she smiled. "Yes, a minor goddess, Mr. Miller, but I'm sorry. I can't help you."

"Doesn't Madame O let you do séances yourself?"

"I don't have the gift, you see. Not just anyone can contact the spirits."

He considered this amazing statement for a moment. "I guess that's probably right. Otherwise, everybody would be doing it, and I wouldn't be chasing after pretty girls in the street in the dark of night to beg them for help."

She lowered her gaze at the pretty-girls comment, and he thought she might have even been blushing. He couldn't tell for sure in this poor light. "I'd like to help you, Mr. Miller, but I'm afraid I just can't. You can come to see Madame Ophelia, though."

"She's not always there in the evenings, though, is she? I tried the other night and no one was there."

"No, she mostly sees clients during the day."

"I guess her clients don't have to work for a living," he said sadly.

"No, because she sees mostly ladies."

He nodded in resignation, then seemed to remember his original mission. "Which way do you go from here?"

She pointed to the opposite corner, and after checking the light traffic, they crossed the street.

"What do you do for a living, Mr. Miller?" she asked him.

"Nothing very exciting. I work for a brokerage house."

As he had expected, she perked up at that. "What does one do at a brokerage house?"

"I advise people on how to invest their money."

Now he had her full attention. "You seem young to be doing such important work."

"I have the whole brokerage house behind me. They tell us what to recommend, and if we get it wrong, well, our clients don't expect to win every single time, do they?"

"I don't suppose they do."

"Say, it just occurred to me that your Madame O could really do well if the spirits could tell her what to invest in."

That seemed to amuse her. "And *you* could do very well if they told you how to advise your clients."

"I never thought of that, but you're right. Can they do that?" he asked hopefully.

"I don't know. I doubt it has ever been tried."

Jake was pretty sure it had been, but he grinned. "Maybe I should suggest it to Madame O. If the spirits helped me, I might be able to afford a séance or two."

"Yes, you might."

He'd already taken a few more steps when he realized she had stopped at the entrance to an apartment building. He turned back.

"This is where I live," she said somewhat apologetically. "Thank you for escorting me."

"I was happy to do it, even though you couldn't help me."

"But perhaps I can, after all. I think Madame Ophelia would be very interested in speaking with you. Why don't you come by the shop tomorrow? Could you come around three o'clock? Not for a séance, but just to talk?"

"I could probably do that. Do you think she'd do a sitting for me for free?"

"I think she might do even more than that for you, Mr. Miller."

"How do you suppose she did that spirit writing?" Anna asked. She had arrived at Elizabeth's front door as early as was considered reasonable on Saturday morning. Gideon and Mother Bates had joined them in the parlor while Elizabeth recounted her adventures of the night before to Anna, even though she had already told her

147

husband and her mother-in-law every single detail after she and Gideon got home last night.

"I don't know for sure, but I'd guess it's just a matter of practice, learning how to write without looking," Elizabeth said.

"But she used her left hand," Anna marveled.

"Some people prefer using their left hand," Mother Bates said. "I had a friend who always wanted to write with her left hand, but the teacher would come by and smack her with a ruler and force her to use her right."

"That happened to some friends of mine as well," Gideon said. "But of course everyone must use their right hand to write, so they had to conform."

"I wonder who decided that," Elizabeth mused.

"Some man," Mother Bates guessed.

"So maybe Madame Ophelia is one of those people and she uses that ability to amaze people," Anna said.

"Or maybe she just trained herself to write with her left hand," Elizabeth said. "It doesn't really matter. I'm more concerned with why she chose to confirm my prediction."

"Yes," Gideon agreed, "especially because it will affect her credibility if it turns out you're wrong."

"I wondered about that, too," Mother Bates said. "She's taking a big chance, isn't she?"

"Not really," Elizabeth said with a smile. "First of all, as we know, I won't be wrong."

"She doesn't know that, though," Gideon reminded her.

"And secondly, no one will remember she confirmed my predictions. They might not even remember if my predictions turned out to be wrong."

"Are you serious?" Mother Bates scoffed. "Of course they'll remember."

"People only remember what they choose to remember, and most people choose to remember the things that confirm what they want to believe. Everyone at the séance wanted to believe I knew where the uncle's will was hidden, so they'll remember that."

"And I imagine they'll be thrilled when it turns out you were right," Anna said.

"And they'll tell all their friends, thereby increasing Madame Ophelia's reputation," Gideon said with more than a hint of disapproval.

"Which I suppose is why she's so anxious for you to be right," Mother Bates said.

"How is Cybil going to prove she found the will?" Anna asked.

"Most people will simply take her word for it, but she's going on a journey today, mainly to find out if she's being followed. If she is, she will lose her pursuer and disappear for several hours before returning home. That will verify for anyone who doubts that she went to her uncle's house and found the will."

"How will she know if she's being followed?" Mother Bates asked.

"Cybil would probably know if someone was following her, but the Old Man will be traveling the same route behind her just in case. Between the two of them, they're bound to notice."

"This seems like a lot of trouble to take," Gideon said. "Why would someone follow Cybil at all?"

"Madame Ophelia probably doesn't trust me yet," Elizabeth explained patiently. "She'll want to make sure I'm not in cahoots with Cybil somehow."

"I suppose that means you won't be attending the salon for a while," Anna said.

"What a tragedy," Gideon said with a sly smile.

"You should probably stay away as well, Anna," Elizabeth said. "Madame Ophelia might well discover that Cybil is a professor at Hunter, but there's no reason to encourage her to think you are close friends with Cybil and Zelda."

"Speaking of Miss Goodnight," Gideon said in all innocence, "will she be participating?"

"I thought she might be your maiden aunt, darling," Elizabeth teased him back. "She's trying to contact her lover who died in the Spanish-America War."

"She would love that," Anna said with a grin.

"But I'm afraid Madame Ophelia wouldn't trust anyone closely related to Gideon," Elizabeth said.

"Thank heaven," Gideon said fervently. "So what happens next?"

"That depends on Madame Ophelia," Elizabeth said. "I know what we'll be doing."

"Won't you have to adapt to what Madame Ophelia does, though?" Anna asked.

Elizabeth smiled. "Perhaps, but I'm pretty sure I already know what she is going to do."

Gideon nodded sagely. "The spirits probably told her."

Elizabeth rewarded him with a kiss on the cheek. "Of course, they did, darling."

Jake entered Madame Ophelia's lair just as the city's clocks were chiming three. He was a little surprised at how grim the place was. He'd expected something fancy with scrolled couches and artwork on the walls. But maybe mediums didn't like to flaunt their ill-gotten gains. The Old Man's offices behind Dan the Dude's saloon weren't the least bit fancy, either, now that he thought about it.

The room was empty, as he'd expected. He'd seen the afternoon séance attendees leaving a little while ago. He fidgeted a bit, rubbing his hands on his pant legs as if they were sweaty, and looking around uncertainly. After a few minutes,

151

one of the two doors opened and Persephone came out.

She was wearing a pea green dress today that made her look a little bilious, but he smiled as if he thought her enchanting.

"Hello, Mr. Miller," she said, apparently finding him enchanting as well.

"Hello, Miss Highland. I hope this is a good time."

"It's exactly the right time," she assured him. "Madame Ophelia is anxious to meet you."

She led him through the other door into the back room, which was obviously where the séances were held. Madame Ophelia was an old bat of a woman all done up in some foreign-looking robe with a ridiculous turban on her head. Some kind of feather was pinned to the front of it and it fluttered every time she moved her head.

"Madame, this is Mr. John Miller, the gentleman I told you about," Persephone said.

"I am so pleased you have come, Mr. Miller. Please sit down here so we can converse."

She patted the table in front of the empty chair immediately to her left, so he sat down. Persephone, he noted, had slipped out, leaving them alone. "Thanks for seeing me," he said, glancing around. This room was even less appealing than the waiting area, and the dim light from the single lamp cast unflattering shadows over Madame Ophelia's face.

"Persephone said you are interested in contacting your dear mother," Madame said.

"That's right. She . . . Well, I need to ask her something."

"It is unfortunate that so many of us find ourselves in exactly that situation, but I suppose we never expect our loved ones to pass. We always think we will have plenty of time with them."

He brightened at that. "You're right. I never thought I'd lose her so soon."

"How long has she been gone?"

"Uh, about five years now, I think." He took a minute. "That's right, five years in a few months."

"You must have been very young when she died."

He hadn't felt young then, but he supposed he had been. "She was young, too. Too young to die anyway."

"You must miss her very much."

Not really. Sometimes he'd recall something happy, but not often. Lizzie had good memories of her mother, but Jake hadn't been so lucky. "I have my memories," he managed.

"I'm sure you do, and you want to know that she is at peace."

If she was, it would be the first time, but he said, "That would be a comfort."

Madame nodded sagely. "Persephone also mentioned you were concerned about the cost of a séance."

He shifted in his chair, as if mention of his financial situation was uncomfortable. "I do have a good job, and I make a good salary, but . . ." He shrugged.

"I understand completely. You are a young man, just starting out in life. I understand you work for some sort of bank."

"A brokerage house. We help our clients invest their money."

She smiled her understanding. "So *they* are wealthy enough to afford many séances."

"I never thought of it like that, but yes, I suppose you're right."

"And if your clients do well, you do well, too. Is that not right?"

"Yes, I . . . I get paid a commission on what they invest."

She nodded. "And suppose you knew confidential information about what investments would be especially profitable?"

He hadn't really expected this, so he didn't have to pretend to be surprised. "Are you saying you can . . . ?" He caught himself before blurting out the unvarnished truth and chose diplomacy instead. "Where would I get this confidential information?"

Madame smiled benignly. "If you are thinking the spirits would reveal it, you are mistaken. The spirits take no interest in such things."

"Why not?"

She blinked in surprise but quickly regained her composure. "Perhaps I spoke too bluntly. The spirits are interested in helping their loved ones, but they do so by sending emissaries to them."

"What's an emissary?"

"A representative, someone who can advise them in certain matters."

"Somebody like you, you mean?"

"I do not give that kind of advice. As I said, the spirits do not know these things. But they send the emissaries to their loved ones. My task is only to announce them."

"And how do you do that?"

"I see you do not understand how these things work. The spirits speak through me. They send messages to their loved ones. They tell them that someone will enter their lives and present an opportunity to them."

Jake shook his head, as if none of this was making sense. "What does any of this have to do with me?"

Madame reached over and patted his hands where they were folded on the table. "You, my boy, may be an emissary."

Jake frowned. "You mean the spirits could tell me how to advise my clients?"

"Yes, the spirits would tell you through me."

"So they do know these things," he concluded.

Madame waved that thought away. "In a manner of speaking. It is all very mysterious.

All I can tell you is that if you will advise your clients to see me, the spirits will benefit them and you as well."

Jake rubbed a hand over his face. "I don't understand any of this."

"As I said, it is all very mysterious. I can tell you only what I have seen. Others have made themselves available, and they have profited from it."

"I didn't come here to find out how to make more money," he protested.

"Why did you come?" she asked gently.

"I told you. I need to contact my mother."

"To ask her a question, yes. What is that question?"

"I . . . I'd rather wait and ask her directly," he said, not quite meeting her gaze.

"Ah, I understand. It is an embarrassing question, then."

"Not embarrassing, just . . . Well, I'd just rather wait."

"Then you must attend a séance and ask your question. We will see if your mother can answer it."

"But I already told you—"

"Yes, I know. You cannot afford it, but I will do this as a gift to you. I will not charge you at all. You can come to one of my séances and ask your question. If you receive your answer, you will know the spirits are real and you will believe me when I tell you how you can help them."

"You'd let me come to a séance for free?" Jake said skeptically.

"It would be an honor. I believe you were sent here for a reason. Nothing gives me greater satisfaction than helping people find the answers they seek."

Jake doubted that very much. He asked her a few more questions but received little new information. Finally, Madame Ophelia sent him back to the waiting area to make arrangements with Persephone to attend a séance in the coming week.

He'd have to check with Lizzie to make sure no one he knew would be attending at the time Persephone scheduled him, but he thought he'd managed to avoid any conflicts by agreeing to attend the Monday afternoon session.

"I'm still a little worried about all this," he confided to Persephone when she had written his name in the appointment book. He'd managed to peer over her shoulder and didn't recognize any of the other names for that session, but people didn't usually use their real names when they were running a con.

"You don't need to be apprehensive, Mr. Miller," Persephone said.

"I know but . . . Do you suppose you could explain to me what's going to happen?"

She glanced uneasily at the door that led to the séance room, signaling her reluctance.

"Not here," he quickly added. "I could . . . I mean, if you'd like, I could buy you supper or something. I know a nice quiet restaurant where we could talk. If I just knew what to expect . . ." He gave her the smile that usually worked on females.

It worked on Persephone, or else she wanted to have supper with him, too. "That would be very nice. I'm sure Madame wouldn't mind if I described a typical séance to you."

"I'd be very grateful, Miss Highland. And I wouldn't have to eat supper by myself. I don't know many people in the city, and it can get pretty lonely."

Her expression softened or perhaps it just grew more interested. "We can't let you be lonely, can we?"

"Should I call for you here?" he asked eagerly.

She glanced at the door again. "Uh, no. Do you remember which building I live in?"

"Sure."

"Call for me there at six thirty. I'll look forward to it." She smiled.

"I'll look forward to it, too."

CHAPTER SEVEN

Persephone had changed into something much more becoming by the time Jake called for her at her apartment house. Plainly, she considered this an occasion. He'd wondered how he would find her, but she was waiting by the door when he arrived. That way he wouldn't know which apartment was hers, he supposed. Women had to be careful.

"It's very nice of you to do this," he said as they started down the sidewalk. The city was crowded with pedestrians returning home or going out for the evening, and the streets were clogged with horses and wagons jostling for position between the motorcars whose drivers obviously felt sounding a horn entitled them to do anything.

"I told you. I'm happy to help. Not many clients offer to take me out to dinner, after all."

"Since you told me most of your clients are wealthy ladies, I'm not surprised."

She smiled at that. "You said you don't know many people in the city. How long have you lived here?"

"Only a few months."

"Where are you from then?"

"South Dakota," he said with an apologetic grin.

Her eyes widened in surprise. "That's a long way. How did you end up in New York?"

"My father had some . . . some business contacts here. One of his old friends gave me a job."

They had to stop conversing to concentrate on crossing the street without being run over, and when they reached the other side, Jake directed her to a small Italian restaurant he had discovered. He had already tipped the waiter to greet him like a regular customer and show them to a table in a quiet corner. Persephone seemed impressed.

"They know me here," he whispered unnecessarily. He ordered a bottle of wine, thinking that might help loosen Persephone's tongue a bit, and spaghetti and meatballs for both of them.

When the waiter delivered the wine, Jake poured them each a glass.

"So," Jake said, leaning forward to demonstrate his interest, "what happens at a séance?"

Persephone briefly explained the procedure of sitting around a table, writing the questions, and burning them.

"If you burn them without looking at them, how does Madame Ophelia know what questions were asked?"

"She doesn't need to know. The spirits know and they are the ones who answer."

"I thought Madame Ophelia answered."

Persephone gave him a smile reflecting infinite patience with his ignorance. "The spirits speak through her."

"That must be strange."

"She does speak in a different voice, or maybe that is the spirit's voice. At any rate, you can tell when it's the spirit. Her spirit guide is a German monk."

Jake didn't have to pretend to be surprised by this. "What does a spirit guide do?"

She pretended to consider this question. "I'm still learning about this myself, of course, but there are millions of spirits from all the people who have already died. It would be impossible for a mere mortal to commune with all of them, so the spirit guide relays the messages from the appropriate ones."

"Oh, that's kind of what I do."

Persephone thought this was amusing. "Are you a spirit guide, Mr. Miller?"

"Please call me John, and no, I don't guide spirits, but I do guide my clients in a way. There are many ways for them to invest their money, so I investigate them and direct the clients to the soundest opportunities."

"That must be a huge responsibility."

He shrugged. "Let's just say my clients don't tolerate too many mistakes."

"And you have others helping you, I think you said."

"Yes, men with more experience. They advise the younger men."

"What would happen if you discovered an opportunity yourself? Would the more experienced men take your advice in return?"

He pretended to consider this. "I . . . I haven't encountered anything like that, but if it looked good, they probably would."

"And would they advise their clients to invest as well?"

"Probably." Then he grinned. "Is this what Madame Ophelia was talking about? Does she think the spirits will tell me about some great offering that I can pass along to my clients?"

"I just know that several of Madame's clients have received messages that helped them financially."

The waiter delivered their dinners at that moment, so Jake had some time to decide what to say next.

"This looks delicious," she said.

Jake hoped it was since he was supposedly a regular customer. "Let's make a toast," he said, raising his glass. Persephone, he'd noticed, hadn't touched her wine. "To the spirits and prosperity."

She lifted her glass and clinked it with his, but she took only a small sip. She was obviously too well trained to take a chance on losing control.

He gave her a few minutes to get started on her

dinner. The food was better than expected, and he enjoyed it himself.

"You must have been very close to your mother," she said to break the silence.

" 'A boy's best friend is his mother,' right?" he quoted wryly.

"Are you saying that isn't true for you?" she asked with apparent surprise.

"No, but I wasn't as close to her as you seem to assume."

She laid her fork down and frowned in concern. "I suppose it's a natural assumption, since you said you wanted to contact her."

"I only said I wanted to ask her a question. You were the one who said your clients like to come back again and again to talk to their loved ones, but I don't think I'll want to."

"Oh my, I'm sorry. I had no idea."

"Do your clients usually have happy reunions with their dead family members?"

Plainly, she didn't want to answer that. "Sometimes it can be . . . painful," she admitted. "Do you think your reunion with your mother will be painful?"

"I hope not, but that depends on her, doesn't it?"

"Was she, uh, difficult?"

"Difficult" was a good description, but he didn't want to give too much away. "She wasn't easy to get along with, but she's been gone a long time now."

"And you've come to terms with her memory. I'm glad you're trying to reach her. That can help a lot. Often you discover that the departed person is sorry for what they've done in life."

"Is there still a chance for them to get into heaven if they make amends?" he asked with a smirk.

"There is no heaven or hell in the afterlife," she said so solemnly that he knew this must have been a sacred tenet of spiritualists or at least something they spouted to their clients to make them feel better.

"Are you saying there's no point in trying to be good, then?" he teased.

"I think you will be happier in the afterlife if you have no regrets," she said with a small smile. She picked up her fork and started eating again.

"But if it wasn't for the regrets, you and Madame Ophelia would be out of business," he said, startling her.

"I never thought of it that way before."

"Neither did I, but I never thought about spirits and afterlives before, either."

She frowned thoughtfully. "I guess it's just human to have regrets. We can't be perfect no matter how hard we try."

"No, we can't, but if we aren't sorry for what we do, we won't have any regrets, either."

"Is that how you usually live your life?" she challenged.

It was, of course, but he managed a sheepish smile. "I'm afraid not. I usually regret most of the things I do."

She gave him an encouraging smile. "I'm sure you won't regret consulting Madame Ophelia."

Since he had rarely regretted helping Lizzie with her do-gooder projects, he had to agree.

Elizabeth, Gideon, and Mother Bates had just settled into a pew the next morning at church when a familiar young man sat down in front of them.

"Aren't you afraid lightning will strike you?" Elizabeth asked her brother softly, knowing the somber tones of the organ prelude would enable her to speak to him without being overheard.

"I needed to see you, and I couldn't take a chance in case they're watching one or both of us," he said without turning around.

"Why would they be watching you?" Gideon asked, but Elizabeth had already guessed.

"You're not supposed to get involved in this," she reminded him fiercely.

He shrugged one shoulder. "I can't help myself. Your charity cons are so much fun."

"And so profitable for you, too," Elizabeth reminded him, in case he wanted to pretend to be righteous because he was in church.

He glanced at her over his shoulder, not looking a bit chagrined. "I took Persephone to dinner last night."

Elizabeth glared at the back of his head, which was totally wasted since he couldn't see her.

"Your brother is turning into a regular . . . What's the word I'm looking for?" Gideon said.

"Gigolo," Elizabeth said, taking pleasure in Jake's shoulders hunching in reaction.

"I don't think so," Mother Bates said sweetly. "Perhaps 'ladies' man' is more appropriate."

"I told her I work for a brokerage house and I want to contact my mother, so she's going to try to con me. Madame Ophelia has already started telling me the tale," Jake said, ignoring Elizabeth's jibe.

"You can't go to a séance," Elizabeth whispered anxiously, leaning forward a little until Gideon nudged her back to awareness. "Too many of the clients know you."

"I'm going on Monday afternoon, and nobody scheduled then knows me."

Her mind was racing with visions of how this could all go very wrong, but before she could say another word, the congregation rose for the opening hymn and all opportunity for discussion passed.

Elizabeth heard very little of the sermon as she considered what Jake's involvement could be and whether it would help or hurt her scheme. By the time the closing hymn ended, she had reasoned herself into acceptance.

After the benediction, Jake turned to go and

166

Gideon stopped him to shake hands, pretending to introduce himself and welcome Jake, who was obviously a visitor. Then he introduced Elizabeth and Mother Bates.

"Just don't show up on Tuesday evening," Elizabeth said as she shook his hand. "Cybil will be there, and we don't want to surprise her."

"The Old Man will warn her I'll be around."

Gideon coughed to cover a laugh. "Have you got him involved in this, too?"

"Just to deliver my messages," Jake said with a smirk. "So nice to meet you," he added loudly enough to be overheard by people passing down the aisle on their way out.

"We hope to see you again," Elizabeth replied with just a hint of sarcasm.

"I'm sure you will," he said smugly, and sauntered out.

"This is like a family reunion," Gideon remarked.

"I should have known Jake couldn't just sit by while Anna was being cheated," Elizabeth said.

"You're right," Mother Bates said. "I hadn't thought of it that way, but of course Jake would want to help her."

"Yes, it's quite noble of him to cheat the medium out of a lot of money to protect his good friend," Gideon said.

"Really, darling, when you say it like that, it

doesn't sound noble at all," Elizabeth told him with a grin.

"I didn't think so, either," Gideon assured her.

Jake pretended to be nervous when he arrived at Madame Ophelia's storefront on Monday afternoon. Actually, he was excited.

Persephone greeted him with a big smile. "You made it."

He glanced around as if checking for spies. "I had to tell my boss I was seeing a client. If they catch me, I'll be fired."

"They won't catch you, and you won't be fired, not after . . . Well, I'm sure you won't be sorry you came. Have a seat. We're just waiting for everyone to arrive."

Persephone moved away to greet two old ladies who had just arrived, walking arm and arm. They might have been holding each other up. A couple middle-aged ladies were already there. They sat on opposite sides of the room, carefully not making eye contact with anyone else, especially not with each other.

Jake wondered what the etiquette was for séance attendees. Should he introduce himself or would that be considered forward? Or was it rude not to? He tried smiling at one of the middle-aged ladies, but she just averted her eyes, as if he'd done something obscene, so he chose a chair a respectable distance from her and ignored her in return.

The two old ladies took chairs beside each other and started jabbering to each other about things that only made sense to them, he supposed. As the appointed time came and went with no new arrivals, he had to assume he would be the only male in the group. So much the better.

After a while, Persephone went around and collected a fee from everyone except him. Did the ladies wonder at that? He did earn some sharp glances. Then she called them into the séance room.

Jake was seated across from Madame Ophelia. The two old ladies were on his left and the middle-aged ladies on his right.

"We have someone new with us today," Madame Ophelia said. "Mr. Miller is hoping to contact his mother."

All the ladies turned to him, but he saw no welcome in their eyes. Instead, they looked at him as if they had just learned the special pie would be divided five ways instead of four, and they weren't happy about it.

After being instructed to do so, they all wrote down their questions. Jake had given his question some thought, and he scribbled *Why did you do it?* on the paper. It was, he believed, vague enough so he was unlikely to get a specific answer and yet dramatic enough to keep Madame Ophelia interested. He folded it carefully as the others were doing to theirs and dropped it into the bag Persephone passed. He gave her an apprehensive glance as he did so, and she responded with an encouraging smile. She must have thought he could bring them a lot of money.

He had to admit that burning the papers that supposedly had the questions on them was a pretty impressive trick. He even managed a gasp, much to the amusement of the ladies.

Then Persephone left the room and Madame Ophelia asked them to concentrate so she could contact the spirits. Jake didn't bother to concentrate. He was too busy watching the other people around the table. Madame hummed for a while, swaying slightly in her chair to give Persephone time to unfold all the questions and start reading them to her through the telephone line.

One of the middle-aged ladies needed some advice. Would her late husband approve of her selling their house? Of course, he would, because then she would have a nice sum of money to be conned out of. The two old ladies wanted their late brother to guide them in deciding to whom they should leave their fortune. The spirits promised someone would appear to help them.

As he had expected, Madame Ophelia had saved him for last. "John. John," Madame said in a new voice, which was weak and whispery.

"Yes," Jake said uncertainly. "I'm here. Who's there?"

"It is I, your mother," Madame said.

Even though he knew it was all fake and the voice sounded nothing like his mother's familiar screech, he still felt a chill go up his spine. It was all rather thrilling. No wonder people did this. "Mother?" he tried.

"John. My sweet boy. I'm sorry."

Jake had never been a sweet boy, and he doubted that his mother had ever been sorry about anything, but it was certainly nice to hear. "Are you?" he asked a little skeptically.

"Soooo sorry," the voice wailed. "Can you forgive?"

"I . . . don't know," he decided.

Another wordless wail that made everyone jump and Madame threw her head back in reaction. Her turban must have been very securely fastened because it didn't fall off.

"You should forgive her," the old lady on his left said urgently. "Give her some peace."

"She still hasn't told me why she did it," he replied. "If she tells me that, then I'll know if I can forgive her."

Madame moaned and bowed her head, her shoulders slumping wearily. Plainly, she was finished delivering messages.

"Isn't there anything for me?" the other middle-aged lady demanded. She was the only one to whom the spirits had not yet spoken.

"Mother, are you still there?" Jake called out as if he really expected an answer.

Madame didn't speak for a full minute. Then she slowly raised her head and looked around. "Oh my, you do not look pleased. Did someone receive bad news?"

"I didn't receive any news at all," the neglected lady said.

"I cannot control the spirits, you know," Madame said apologetically. "If they choose not to speak, it is not my fault. Mr. Miller, did you make a connection?"

"I guess," he admitted.

"He wouldn't forgive his mother even though she said she was sorry," one of the elderly ladies said venomously.

Madame gave him a sympathetic smile. "Sometimes it is difficult to be reunited with our loved ones. I hope you received the answer you sought."

"Not really," he said.

"I am sorry to hear it, but the spirits can be stubborn."

"She was probably just hurt," the old lady insisted. "I wouldn't talk to you, either."

Jake wasn't sure how he should respond to that, so he didn't say anything.

Madame Ophelia summoned Persephone to see

everyone out. Being a gentleman, Jake allowed the ladies to precede him, and before he reached the door, Madame Ophelia called his name.

"May I have a moment, Mr. Miller?"

Jake returned with a show of reluctance. His experience had been less than satisfactory, so he wouldn't be anxious to stay.

"Please sit down." When he had taken the chair to her left as he had during their first meeting, she said, "Do you believe you contacted your mother?" Jake had to admit she looked like she really didn't know what had happened.

"It seemed like I did, but she didn't really answer my question, so I can't be sure."

"Mrs. Anderson said she asked for your forgiveness."

"That's what it sounded like."

"The spirits don't think the way we do, and sometimes their messages to us are not what we want but rather what we need to hear."

"So you think I needed to hear that she was sorry?" he asked skeptically.

"Perhaps she needed to tell you."

"It's too late to make amends."

"Are you sure? Wouldn't you like to make peace with her even now?"

Which was, he had to admit, a very intriguing question, and the answer could easily lead to many return trips to the land of the spirits at twenty dollars apiece. "I'm not really sure it would change anything even if I really could make peace with her."

"So you still doubt that you were in contact with your mother?"

He made a helpless gesture. "How can I know for sure? Even if that was a spirit talking to me, how do I know it was my mother? There are probably a million spirits, maybe more, and some of them might be troublemakers trying to trick people."

"I can see you are a thinking man," she said, nodding sagely. "You want to believe but you are not easily persuaded."

"I'm not gullible, if that's what you mean."

"You are wise to question. Perhaps your mother will send you a sign to prove her sincerity."

He frowned his concern. "What kind of a sign?" A message in a whiskey bottle, maybe.

"I do not know, but I have seen the spirits take matters into their own hands when they are anxious to make contact."

Jake sighed. "If that happens, I'll be back to see you again. Until then, thanks for an interesting afternoon."

She let him go without another word.

Persephone was waiting in the front room. Everyone else had gone. She smiled wanly. "I guess it didn't go as well as you hoped."

"I don't know what I expected, but I didn't get the answer I was looking for."

174

"Then you'll be coming back," she guessed.

"I don't think so. My mother is just the type to string me along for months. I hated it when she was alive, and I don't have to put up with it now that she's dead, so I'm not going to."

She looked genuinely disappointed. Either she was thinking about the money they would lose or she had started to like him. He wanted to think it was the latter, but he was probably wrong. "What did Madame Ophelia say to you afterward?"

"She seemed to think my mother's spirit would try to contact me some other way to prove she was real or something."

"Yes, that does happen. You would be amazed how involved the spirits can be in our lives."

"I would definitely be amazed because I'm still not sure this is real," he said with a small smile.

She smiled back. "We love convincing unbelievers, and just imagine if the spirits began to advise you in your business. You could be the most successful stockbroker in New York."

"Madame Ophelia already told me the spirits don't do things like that."

"They have their own ways of helping the ones they choose. You just need to have a little faith."

"Right now I don't have very much."

"At least promise me that if you get some sort of sign, you'll return and tell us. Madame Ophelia will want to know, and so will I."

"I promise," he said with mock solemnity.

"And I wouldn't mind seeing you again even if you don't get a sign," she added shyly.

"Really? You weren't just being nice to me because you wanted my business?" he asked with creditable amazement.

"Really." She gave him a hopeful smile.

"Then I'll see you again for sure, but not until I've given the spirits a chance to convince me."

"That's fair enough. I will look forward to seeing you again, John."

Which was good because she certainly would.

"President Wilson has called a special session of congress to vote on the Woman Suffrage Amendment," Mother Bates announced as Gideon entered the parlor. He had just returned home from work, and while Elizabeth had come out to greet him, as usual, she had left it to his mother to make the announcement.

"That's wonderful news," Gideon said. "I assume he's encouraging congress to pass it this time."

"That's what he claims," his mother said. "I'm afraid I don't really trust his change of heart, after he had the protesters jailed so many times, but he says the suffragists convinced him of their patriotism with their volunteer work during the war."

"And don't forget the little girl who supposedly gave him a bouquet of flowers when he returned

176

from the peace talks," Elizabeth said. "He swears that changed his heart."

"Yellow flowers, I assume," Gideon said with a smile. Yellow was the color of woman suffrage.

"Daffodils, I think," Elizabeth said, leading him to the love seat and pulling him down beside her.

"How soon will congress convene?" he asked.

"In a few weeks. Mid-May, I think," his mother said. "We should have the votes this time, at least in the House."

"It's passed the House before," Gideon reminded her. "It's the Senate you have to worry about."

"Times are changing, Gideon," his mother said. "I just know it's going to pass both houses this time. It must."

"I hope you're right," Gideon said. It had been a long fight and many women had sacrificed so much. They deserved to win.

"How was your day?" Elizabeth asked him.

"Uneventful. Not a single suspected con was reported." That made her smile, as he had intended. "Are you worried about Jake? He was going to the séance this afternoon, wasn't he?"

"One should never worry about Jake," she said. "He'll be fine, I'm sure."

Gideon frowned. "Are you really sure?"

She sighed. "I probably would be if I knew what he was up to, but if he's posing as a stockbroker, they'll probably want to use him somehow, if they can. He also has the advantage of already knowing they'll try to con him."

"And he's not likely to give them any money," his mother added with a sly grin.

Gideon still wasn't sure. "You're absolutely right, but how does he expect to get money from them? How do you con a con artist?"

"I've been giving that a lot of thought," Elizabeth said. "I might have to consult the Old Man, and Jake may have already gotten some ideas from him, but between the three of us, I think we can figure it out."

"Do you have any ideas of your own, dear?" his mother asked her.

"Happily, I do."

The look she gave him was apologetic because he couldn't approve of her running a con, but he could hardly object, either. He'd known what she was when he married her, and he'd participated in every con she'd run since he'd met her, willingly and otherwise, so he had no moral standing to criticize. "What do you have in mind, darling?"

She blinked in surprise, probably because she'd expected him to argue, but she said, "Jake came up with a wonderful idea, the one he told me about that night at the salon, but now that he's actually involved, I think we can do even more. I haven't worked out the details yet, but I think Jake can use my role as a real medium to his advantage. The key is to make them believe I can really predict the future."

"I wish you could predict the Woman Suffrage Amendment will pass," his mother said.

"I would if it were guaranteed," Elizabeth said wistfully.

"But how can you be sure something is guaranteed to happen?"

"Probably by making it happen," Gideon guessed. "Am I right?"

"Have I told you how brilliant you are, darling?" Elizabeth asked with an adoring smile.

"Not nearly often enough."

"Oh, Mrs. Bates, you were right! You were exactly right!" Cybil exclaimed the moment Elizabeth and Gideon entered Madame Ophelia's storefront on Tuesday evening. Everyone else from the previous séance was already there, waiting, and they all jumped to their feet as they shared Cybil's excitement.

Elizabeth smiled uncertainly because she would have had no idea what she'd said to Cybil when the spirits were speaking through her. "Did you find it, then? What you were looking for?"

"My uncle's will, yes. It was just as you said. I went to the fireplace in his bedroom and found a loose brick right where you said it would be. I never would have noticed it. It looked exactly like all the others, and nobody goes about pulling on the bricks in a fireplace to see if they're loose, do they?"

"No, I don't suppose they do," she allowed.

Cybil continued as if she hadn't spoken. "I pulled out the brick and found a metal box. It was locked, of course, but I pried it open because I knew what would be inside. You'd already told me that! So I opened it and there was my uncle's will."

"I'm so glad," Elizabeth said without much joy.

"Why was it so important to you to find the will, Mrs. . . . ?" Gideon asked, purposely using the wrong title.

"It's Miss. Miss Miles," Cybil said. "And you must be Mr. Bates."

"Yes, and I'm also an attorney, so I'm naturally interested." He sounded as if he really didn't know Cybil, which made Elizabeth absurdly proud.

"It's rather a silly story because my uncle was so eccentric," Cybil explained somewhat apologetically. "Uncle was quite wealthy. His wife died many years ago, and his only son is somewhat of a . . . Well, I suppose you could call him a black sheep and a bit of a wastrel. Uncle had told my cousin he was cutting him off without a cent and leaving all of his fortune to me."

"Why would he leave his fortune to a woman?" the only other male in the room asked. Elizabeth remembered him as Cindy's unbelieving father.

That earned him a black look from Cybil and Elizabeth, but his wife said, "She told you he was eccentric."

"There's a difference between eccentric and foolish," the man said.

Even Gideon glared at him this time, but he seemed oblivious.

"I also said my cousin is a wastrel," Cybil said patiently. "He would have squandered his father's fortune, but my uncle wanted it used for a worthy cause. He trusted me to carry out his wishes."

"What worthy cause did your uncle want you to support?" Persephone asked. Elizabeth hadn't even noticed her enter the room.

Cybil turned to her, her cheeks still flush with excitement. "He left that to my good judgment. I told you. He trusted me."

"I assume you have registered the will for probate," Gideon said.

"Oh yes. I consulted an attorney when my uncle died, and he told me exactly what to do."

"What would have happened if you hadn't found the will?" the young woman named Tilly asked.

"Then the uncle would be considered to have died without a legal will and the rules of intestacy would have applied," Gideon said.

"What does that mean?" Tilly asked with a confused frown.

"It means my irresponsible cousin would have

181

inherited everything, as my uncle's only child, so you see how important it was to find the will." Cybil turned back to Elizabeth. "That is why I cannot thank you enough for helping me."

"I really didn't do anything," she said.

"You are far too modest, Mrs. Bates," Persephone said. "You have now made two accurate predictions."

"Two?" the other gentleman said. "What was the first?"

Elizabeth waved his question away. "Nothing important." But Elizabeth noticed Persephone hadn't counted her recognition that the two women at the trial séance were fakes.

Gideon grinned. "The other one was something about who would win a horse race."

"Now, that would be a good talent to have," the man said. "Does she do that often?"

"Never before," Gideon said.

"Or since," Elizabeth added. "So embarrassing."

"You need not be embarrassed about helping *me,* though," Cybil said, her enthusiasm undimmed.

"Do you have any ideas for how you will use your uncle's money?" Elizabeth asked.

"Not yet, but I'm sure I will find the perfect project. The city has so many needy people."

"Perhaps the spirits will help you decide," Persephone said.

Elizabeth didn't dare meet Gideon's eye,

182

because they both knew the spirits definitely would.

"I believe Madame is ready for you," Persephone said. "Will you step into the séance room?"

CHAPTER EIGHT

The séance itself was somewhat of a disappointment since Elizabeth did not receive any messages from her spirit guide. Madame gave her every opportunity, indulging in long silences punctuated by her annoying humming, but Elizabeth remained silent. The other participants received the usual messages, and Cybil's uncle was happy that she had found his will. He did, as expected, promise to send someone to advise her on how to use his money.

The couple Elizabeth had come to think of as Cindy's parents was obviously dissatisfied with the session since they received no special revelation and also didn't witness anything remarkable from Elizabeth. Tilly was taking no pains to hide her growing skepticism of the whole process and her mother seemed dismayed by her attitude, especially since Tilly's brother, Andy, had managed to convey a few words encouraging his sister to follow the advice of the man he was sending to help them. Elizabeth was naturally subdued, so Cybil was the only participant pleased by the experience. She began chattering the moment Madame Ophelia ended the session.

"Having Uncle's money is such a huge responsibility," she said, her gaze taking in all of those still seated around the table.

"But your uncle said he would send someone to help you," Tilly's mother reminded her.

"Perhaps he already did," Cybil said. "Mrs. Bates, your husband seemed to know a lot about wills."

"Yes," Elizabeth admitted reluctantly. "He told you. He's a lawyer." As he had been the last time, Gideon was waiting for them in the front room.

"Could he advise me?"

"I . . . You'd have to ask him," she hedged.

"But he could if he chose to, couldn't he?" Cybil pressed.

"I suppose so. He does help people manage their estates." She tried to sound almost apologetic.

"How fortuitous! He must be the one my uncle sent to help me." She jumped up from her chair. "I'll ask him at once."

Madame's expression had remained calm throughout this exchange, but she cried, "Persephone!" quite loudly before Cybil could reach the door.

Persephone must have been waiting just outside because the door opened at once. Persephone expressed surprise at coming face-to-face with

186

Cybil in her rush to leave, but she bravely blocked the door, instinctively knowing she shouldn't allow Cybil to run out.

"Miss Miles wishes to speak to Mr. Bates," Madame said. The words seemed to convey a silent warning.

Persephone still looked uncertain, but she stepped out of the way, allowing Cybil to exit. The others rose and slowly filed out to the waiting area.

"Mrs. Bates?" Madame Ophelia said, stopping her when she would have followed them.

Elizabeth turned back and managed a wan smile. "Yes?"

"Are you feeling all right?"

"I'm fine," Elizabeth said. "Or at least as fine as someone can be when they have discovered spirits speak through them."

"I understand completely. I felt the same way when I first discovered my powers."

Elizabeth was sure she had. "If you're wondering why I didn't, uh, have anything to say this evening, I'm afraid I have no idea."

"Then you didn't receive a message that you decided not to convey?"

Was that an accusation? Elizabeth chose not to think so.

"I admit I was extremely reluctant to have another *experience,* but I also felt nothing unusual this evening."

"Perhaps the spirits had nothing to say," Madame said with a small smile.

"I can only hope they remain silent, at least to me."

"I hope you will continue to see me. I know you are not pleased to discover your talents but resisting them is futile. Please continue to attend my séances at no charge. I believe you are a kindred spirit and will consider it a professional courtesy."

"That is very generous, but I don't wish to make a spectacle of myself," she protested.

"I assure you, that will never happen. I would be honored if you will let me assist you in learning about your abilities and how to control them."

Was that a kind offer or a self-serving one? Elizabeth chose to be gracious. "You are indeed very generous. I'll have to discuss it with my husband, of course."

Madame merely smiled, as if confident of what Elizabeth's ultimate decision would be.

Elizabeth wandered out to the waiting area, where everyone stood around watching Cybil's conversation with Gideon. He looked genuinely nonplussed and was just passing her his card with apparent reluctance.

"I'm sure the attorney who is already advising you could be just as helpful as I could," he was saying, probably to avoid any hint that he was trying to steal a client from a colleague.

"Perhaps, but his wife isn't the one who made it necessary for me to seek guidance in the first place," Cybil replied. "My uncle's spirit said he would send someone to advise me, and I can't help thinking he must have meant you."

Poor Gideon didn't even have to pretend that the compliment made him uncomfortable. He managed a smile, but it was painfully stiff.

"I'm sure my husband will do his very best, if you choose to employ him," Elizabeth said to rescue him. "Darling, I'm ready to go now."

"If you'll excuse us," he mumbled to Cybil.

"Of course. I'll telephone your office for an appointment," she called after them as Gideon escorted her to the door.

The street outside was quiet as they walked down to the avenue, where they could find a cab. When they were far enough away, Gideon whispered, "What was Cybil up to? I hardly knew what to say to her."

"You did beautifully, darling. And Cybil is so clever! I never even thought of it myself. She just gave herself a reason to visit you from time to time in case we need to communicate. We don't dare go to one another's houses in case Madame Ophelia has someone watching us."

"Why would she have someone watching us? I know Jake was concerned, but she can't have

189

people following all of her clients around the city all the time."

"She wouldn't need to, although I'm sure she does it sometimes to get information about them that she can use in her predictions. But I'm different. I'm trying to convince her I'm a real medium, and she'll naturally be at least a little suspicious that I'm faking it. If she knew Cybil was my aunt, she'd know for sure that I'm a fake."

"I see, so you don't dare go visit her or speak to her outside of Madame Ophelia's sight."

"Exactly, but now Cybil can go to see you whenever she needs to."

"And I suppose all that nonsense about her uncle sending someone to advise her didn't refer to me."

"Not at all. I'm sure Madame is quite put out that Cybil has already fixated on you, but that was also very clever of Cybil. Ordinarily, they would probably let some time go by before Cybil encountered the person who is going to con her out of her uncle's money, but now they'll have to speed things along so you don't find a legitimate place for her to spend it before they get to her."

"I'll have to instruct Smith not to be too prompt in scheduling her appointment, then."

"Yes, give them a few days. I'm sure someone will be along soon to convince Cybil he knows exactly how she should spend all that lovely money."

Jake couldn't help yawning as he walked to his office the next morning. Why did people think having a job was such a great thing? No matter how much fun you had the night before, you still had to get up early, get shaved and dressed, and go to some business where people expected you to be pleasant and do some work. Going to an office was bad enough. At least he didn't have to actually do any work.

The building was nondescript and located far enough from Wall Street that the rent was low but close enough that it was still believable. The Old Man kept it for his out-of-town colleagues to use and they paid him handsomely to do so. The rest of the time, it sat empty. At least he wasn't charging Jake to use it, since this was for one of Lizzie's projects.

He trudged up the three flights of stairs to a door marked ABERNATHY AND ASSOCIATES BROKERAGE. It was one of several such signs available for use as needs dictated. Inside was a reception area where a hatchet-faced woman sat. A large ledger sat open on the desk in front of her, although he knew the numbers written in it were meaningless. A broken ticker tape machine sat in the corner, and a few chairs lined the walls for clients who would never appear.

"Good morning, Harriet," Jake said, trying his most charming smile.

Harriet did not return it. "You're late."

Jake sighed. "Dock my pay, then, will you?"

She shook her head, refusing to be amused. "If you're trying to fool somebody, you need to be good at it."

She was right, of course. Jake knew someone had been following him off and on since his last séance. They'd followed him from Madame Ophelia's to his rooming house, which made him uneasy, but no one there knew what he did for a living, so he was safe, but that meant he had to make a show of going to his job every day, at least until they stopped following him. Luckily, the building had a back entrance, where he could sneak in and out without being seen. He could always go out the front and walk to the Stock Exchange, too. They wouldn't actually let him onto the trading floor, but he could slip into the building and lose his tail if he needed to.

"Shall I hold your calls?" Harriet asked sarcastically.

"Oh yes. Hold them all morning. I need a nap."

Harriet shook her head again and went back to reading the meaningless numbers in her ledger.

Jake went through the other door to the inner office. This room was furnished with desks and papers purchased from a brokerage office that had gone out of business. No one knew what any of the papers meant, but the place looked authentic in case someone needed to fool a mark. Someone had thoughtfully added a sofa to the décor, and Jake slipped off his suit coat to hang it up before stretching out for the planned nap.

As he draped his jacket over the back of a chair, he noticed something white peeking out of the pocket. This wasn't surprising, since he always carried a handkerchief. All well-dressed men did. But Jake's handkerchiefs weren't edged in lace and lace was what was peeking out of his pocket.

Intrigued, he grabbed it and pulled it out. Yes, it was indeed a lace-edged handkerchief and it was embroidered, too. Lots of flowers. Somebody had spent some time on it. But the center-piece of the design was a word that made Jake grin.

Mother.

Anna didn't have classes on Wednesday morning, so Jake snuck out the back door of the building, and when he was certain he wasn't being followed, he made a beeline for Anna's house. He really needed to speak to Lizzie, but he didn't dare approach her directly because she might have been being watched. Anna could be his go-between, though.

A maid answered the door and she seemed delighted when Jake asked if Anna was home. Why did everybody always have the wrong idea about his feelings for Anna? And more important, her feelings for him?

A few minutes later, the maid showed him into the parlor and then Anna came breezing in. Plainly, she hadn't been expecting company. She was wearing some dreary old dress and her hair was coming out of its pins. She had a big smile for him, though.

"Jake, what brings you here on this beautiful morning?"

He reached into his pocket and pulled out the handkerchief. "I found this in my pocket this morning."

She took it and examined the workmanship, but plainly, she did not understand the significance. "This hardly seems like your style."

"I guess Lizzie isn't keeping you updated about what's going on," he said.

"No, sadly. She doesn't want Madame Ophelia to think we're in cahoots."

"Even though you are."

"So sit down and tell me everything," she said, pushing an errant lock of hair out of her eyes and making her way over to a love seat.

He sat down beside her and told her what he knew.

"Oh, Jake, you are making a specialty out of romancing helpless females," she teased.

"It's not a specialty," he protested. "And they certainly aren't helpless."

"I suppose you're right . . . about them not being helpless, at least. Your last victim was little more than a con artist, and this girl actually is one."

"Thank you. I'm glad someone appreciates my work."

Anna rolled her eyes. "Why did you feel it was necessary to romance her at all, though?"

He shrugged. "Just a little incentive for her to pay me extra attention. They have lots of marks. I wanted to stand out."

"Oh, Jake, you'd stand out anyway."

He smiled modestly.

"So, what are you going to do?"

"I'm not sure what I *should* do," he said. "That depends on what Lizzie has planned."

"I thought you knew. Weren't you the one who came up with the idea in the first place?"

"Yes, but she hasn't let me know when she wants to do it."

"I feel certain she will."

"But now she can't wait too long because I got the handkerchief."

"Supposedly as a sign from your dearly departed mother," Anna said.

He pulled out the handkerchief and looked at it again. "I have to admit, it's a very nice touch. Not even something I could miss."

"Absolutely not. You couldn't misunderstand or ignore it, either."

"I thought they'd be clever but more subtle," Jake admitted.

"I don't think Madame Ophelia would waste her time on anything subtle. And I suppose it was also designed to be dramatic enough to get you back to her quickly."

"Which is why I can't delay too long. I suppose it might take me a day or two to find it, but not any longer than that. This is too obviously the sign Madame Ophelia predicted, so I'd run to her as soon as I found it."

"I can go see Elizabeth today and let her know."

"I'd appreciate it. She can telephone me at home this evening."

"You could have just telephoned her about finding the handkerchief, couldn't you?"

"Not with operators listening in. I'd have to explain too much, which is why I need your help."

Anna sighed with feigned disappointment. "And here I thought you'd just been looking for an excuse to come and see me."

"Well, I have missed you." He frowned. "Which reminds me, how is Miss Quincy?"

"She's quite well. I'll be sure to tell her you inquired," Anna said with a smirk.

He gave her an exaggerated glare. "Don't you dare. Besides, isn't she . . . I mean, she doesn't like boys, does she?"

To his delight, Anna blushed at that. "I really couldn't say."

"I could find out for you," he offered with a knowing smile. "It *is* my specialty."

"Don't you dare," she echoed his warning.

He raised both hands in surrender. "Don't worry. One pretend girlfriend at a time is plenty for me."

"Do you think she really likes you? Persephone, I mean," Anna asked.

"It's hard to say, but it doesn't matter. She won't like me at all when this is over."

"How do you suppose they want to use you?"

Jake frowned. "I've been trying to figure it out. I'm thinking they'll want me to tell my clients about some kind of sure-thing investment scheme, but I can't figure out how they'll convince me it's a sure thing."

"You never have that problem, do you?" she teased.

"I have that problem all the time, Anna. My business isn't easy," he said, deeply insulted.

"Forgive me for making assumptions," she said, still smirking. "But I'll go visit Elizabeth and have her telephone you, although I'm surprised to hear that you'll be at home this evening."

He sighed with long-suffering. "I have to get up every morning and pretend to go to work in case they're watching me."

"You poor darling."

"I don't know how people do it."

"Maybe you should ask Gideon. He seems to thrive in that sort of life."

"But he probably would have died of boredom by now if he hadn't met Lizzie."

"So would I," Anna assured him.

That made him smile. "Now that I think of it, tell Lizzie not to call me too early. I may want to stop off for a drink on my way home from the office."

Elizabeth was delighted to see Anna, who stopped by on her way to her afternoon classes.

"Jake came to see me this morning," she explained when the maid had left them alone.

"How presumptuous of him," Elizabeth teased. "I assume he had a message for me."

Anna explained Jake's séance experience and how he had found the handkerchief in his pocket. "How did it get there, though?" Anna asked. "I was embarrassed to ask Jake. He seems to think I'm just as knowledgeable as he is about these things, and I don't want to disillusion him."

Elizabeth laughed at her. "One of the first things I learned was how to pick pockets. It's a skill that comes in handy, especially if you want to put something *into* someone's pocket."

"How clever! I never would have thought of it. I thought pickpockets just stole things. I see the warning signs on the trolleys all the time."

"Yes, pickpockets love those signs. Every time someone sees them, he pats his wallet to make sure it's still there, so the pickpocket knows exactly where it is."

"How awful!" Anna cried, aghast.

"So yes, pickpockets do just steal things, but no con artist worth his salt would even consider such a thing. The risk is far too great for such a small reward."

"I suppose you're right. Stealing someone's wallet is pathetic when compared to emptying his bank account."

Elizabeth shook her head in dismay. "Oh, Anna, I'm afraid we have totally corrupted you."

"I hope so. Jake thinks Gideon would have died of boredom if he hadn't met you, and so would I."

Elizabeth sighed in mock despair. "I hope not!"

"But I'm sure of it, so you must do what you can to keep saving me by telling me what you and Jake have planned."

"You'll be horrified," Elizabeth protested.

"I'm counting on it," Anna replied.

Jake had made it back to his office after his visit with Anna without being followed, and he filled the afternoon hours with his delayed nap. By the time he could reasonably leave the building, he was refreshed and ready to go. He made no effort to notice if he was being followed or not, and he stopped into a saloon where many of the Wall

Street denizens enjoyed a libation after a busy day of making money.

Jake made sure to sit at the bar with an empty seat to his right, just in case, and he wasn't disappointed when a well-dressed gentleman carrying an expensive-looking briefcase sat down beside him. He looked to be around fifty, with dark hair lightly threaded with silver and an impressive set of side-whiskers. He laid the briefcase on the bar and folded his hands over it, as if the contents were precious or at least valuable. He ordered a double whiskey.

"Rough day?" Jake inquired casually.

The man smiled wanly. "Not exactly. I'm just . . . I'm new to the city, and I'm afraid I find it all a bit overwhelming."

"What brings you here, Mr. . . . ?"

"Waterson," the man said, reaching out a hand.

Jake took it and shook. "Pleased to meet you and welcome to our fair city, Mr. Waterson. I'm John Miller."

"Thank you, young man. I appreciate your friendliness. I haven't encountered much of that since I arrived."

"You've just been going to the wrong places, then," Jake said. "New York can be a very friendly city."

Waterson smiled. "You must be in sales."

"Is it so obvious?" Jake asked good-naturedly. "And I'm also new to the city."

"So you haven't yet become jaded," Waterson said. "What do you sell?"

"Stocks," Jake admitted with a grin. "It's the coming thing, I'm told."

Waterson shook his head. "Nothing will ever replace land. They aren't making any more of it, you know."

This was truly something Jake had never considered, so he didn't have to pretend to be impressed. "I guess you're right. I hadn't thought of that."

Waterson glanced around as if to make sure no one was listening. Then he lowered his voice and said, "Especially if that land is on top of a whole bunch of crude oil."

Jake widened his eyes. "Sounds like you aren't just shooting the breeze, Mr. Waterson. Do you really have some land that's sitting on an oil deposit?"

Waterson looked around again and then nervously picked up his glass and took a large sip. Plainly, he was quite used to drinking straight whiskey. "I'm afraid I've already said too much. Anyone could overhear us."

"Then why don't we go somewhere more private? I wouldn't mind hearing all about this land of yours."

"Oh, it's not mine. I'm just the agent, you see."

"Agent? You mean, you're going to sell it for somebody else?"

Waterson winced. "That is my mission, yes, but I've found it very difficult to make the right contacts here in the city. The wealthy men who might have the means aren't interested in even seeing me."

"What you need is somebody to make the contacts for you."

Waterson's eyes narrowed skeptically. "And I suppose you're just the man for the job."

"As a matter of fact, I am. I'm a stockbroker, so I have lots of clients who might be interested in your land."

He frowned, still skeptical. "Lots?"

"Well, I have a few, but you only need one, don't you?"

"I suppose you're right."

"So can we go somewhere private and you can explain the deal to me? Then I'll know better if any of my clients would be interested."

Waterson considered Jake's offer for a long moment. "I don't suppose it would hurt anything to explain it to you."

"We could go up to my office," Jake offered.

"My hotel is nearby and we can order up some supper," Waterson countered.

Jake waited while Waterson drained his glass and then followed him out. The hotel was only a block away. It was a small one but elegant. Waterson had a suite and he was as good as his word about ordering supper. He asked for two steak dinners. While they waited, Waterson opened his briefcase and pulled out some maps and other important-looking papers.

The map he spread on the dining table was most impressive. It was, Jake was surprised to note, a map of Texas.

"Is that where you're from?" Jake asked.

"Oh no. I'm from Phildelphia."

"And you own land in Texas?"

"Not I, no. As I said, I'm not the owner. I only represent the owners. They hired me to sell the property for whatever I can get for it."

Jake frowned. He didn't understand much of the map, but he could clearly see the property in question outlined and a large black lake marked "mother pool" that overlapped a portion of the property. The little triangle shapes scattered over the state were clearly meant to be oil wells, and several of them were located within the property lines. To make the map even more intriguing, the adjoining properties were marked as owned by Standard Oil and the Texas Company, both major producers of gasoline products.

Waterson poured them each a generous measure of whiskey from a decanter on the sideboard, and Jake took a tentative sip. Cheap rotgut, which was probably why he'd put it into a decanter, but Jake said, "Good stuff."

Waterson smiled, sure he had a rube well in hand. "As you can see, the property in question is located in an oil-rich section of the state. For reasons known only to them, the other oil companies have not chosen to purchase this particular property."

"Have you contacted them about buying it?" Jake asked. "It looks like the oil deposit could be worth developing."

"My clients prefer to sell to private individuals." Waterson looked a bit uneasy.

Jake was suspicious now, as he was meant to be. "Who are your clients?"

Waterson cleared his throat. "They are, uh . . . They live in Germany."

Jake whistled his amazement. "I can see why they don't want to approach the oil companies, then."

"Exactly. Those companies wouldn't want to be seen doing business with Germans so soon after the war, particularly if they are sending money to our former enemies."

"We don't have a peace treaty yet, so they're *still* our enemies," Jake reminded him.

"Ahem, you're right, of course, so you understand why it is necessary to keep the sale of this property private."

"I understand completely," Jake said solemnly, impressed by the detail Mr. Waterson had given this project.

"So do you still think you have a client who might be interested in purchasing this land?"

Jake rubbed his chin thoughtfully. "I might. I'll have to give it some thought and ask a few questions, but I do have a client or two who aren't deeply concerned about, uh, following the rules."

"I'm sure there are no rules about buying property owned by German nationals," Mr. Waterson said hastily.

"No rules, but public opinion can be brutal, as you reminded me yourself. Can you give me an idea of how much acreage we're talking about here and what would be a reasonable price?"

Waterson sighed. "My clients are not in a position to be greedy, of course, but I'd think ten dollars an acre seems fair."

"And how many acres are we talking about?"

"Twenty-five thousand."

Jake whistled again. "I don't know if we could get that much, but let's see. You'll get a commission and so will I."

"Naturally, Mr. Miller. Ten percent is the usual fee."

"Each," Jake clarified.

"Each," Waterson confirmed. "How soon do you think you might find me a buyer?"

"Give me a few days." He gave Waterson one of his business cards with the address of his fake office and a phone number that Harriet would answer.

"I will look forward to hearing from you, Mr. Miller."

• • •

"Did you have an enjoyable evening?" Elizabeth asked Jake when she was finally able to reach him on the telephone later that night.

"As a matter of fact, I did," he replied. He sounded a little less than sober, although she knew he rarely got genuinely drunk. It was bad for business. "I met a very interesting gentleman who owns some land in Texas that he'd like to sell to one of my clients."

"I suppose that explains your late evening, then."

"Yes, it does. My only regret is his choice of whiskey, but I believe I have met the man I was supposed to meet."

"I wonder if Cybil will meet the same man."

"It will be interesting to see. Are you ready to schedule our entertainment?"

"I think so. I will let you know when I do. I just don't want to look too eager."

"Maybe Cybil can be of use."

Elizabeth was glad they weren't face-to-face because she would have had to acknowledge this was a good idea. "Perhaps she can. I'll investigate."

"And I will look forward to hearing from you," Jake said.

They bid each other good night, satisfied they had said nothing that would be of interest to any nosy operators.

"Did you finally reach Jake?" Gideon asked when Elizabeth returned to where they had been sitting in the parlor. Mother Bates had already retired for the night.

"Yes. He met the man who is going to con him," she said, sitting down beside him on the love seat.

"How does he know that?" Gideon asked with great interest.

"Because the man owns some land in Texas that he wants to sell to one of Jake's clients."

"I see."

"Do you, darling?" she asked with interest.

"Oh yes. It's simple really. The man Jake met probably doesn't even own any land in Texas."

"That seems likely, although he might. That's something Jake will need to find out, because if he doesn't actually own the land, it will be difficult."

"What will?"

"Everything, darling. Everything."

Gideon looked far less sure of himself now. "And if he doesn't own the land?"

"Then Jake will need to figure out a way to con him instead."

"And if he does own the land?"

"Then he can just outcon him."

"Why didn't you say so? It's all so clear now," Gideon said, pulling Elizabeth over to sit on his lap.

"You really shouldn't try to understand these things, darling. I know it just upsets you," she chided while he nuzzled her neck.

"I can't help myself. Besides, I know sooner or later, you're going to pull me into something."

"Do you think understanding it will help you?" she asked with a knowing grin.

"Not at all, but I think it's human nature to want to be prepared."

"Can anything really prepare you to participate in a con?"

"Probably not. At least there seems very little danger that anyone will kidnap or try to murder you this time."

"Murder is always an option, you know, if things get really bad," she reminded him. She'd been murdered once herself, as he well knew.

"Surely things can't get really bad with this one."

"Not for me. I'm the one with the powers, remember. And don't worry, darling. If I do get killed, I'll be sure and come back to visit you from time to time."

"Don't joke about that," he said, growing very still as his arms tightened around her.

"I'm sorry. I guess . . . I'm not used to having someone care so very much about me," she said, stroking his face lovingly.

"You should get used to it, then, because you're going to have to put up with it for many more

208

years. And in the meantime, I want you to tell me exactly what Jake has planned."

Elizabeth sighed. Anna had taken it very well, so perhaps Gideon would, too. "All right, but don't say I didn't warn you."

CHAPTER NINE

E lizabeth wasn't at all surprised when her
maid told her Persephone Highland wished
to see her on Friday morning. The maid escorted
her into the parlor, where Elizabeth and Mother
Bates had been busily writing letters to various
legislators, encouraging them to vote in favor
of the Woman Suffrage Amendment that would
be presented at the special session of congress
convening soon in Washington City.

"Persephone, how nice to see you," Elizabeth
said.

Persephone was looking around a little uncertainly. "Thank you for seeing me. Oh, hello, Mrs.
Bates."

Mother Bates returned her greeting and said,
"Would you like to see Elizabeth alone?"

"Oh no, I just . . . It's not private or anything,"
Persephone stammered.

"Please sit down. Can I offer you some tea or
something cool to drink?"

"Thank you, no, I just need to speak with you
briefly." Persephone joined Elizabeth on the love
seat and Mother Bates took a chair opposite,
smiling expectantly.

"I know you aren't . . . well, convinced of your powers, but others are. Miss Miles, for example."

Elizabeth smiled politely. "She would be, I suppose."

"Yes, well, she is most eager to contact her uncle again, and while Madame Ophelia assured her that her spirit guide could most certainly be of assistance, Miss Miles will only trust you."

"Oh."

"So, Madame Ophelia would consider it a personal favor if you would agree to attend a séance this evening. It would be the same group as before, assuming they can all attend. Miss Miles will certainly be there."

"May I come, too?" Mother Bates asked guilelessly.

Elizabeth needed all her fortitude to resist giving her a quelling glare, but fortunately, Persephone said, "I'm afraid Madame Ophelia limits the séances to six guests. She has determined that any more just confuses the spirits and the messages get garbled."

"But if someone else is unable to come, could I sit in?" Mother Bates asked hopefully.

"I . . . I suppose so, although we won't know until this evening."

"If you can make room for her, you can telephone us," Elizabeth said, ending the discussion. She doubted anyone involved would miss this.

"What do you suppose Miss Miles wants to know from her uncle?"

"I really don't know. More advice, I believe, is what she asked for."

"On how to use her uncle's money, I assume," Elizabeth said. "I wonder if she has consulted my husband yet."

"Don't you know?" Persephone asked in surprise.

"My husband never discusses his clients with us. Attorneys must maintain confidentiality. Sort of like mediums, I imagine," Elizabeth added.

"I suppose," Persephone said faintly. "So I can tell Madame Ophelia that you'll attend the séance this evening?"

"Yes. I don't want to disappoint Miss Miles, although you understand I can make no promises. I do not control what happens, and I had nothing at all to contribute at the last séance, you will recall. It's entirely possible that my so-called powers have vanished as suddenly as they first appeared."

Persephone gave her what was probably intended to be a reassuring smile. "Madame Opheila considers that highly unlikely. She has every confidence in you, Mrs. Bates."

"That's sweet of her," Elizabeth said, not daring to glance at her mother-in-law.

Persephone was as good as her word. As soon as they had arranged the time of the evening's séance, she took her leave. The moment the front door closed behind her, Elizabeth turned to her mother-in-law. "That was very sneaky of you, Mother Bates."

Mother Bates made no attempt to pretend she didn't understand. "I saw an opportunity to attend the séance and didn't want to let it pass. You can't blame me. You're having all the fun and I'm sitting home writing letters no one will even read."

Elizabeth conjured up some outrage. "If no one reads these letters, why are we writing them?"

"Oh, I suppose someone glances over them to see the subject and puts them in a pile. It's not what the letter says that matters so much. What matters is how many of them there are. The legislators need to know how much people care and how important it is. And stop trying to change the subject. You know I'm dying to attend another séance."

Elizabeth actually winced. "Please don't say 'dying' and 'séance' in the same breath."

Mother Bates laughed. "You know what I meant. I could understand if it were real or if you thought it was real, but you know it's all fake."

"Which is why I don't understand why you are so anxious to attend another one!"

"But it's so interesting, although I do feel sorry for the people who really believe."

"And sadly they'll continue to believe. Even if we expose Madame Ophelia as a fake, they'll probably just find another medium."

"But surely not all mediums are cheating their clients out of such large sums of money," Mother Bates said.

"We can hope not, and we can take comfort in knowing we have put one of the worst ones out of business. But only if we succeed."

"I understand, my dear," Mother Bates said. "And you'd rather not have to worry about me while you go about it."

Elizabeth sighed. "I really would worry about you, you know."

"Then I'll try to comfort myself with that fact and take solace from hearing all about it later."

"I'll make sure Jake entertains you with stories about his romance with Persephone, too."

"What a rogue he is. I assume that is progressing well."

"She seems to be returning his interest, but she may also just be keeping an eye on him while they use him to get to his wealthy clients."

"Does Jake have wealthy clients?" Mother Bates asked in surprise.

"He's pretending to be a stockbroker."

"Oh, of course. I should have known it would be something like that. Perhaps she just thinks he's a good catch."

"Jake?"

"He's a handsome boy, and if he had a respectable job, he would be."

"I suppose you're right. I guess I just know him too well."

"Familiarity breeds contempt, as they say."

"Especially where brothers are concerned," Elizabeth said with a wry grin.

"Is this the night Jake will do whatever it is he's going to do?" Mother Bates asked.

"Oh dear, yes, it is. I need to telephone him right away."

The cab dropped Gideon and Elizabeth off in front of Madame Ophelia's shop, and Elizabeth was already breathing rapidly.

"What is it, darling?" Gideon asked, anxious even though he knew it was all an act. She really did look distressed.

"I don't know. I just got this horrible feeling as we drove down this street."

"Let's get inside so you can sit down." He slipped an arm around her waist as her step faltered so she wouldn't fall.

He managed to get the door open to find the other participants already waiting. Their eager smiles of greeting quickly evaporated when they saw the state Elizabeth was in.

"Mrs. Bates, are you all right?" Cybil asked, hurrying to assist Gideon. Together they led her to the nearest chair and lowered her into it.

"What's wrong?" she asked Gideon as the others rushed over to see for themselves.

"I don't know. She started to feel unwell just as we arrived."

"Would you like a glass of water?" Tilly asked. "Persephone, can you get Mrs. Bates some water?"

"What is it?" Tilly's mother asked. "Would you like some smelling salts?"

Elizabeth shook her head. She had wrapped her arms around herself and leaned forward slightly, as if in pain.

"Darling, what is it?" Gideon asked, laying a hand on her back to comfort her. "What can I do for you?"

"Nothing," she murmured. "I just . . . I suddenly got this horrible feeling of . . . of foreboding as we arrived here, as if something terrible had happened."

Everyone glanced at one another, but no one seemed aware of anything having happened, terrible or otherwise. Persephone pushed her way through the cluster of bodies surrounding Elizabeth to present her with a glass of water, which she took with both hands.

"Nothing has happened," Persephone assured Elizabeth. "We were all just waiting for you to arrive."

Elizabeth sipped the water and then sighed and handed the glass back to Persephone. "Thank you. I don't know what came over me. I'm feeling a bit better now. I'm sure it was nothing."

Plainly, it was not nothing, and no one was convinced it was.

"If you aren't well, we can postpone the séance," Cybil said, but the involuntary sounds of protest from the others that followed this assertion proved she was the only one willing to be so generous.

"I don't want to disappoint anyone," Elizabeth said a little unsteadily. "I'm sure I'll be fine. I'm . . . It was just a silly notion, I'm sure. I have no idea what could have upset me."

"Let's give the poor girl some air," Cybil suggested, motioning for everyone to step back, which they reluctantly did. "You didn't have a vision or anything, did you?"

"A vision?" Elizabeth echoed in surprise. "No, nothing like that. Just an overwhelming feeling of dread, but it has passed now."

"Perhaps something happened here in the past," Persephone suggested eagerly. "People with the gift can be sensitive to such things."

"Can they?" Gideon asked skeptically.

"Of course, they can," Tilly's mother said, although Gideon had no idea why he should take her word for it.

Gideon glanced at the other couple, who had yet to express an opinion. "It's possible," the woman assured him. The man said nothing.

"There," Elizabeth said, straightening in her chair and laying a hand on her heart. "It's gone now. I feel perfectly normal again."

"Are you sure?" Cybil asked with a worried frown.

"She wouldn't say so if she wasn't," Tilly's mother said testily.

"Do you feel up to participating in the séance?" Persephone asked with apparent concern. Perhaps she was afraid of losing business if Elizabeth fainted or something.

"I do. In fact, now I'm actually more eager. I want to see if I can figure out what I was feeling. Perhaps the spirits will reveal it to me." She sounded amazingly sincere, and Gideon managed not to roll his eyes.

Everyone seemed relieved to hear this, especially Persephone, who probably hadn't relished the thought of explaining to Madame Ophelia that they had to cancel the séance.

"I'll go see if Madame is ready for you," Persephone said, hurrying off.

"What did it feel like?" the other woman asked. "You said it was dread and a feeling of foreboding."

"I don't think I can describe it," Elizabeth said. "But it reminded me of how I felt when I thought Gideon was going to die of the flu." She looked up at him lovingly and took his hand in hers to squeeze it.

A murmur of sympathy came from all the others, and they looked at Gideon with new eyes. He straightened, feeling somehow obligated to look healthier, as if he deserved to have survived when so many others had not.

"My Andy died of the flu," Tilly's mother said.

"I'm sorry," Gideon said. No one else spoke. They had probably already offered their condolences long since.

An awkward silence fell until Persephone returned and announced that Madame was ready for them. She collected the fees from everyone except Elizabeth, who was the last to file into the room.

"I'll be right here if you need me, darling," Gideon said, surprised at the apprehension he felt, even though he knew Elizabeth was in no danger whatsoever.

She gave him a wan smile and entered the séance room.

Everyone had taken the same seats as before, leaving Elizabeth to face Madame Ophelia across the table. They all looked at her expectantly, even Madame Ophelia. She said, "I'm fine, really."

"Persephone said you were overcome by a feeling of foreboding," Madame said in an accusatory tone that Elizabeth found unnecessary.

"That's how I would describe it, but it passed. Perhaps I'm just a bit nervous since you all

220

obviously have great expectations that I don't think I can fulfill."

"We have no expectations," Madame insisted, although Elizabeth could tell the rest of them were disappointed to hear her say so. "The spirits will speak if they choose. It is not our decision to make, and we cannot force them or stop them."

"Thank you," Elizabeth said, settling more comfortably in her chair. She let her shoulders sag in relief.

Madame nodded once as if glad to have that settled. Then she said, "Write down your questions, please."

They did so, dropping them into the bag and witnessing the ritual burning. When Persephone had gone, Madame instructed them to place their hands on the table and clear their minds. The séance proceeded as usual, with Madame answering some of the questions or at least offering platitudes until Elizabeth interrupted her with a tortured moan.

She'd closed her eyes, but she could actually feel the sudden tension in the room. She moaned again.

"Who is it? Who is there?" Madame demanded.

"No," Elizabeth groaned, swaying a bit in her chair. "No, stop!"

"Stop what? What do you see?" Madame asked.

"Horses. Stop them! No!" Elizabeth cried desperately.

"What is happening?"

"No, stop!" she screamed, not a female scream but a deeper one of agony.

"What is it?" one of the other women demanded. "*Who* is it?"

"Aaahhhh!" Elizabeth cried. "It hurts! It hurts! Save me. I'm dying!" Another guttural scream and she fell sideways onto Cindy's mother, who let her slip to the floor, unconscious.

A moment of stunned silence became a cacophony of questions and commands and distress as Madame called for Persephone and everyone around the table began to argue about the best way to revive her.

Eventually, Gideon's voice demanded to know what happened and his strong hands lifted her to a sitting position. Someone waved the smelling salts beneath her nose. She turned away and moaned and finally had to bat it away before they suffocated her with it. She allowed her eyes to flutter open, and then she moaned in dismay. "Not again."

"What did you see?" Cybil demanded. "Do you remember?"

"Let her get up off the floor, at least," Gideon said, his annoyance apparent.

She let him help her up to sit in her chair. The rest of the participants were clustered around her except for Madame Ophelia, who would be stuck in her seat because of the telephone connection.

Elizabeth looked up at Gideon and blinked. "I think I'd like to go home."

"We'll go at once," Gideon said, but the others drowned him out with their protests.

"You have to tell us what you saw."

"It must have been awful!"

"Can you remember anything at all?"

The questions came one on top of the other so that she couldn't even keep track of them.

"I don't know," she said finally, rubbing her temples with her fingertips. "I just remember being terrified and then pain and . . . and darkness."

"You said you were dying," Andy's mother said.

"No, not *me*," Elizabeth said, then covered her mouth with both hands. "I mean . . . Gideon, will you take me home?"

"Who was it?" Cindy's father demanded. "Whose death did you see?"

"I don't know," she cried, pushing to her feet. "Please, Gideon."

He wrapped an arm around her shoulders and escorted her out with the others in their wake, still demanding answers. They had all just reached the waiting area when they heard a disturbance out in the street. Horses running much too fast for city driving, especially since they had to make their way through motorcar traffic. Frantic cries of the driver and another voice shouting,

"Stop!" Horses whinnying in terror, and finally the screams of pain.

"What on earth . . . ?" Gideon muttered, but they couldn't see a thing because of the heavy draperies over the windows.

"No, no," Elizabeth pleaded, backing away from the door as the others surged toward it, anxious to see what the commotion was. *"Don't look!"* she warned when someone tried to push back the draperies.

Cindy's father had just reached the door when it flew open and Jake came in, looking around frantically.

"Do you have a telephone here?" he asked, glancing at each of them as if searching for a familiar face. "There's been an accident." Then he saw one. "Persephone, do you have a telephone?"

"No. What happened?" she said, coming to meet him.

"Someone has been run over by a wagon," Cindy's father shouted to them from the doorway. Since he was holding the door open, they could hear the victim's agonized screams quite clearly now.

"There was a terrible accident," Jake was telling Persephone. "I was just coming to tell you. . . ." He reached into his pocket and pulled out a lacy handkerchief and held it up. "I found it, the thing you told me about or rather Madame

Ophelia told me about, and I was coming here to show you and this man walked out into the street and the horses were going so fast and . . ." He stopped and drew a calming breath. "I said I'd telephone for an ambulance."

"But we don't have a telephone," Persephone reminded him.

"Yes. I . . . I should go help." He turned and pushed his way past Cindy's father back out to the street.

"It looks like the poor man was crushed," Cybil reported from where she was peering out the front window now that someone had pushed open the drapes. The other women were crowded around her and Persephone joined them. They cupped their hands around their faces in an attempt to see through the glass into the darkness.

"I should help, too," Gideon said.

"Don't leave me! Besides, you can't help him," Elizabeth cried. "He's dying!"

All the women and even Cindy's father turned to stare at her, and then the victim's renewed shrieks of agony drew their attention again.

"What in heaven's name are they doing to him?" Gideon demanded.

"Putting him into the wagon," Cindy's father reported.

"Which is probably the quickest way to get him to a hospital," Cybil reported tartly, "but they could have been gentler."

"It's no use," Elizabeth said. "He's going to die."

They all turned back to her again, even Cindy's father, who gave her his full attention now that they could hear the wagon pulling away.

"She's probably right. The way the blood was pouring out of his mouth—"

"Horace!" his wife chastened him.

Horace shrugged apologetically.

"Is that what you saw?" Tilly asked, coming toward Elizabeth with her eyes wide in amazement. "You saw this accident."

"You did, didn't you?" her mother said. "You saw horses and someone screaming."

Elizabeth was shaking her head and backing away from them, but Gideon wrapped his arm around her again to stop her.

"Leave her alone," he said sharply, halting them in their advance, but their expressions revealed their determination to learn the truth.

"Tell us," Cybil urged. "What good will it do to keep it a secret?"

Elizabeth drew an unsteady breath. "I don't know if it was that exactly," she hedged.

"But something very similar," Cybil guessed.

"I saw horses running toward me," Elizabeth admitted.

"Toward *you?*" Tilly echoed.

"Not me exactly, but . . . it was like I could see it through his eyes, the man who was struck."

226

"Did you feel his pain?" Cindy's mother inquired a little too curiously.

But Elizabeth shook her head. "Not really, but I . . . I knew he felt it and he was screaming. Did I scream?"

"You did," Gideon informed her with a disapproving frown. "It took everything in me not to rush in there."

"I'm sorry, darling. I didn't do it on purpose," she lied.

"How do you know he's going to die?" Persephone asked. Something in her voice betrayed more than a casual interest.

"I don't," Elizabeth insisted. "I mean, I pray he doesn't but . . ."

"What made you *think* he was going to die?" Gideon asked, framing the question he assumed Persephone wanted to ask. "Because that's what you said."

Elizabeth closed her eyes against an unpleasant vision. "I knew he was in terrible pain and then . . . then everything stopped and went black. He was . . . at peace somehow."

"I don't suppose we'll ever know what happened to him, though," Tilly's mother said with regret.

"Maybe we will," Cindy's father said. "Did you know that young man who came in to ask about the telephone, Persephone?"

Persephone seemed startled to be consulted. "I . . . Yes, I know him."

"Is he a client?" Tilly asked. "From what he said, it sounded like he was."

"Yes, he . . . Yes, he's a client."

"So you can find out what happened from him," Tilly said. "He went with the man in the wagon."

Cindy's mother had been staring at Elizabeth with an unnatural intensity for a few moments. "You knew this was going to happen even before the séance, didn't you?"

Elizabeth shook her head, but the woman ignored her silent denial.

"You knew," Cindy's mother insisted. "That's why you were upset before you even came in. Your husband said you started to react as soon as you arrived."

"That's right," Tilly said. "Which would have been when she reached the place where the accident actually happened."

"So you knew it was going to happen even then," Cindy's mother insisted.

"Not really," Elizabeth protested. "Not exactly, I mean. I just knew something bad was . . . was somehow associated with that place."

"You cannot deny it now," Madame Ophelia said, startling them all. She had extricated herself from her chair while their attention was diverted and now stood in the doorway to the séance room. "You have the gift."

"But I don't *want* it," Elizabeth insisted.

"We cannot choose. The gift chooses us and we must accept it."

"You should be grateful," Persephone assured her. "Few are so blessed."

"I don't believe it is a blessing," Elizabeth said. "How can it be if I see how other people are going to die?"

"Not all your visions will be so upsetting."

"And you'll be able to help other people the way you helped me," Cybil said.

Elizabeth clapped her hands over her hears. "Stop! You don't even know if I'm right about that poor man. Perhaps he'll recover and you'll see that I can't predict the future at all."

But she hadn't convinced them. They all stared back at her with condescending smiles, certain they were right and she was wrong.

"Come along, darling," Gideon said. "I'll take you home."

She gratefully accepted his offer and allowed him to escort her out. They could hear the hum of conversation as everyone left behind began to rehash the evening's events and embellish their memories of them. Embellishing memories was simple human nature, and in this case, Cybil would help the process along.

Elizabeth wouldn't let Gideon discuss a single thing about the evening until they were in the privacy of their own home, since one never knew who might be in Madame Ophelia's employ.

Besides, Mother Bates would want to know every detail, too.

They found her reading by the light of an electric lamp in the parlor. "So," she greeted them, "did Jake die?"

"Jake wasn't supposed to die," Elizabeth said with a laugh. "He only witnessed the accident."

"I still don't understand how someone can pretend to be trampled by a team of horses," Mother Bates said.

"It's a rather risky con, but these men do it all over the country," Elizabeth said, sitting down on the love seat.

Gideon sat down beside her and took her hand in both of his. "I know how he managed the blood."

"Yes," his mother agreed, obviously proud of her knowledge, "a cackle bladder."

Gideon had seen the rubber bladder filled with chicken blood used more than once. "He must have used several if there was as much blood as Horace claimed."

"It doesn't take much blood to make a mess," Elizabeth said from experience.

"How would he fit more than one in his mouth, though?" Mother Bates asked.

"If he needed another one, he would palm it and make the switch when he put his hand up to his mouth to cough or whatever," Elizabeth explained.

"I know Jake must have paid the man for doing

this tonight, but there can't be a lot of opportunities for pretending to be killed by a wagon, so how do they make money doing it?" Mother Bates asked.

Elizabeth didn't so much as glance at Gideon, who was probably trying very hard not to groan in dismay at his mother asking about the way con artists made money. "From what I understand, the victim doesn't usually die, because that would ruin the whole thing. He pretends to be injured and the driver—he usually does this with a motorcar and pretends to be hit—is anxious to forget the whole thing, so he gives the victim whatever money he has in his wallet to pay for medical treatment."

"But in this case, his partner was driving the wagon instead of witnessing the accident and insisting the driver do the right thing and give the poor victim some money," Gideon added.

"But how on earth do they keep the poor fellow from really getting trampled?" Mother Bates asked.

"In this case it was easy, because no one actually witnessed the accident," Elizabeth said.

"Except Jake," Gideon reminded her.

"Yes," she agreed with a grin, "Jake, whose legendary honesty bore witness to how awful it was. So all the victim had to do was lie down on the street, bite his cackle bladder to get the blood flowing and scream his head off."

"He was quite convincing," Gideon said. "It gave me chills just to hear him."

"I assume he's had a lot of practice," Elizabeth said.

"Elizabeth, I will never forgive you for not allowing me to attend tonight," Mother Bates said with mock fury.

"It was the work of a moment," Elizabeth said. "The rest of the evening was deadly dull, I assure you."

"Except for Elizabeth screaming. You did a remarkable job of foreshadowing the poor man's agony, darling," Gideon said.

"Thank you. I've had a lot of practice myself."

"Practice with screaming in agony?" Mother Bates marveled.

"Oh yes. I had a brother, you see. I could get him in all kinds of trouble if he hurt me."

"Poor Jake," Gideon said, shaking his head.

"He deserved every bit of it," Elizabeth insisted.

"He probably did."

"What comes next?" Mother Bates asked with renewed interest.

"That depends on Madame Ophelia and her associates," Elizabeth said. "Jake has already been approached, but I don't know about Cybil. I assume it won't be long."

"I can hardly wait to see what kind of charity they suggest for Cybil."

Gideon grinned. "Perhaps they'll suggest rehabilitating people who are injured in motorcar accidents."

"I still don't see why I can't go to the séances with you," Zelda said the next morning over breakfast.

"Because you'd take up a seat that a real victim would occupy," Cybil explained, not for the first time. "If it makes you feel any better, we don't let Gideon's mother attend, either, and she is just as eager as you are to help."

Zelda sighed and assumed her most put-upon expression, which Cybil thought looked awfully cute but still left her unmoved. Too many of her loved ones were already involved in this. She wasn't about to allow Zelda to be exposed.

Cybil had just risen to start clearing the kitchen table when they were both startled by a crashing sound on their back porch.

"What on earth—" Zelda said, jumping up.

They both ran to the back door and peered out to see a rather ragged-looking girl poking through the contents of their overturned garbage pail. Zelda threw open the door before Cybil could caution her.

"What are you doing there, child?" she asked in her sweetest voice. "If you're hungry, all you have to do is ask."

The girl scrambled backward, peering up at them apprehensively from where she crouched on

233

the porch. "I ain't hurting nothing." She looked to be around thirteen, but appearances could be deceiving, as Cybil knew.

"Of course, you aren't," Zelda said gently, "but you don't have to dig through garbage. Come inside and we'll fix you something to eat."

"Who are you? What kind of place is this?" the girl asked suspiciously. Her face was dirty, although Cybil noticed her neck didn't seem to be, as if she'd smeared the dirt on her face for effect.

"It's just a house," Zelda said. "We live here. We're teachers."

"Teachers?" she scoffed. "Who do you teach?"

"Young women," Zelda said with a smile.

"I knew it!" the girl cried triumphantly. "You run a brothel, don't you? You're trying to lure me in."

Even Cybil was shocked by the accusation. "We are just offering you a meal," she said.

"I've heard of that. You tell a starving girl you'll feed her, and once she's inside, you tell her she's got to earn her keep. Well, you're not tricking me."

With that, she sprang up and darted away, slipping out the back gate, which she had left standing open into the alley beyond.

Zelda would have followed, but Cybil caught her arm. "Let her go."

"But she's just a child," she protested.

"So it seems, but I don't think we've heard the last of her."

Zelda's eyes widened. "What do you mean?"

But Cybil only smiled. "You'll see."

CHAPTER TEN

Jake hoped he would find Persephone in the shop this morning. He knew they had séances on Saturdays, but probably not this early. He needed to see her alone, if possible. It would be hard to work his charm on her if she insisted Madame Ophelia be included in their conversation.

The shop door was unlocked, and when he stepped inside, the waiting room was empty and the séance room door was open, so he knew no business was being conducted here yet. "Hello?" he called.

As he'd hoped, Persephone came out of the other room, the one where they obviously kept the equipment they wanted to conceal from the customers.

"John, I'm so glad you came by. How is that poor man?" Persephone asked. She seemed genuinely concerned.

Jake had snatched off his hat as he entered and now he worked the brim nervously. "I don't even like to think about it, but I thought you'd want to know. He . . . he didn't make it."

"I'm so sorry," she said quickly and with apparent sincerity.

"So am I, but the doctor said . . . We took him straight to a hospital, you see—but he was already dead when we got there. The doctor said there was nothing he could've done anyway, but I can't help feeling bad about it."

"Of course, you do, but if the doctor couldn't have helped him, there's nothing you could have done, either."

"I could've stopped him from crossing the street," Jake said glumly.

"Could you really have stopped him?" she asked in surprise.

"Well, no, I don't think so, but I keep thinking that if I'd been just a minute sooner, maybe I could have."

"You mustn't torture yourself over it. You had no idea what would happen, and you did all you could. Not many people would have gone with him to the hospital."

"I don't even know why I did. I think I was afraid the driver might just dump him into the street as soon as he was out of sight, not wanting to be bothered. It wouldn't be right to leave a man to die alone in the gutter."

"You're very kind," Persephone said, giving him a sweet smile.

"I don't know about that." He really didn't, either, but he was willing to take her word for it.

"Well, I do, and I think you are. Now you said something last night about coming to see us because you'd gotten a sign, I think."

"Oh yes, I almost forgot in all the excitement. Madame Ophelia told me I'd get a sign from my mother."

Persephone's sweet smile bloomed again. "I believe your mother's spirit told you that, not Madame Ophelia."

Jake nodded his understanding. "Right. I guess I'm not used to this spirit thing yet. Anyway, I was supposed to get some kind of sign, and I found this in my pocket yesterday." He pulled out the handkerchief and handed it to her.

"You just found it yesterday?" she asked, probably surprised that it had taken him so long. She unfolded the cloth square to read the embroidery. "Oh my!"

"Yes, it's amazing, isn't it? I couldn't imagine what kind of a sign my mother could send me so I'd be sure it was from her."

"This is pretty obvious, though, isn't it?" Persephone said, plainly pleased. "Do you know what it means?"

"I think it means that I'm supposed to take advantage of the opportunity she sent me. It came as a surprise, but I'm going to make a lot of money on this deal, Persephone. For once my mother is going to really help me."

• • •

After their encounter with the mysterious girl, Cybil and Zelda went about their usual Saturday duties, tidying up their house and going to the market. Cybil could tell Zelda was still worrying about the girl and nothing Cybil said could convince her not to. They were finally relaxing that afternoon when someone knocked on their door.

"I'll get it," Cybil said, fairly certain she knew who would be calling or at least the reason for their visit.

Zelda frowned but made no move to follow her out to the foyer. Cybil opened the door to a rather ordinary-looking gentleman in a well-tailored suit and sporting an impressive set of side-whiskers. He pulled off his derby hat when he saw her.

"I'm so sorry to bother you, ma'am, but I was wondering if you'd seen a young girl wandering around the neighborhood alone. She . . . Well, I'm afraid she might be in some danger."

"Danger from what?" Cybil asked.

The man winced. "From being all alone in the city. Any young girl would be in danger in that situation, don't you agree?"

Cybil didn't bother to say if she did or did not. "Is she some relation to you?"

"No, not exactly. You see, she . . . Well, I suppose I should explain. I've started a sort of ministry in the city, a home for wayward girls."

"How magnanimous of you, sir," Zelda exclaimed. At some point she had joined Cybil in the foyer. She would have overheard him and been unable to resist.

"I am just trying to do the Lord's work," he said modestly. "But it isn't as easy as one might think. And now young Sally has run away. She's not very trustful, I'm afraid."

"I think we may have seen her," Zelda said. "She was rooting through our garbage this morning for something to eat."

"Oh dear, that sounds like something she might do. She was living a rather vagabond life of late, at least until I convinced her to come to my refuge. Do you by any chance know where I could find her?"

"We could tell you which way she went after she left us," Cybil said, "but that was hours ago. She could be anywhere by now."

The poor man seemed to sag with despair. "What am I going to do? These poor girls need so much help and I simply can't make them trust me."

Zelda nudged Cybil out of the way. "Why don't you come inside, Mr. . . . ?"

"Oh, I'm sorry. How rude of me. Waterson is my name, but I don't want to impose—"

"Nonsense," Zelda insisted. "You must come in and tell us all about your ministry and how you came to think of it and then maybe we can help you find poor Sally."

Elizabeth and Gideon returned from an afternoon walk in the park to find Mother Bates entertaining a visitor in the parlor.

"Madame Ophelia," Elizabeth said. "What a surprise."

Elizabeth had to feign her dismay since she'd been expecting a visit soon, but Gideon's was very real. "To what do we owe this honor?" He didn't even bother to hide his displeasure.

Madame Ophelia was unfazed. "I knew you would want to know at once that the poor gentleman who was injured last night did indeed pass."

"Oh dear," Elizabeth said, noting that Mother Bates was managing a sympathetic expression.

"I suppose that young fellow returned to tell you the news," Gideon said. His annoyance was very real, which was a good thing since Gideon was a notoriously bad liar. "Didn't you say he was a client?"

"I can see that you don't trust me, Mr. Bates," Madame said with a hint of condescension, "but I assure you I am telling you the truth. Why would I lie about something that can be easily checked?"

Elizabeth knew it couldn't be checked at all, since none of them had any idea who the victim or the driver were, but she was happy to allow

Madame her bold falsehood. "You can't blame my husband for being skeptical," Elizabeth said. She loved saying "my husband."

"Indeed, it is to his credit that he wishes to protect you, but he is powerless to do so now that you understand your gift."

Elizabeth sighed and sank down onto the love seat beside Madame Ophelia. "I'd hardly call it a gift."

"Oh, but it is," Madame insisted. "I have come to help you accept it, if you will give me the opportunity."

"This is ridiculous," Gideon declared.

"Gideon, dear," his mother said, "perhaps you would leave us alone to discuss the matter with Madame Ophelia."

"But I—"

"Yes, darling, please allow me to hear what Madame Ophelia has to say," Elizabeth entreated, giving him a loving smile that he could not possibly refuse, even if they hadn't already discussed the need for him to leave her alone with the medium.

"I will look after Elizabeth's interests," Mother Bates assured him, forcing Elizabeth to bite her lip so she wouldn't grin at her mother-in-law's masterful finagling. She did so want to listen in on this conversation.

Gideon frowned thunderously. "All right, but you know how I feel about all of this."

243

"I believe we do, darling," Elizabeth said. "I promise I won't make any decisions without consulting you."

With a long-suffering sigh, he left them, closing the parlor doors behind him.

Elizabeth turned to Madame Ophelia. "Can you really be sure that man died?"

"I am positive."

"Because you know that young man?" Mother Bates asked.

"Yes. I believe Persephone told you he is a client. He was coming to show us that he had received a sign from his late mother."

"A sign you told him to expect?" Elizabeth asked.

"Of course. He will become very successful as a result of the guidance the spirits have given him. This is how I use my gift, and you have the power to help others in the same way."

"By telling them how to win horse races?" Elizabeth asked bitterly.

Madame smiled beneficently. "That must have been startling to you, but sometimes the spirits make themselves known in odd ways. You might have resisted even longer in accepting your gift if the first manifestation had been less dramatic."

"Nothing could have been more dramatic than the second manifestation," Elizabeth said. "That poor man actually died."

"I think you're forgetting the real second

manifestation, dear," Mother Bates said kindly. "The accident was the third. The second was finding the will for that lady."

Actually, the second one had been Elizabeth accusing Madame's confederates of being fakes, but Elizabeth didn't think it was a good idea to remind her of that. Elizabeth rubbed her temples in feigned frustration. "You're right, of course. I almost forgot Miss Miles and her uncle. I suppose she's waiting for some more guidance as well."

"And she will receive it. The spirits have spoken," Madame said. "I understand your reluctance, Mrs. Bates. I was slow to accept my gift, too."

Elizabeth doubted this very much, but she said, "What finally convinced you?"

"A trusted mentor," Madame said, making Elizabeth want to roll her eyes and forcing her not so much as to glance at Mother Bates, for fear they would not be able to control themselves. "And irrefutable proof that my gift was real."

"I believe you have achieved both of those, Elizabeth," Mother Bates said helpfully.

But Elizabeth couldn't be too easily persuaded. "But what am I supposed to do now that I understand my so-called gift? I can hardly set up shop and start holding séances. What would your friends say, Mother Bates? We'd become a laughingstock."

"You are fortunate that you do not need to earn your living, Mrs. Bates," Madame said in that voice she used to persuade. It had probably proven very useful to her through the years. "So you need not *set up shop,* as you say. I would be more than happy to allow you to attend séances with me so you can use your talents without having to scandalize your society friends."

"And what if Elizabeth decides to do nothing at all?" Mother Bates asked. "She could simply decide not to pay any attention to this gift of hers."

"That is not possible," Madame said. She turned back to Elizabeth. "Last night you knew what was going to happen to that man even before the séance started, didn't you?"

"I . . . Yes, I'm afraid I did," she said quite truthfully.

"You saw it without even trying. You could not help yourself. You cannot control your gift. The best you can do is learn to use it properly."

"And how do I use it *properly?*" Elizabeth asked.

"By sharing it," Madame said gently. "If you attend my séances, you can do this easily, and you will not be overcome by it."

"Did you feel overcome last night, dear?" Mother Bates asked.

Elizabeth sighed in resignation. "Yes, I did. But I'm not sure what I could have done with that knowledge. I didn't even know who was going to be . . . injured, so how could I have used my power to stop it?"

"You will learn to recognize the visions when they come. If you had known what you were seeing last night, you could have waited and stopped that man from stepping into the street, for instance."

"Do you think so? You mean, I could have saved him?" she asked in dismay.

Madame smiled benignly. "It is possible, but you will need more practice to master the skill."

"That would be a wonderful ability," Mother Bates said. "To foresee disaster and stop it, I can't even imagine how amazing that would be."

"And you would accept me into your séances?" Elizabeth asked doubtfully. "Won't people be— I don't know—confused by having two of us giving them messages?"

"I think they will be thrilled," Madame said with certainty. "And I will welcome you as a sister."

"Can I have some time to think about this?" Elizabeth said. "And to discuss it with my husband?"

"Does he control what you do?" Madame asked with what might have been a note of censure.

"Of course, he does," Mother Bates said with a certainty that would have astonished Gideon. "Husbands must have absolute authority over their wives."

"Legally, perhaps, but that hardly applies in this case," Madame said.

"Oh, I think it does. He could forbid her to attend your séances," Mother Bates countered.

"And would you obey him?" Madame challenged.

Elizabeth chose not to address that particular issue, since Gideon was hardly likely to forbid her from doing anything at all.

"My husband will always want what is best for me," she said instead. "Would you like to schedule a particular séance for me to attend or may I visit different ones?"

Plainly, Madame had not expected such an easy victory. She had to give the question a moment's thought. "I . . . Perhaps you would like to visit several different ones. That will give you the opportunity to meet more of my clients." And impress them so Madame could charge them more, since they might get an accurate prediction. "We must determine when and how your gift works best."

"Shall I tell you when I will attend?"

"I would appreciate it. I will have to raise the price for those who come, since you will take a spot at the table." So she had already considered this!

"Let me discuss it with my husband and I will send you word of when I can next attend."

• • •

Gideon was a little surprised when Smith, his clerk, came in after his first client on Monday morning had left to inform him Cybil Miles had made an appointment for later in the day.

When she arrived, Cybil was more conservatively dressed than he had ever seen her. She wore a blue walking suit with a white shirtwaist, and she had chosen a simple matching hat with only a plain ribbon and a small cluster of flowers as adornment.

"Miss Miles, how nice to see you," he said as she came in, using her more formal title in case she was not alone. He had come around his desk to greet her and shake her outstretched hand.

"I was so glad you were able to see me today," she said. "I'm alone, so we can speak freely."

Gideon got her seated comfortably in one of the client chairs and instructed Smith to bring her some tea. "May I assume that you have recently made a new friend?"

"Indeed, I have. It all started out so innocently. We caught a rather wretched-looking child rummaging in our garbage on Saturday morning. Zelda tried to lure her into the house so we could at least offer her some food, but she accused us of wanting to sell her into prostitution and ran off."

"That sounds like something that might happen anytime in the city," Gideon said.

"Sadly, you are correct, and we might not have

thought anything more about it except that a few hours later, a gentleman came to our door to ask if we had seen the child."

"That does sound odd," Gideon agreed. "Did he claim she was his daughter or something?"

"Absolutely not. He was rather well-dressed and a bit too respectable-looking to lay claim to such an urchin, and he openly admitted that she was no relation. He was, he claimed, trying to establish a sort of ministry that would provide a safe haven for the many abandoned female children in the city. It would be similar to the Newsboys' Lodging Houses, except it would only admit girls."

"Are you sure he wasn't just a . . . a procurer?" Gideon asked, choosing the only word he could think of besides "pimp," which should have been shocking to a lady like Cybil.

"I don't have much experience with men who manage prostitutes, but I can't imagine a more unlikely candidate for that position," she reported with amusement. "He was so very, very respectable and apologetic. He also lamented the difficulties he was having in convincing the girls in question of his honorable intentions."

"I'm glad I wasn't the only skeptic."

"I'm sure it's a natural assumption when a man tries to round up girls and put them into a house. He was so despondent over his lack of success that Zelda invited him in for some coffee. When he learned that we are both professors at a college for women, he declared we were the perfect partners for his enterprise. He believes the only thing holding him back was some respectable females to help recruit lodgers and an influx of capital, so he could properly outfit the building he wants to purchase."

"Was he equally astonished to learn about your recent inheritance?" Gideon asked with a knowing grin.

"We didn't mention it to him, but I didn't think we needed to, since it seems likely he already knows about it."

"I suspect you are right. What do you need from me?"

"A little legal advice, actually," Cybil said with a grin.

Gideon returned her grin. "How fortunate. I happen to have a little to spare."

"I just want to be certain I understand the legalities of my inheritance, so I can adequately forestall this gentleman while we finish our work."

"Since you don't actually have an inheritance, that should be relatively simple, but I know you aren't really worried about losing any money, just in holding him off while keeping him on the hook. Is that about right?"

"Not exactly how a con artist would phrase it, but yes, that is exactly what I need to do."

"I don't really see a problem. You only dis-covered your uncle's will a few days ago. You said you had filed it for probate, and ordinarily it would just be a matter of time before you received your inheritance. However, your imaginary cousin will probably contest the will since he is the direct heir and was completely disinherited, so that could delay the distribution of the funds indefinitely."

"I hadn't thought of a discontented, disinherited heir to delay things. That is exactly what I need," Cybil said, obviously delighted.

"I'm happy to help."

"I just wish this didn't sound like such a worthy cause. They could hardly have come up with anything more likely to appeal to me."

"I believe Madame Ophelia is so successful with her séances because she is so good at judging people and figuring out what matters most to them. You are an unmarried college pro-fessor who teaches other women, so naturally you would be well aware of all the hazards facing young women in this city."

"Yes, I am, and someone should have seen this need long ago and taken steps to meet it."

"I'm sure some people have, although they have obviously not succeeded in any meaningful way, but this gentleman is not one of them, so we needn't worry about hurting his efforts."

"I'm sure you're right. I certainly hope the child we saw was in his employ."

"She probably was, at least temporarily. She may not even be a street urchin."

"I sincerely hope not. We've been keeping an eye out for her, but she hasn't returned."

"I doubt she will. She served her purpose. Now, tell me what this fellow's name is and what he looks like."

"His name is Waterson and he's rather non-descript except for his side-whiskers, which are quite impressive." She gave him the rest of Waterson's description and it could have fit half the men in the city. Still, Gideon made notes.

"I'll pass that information along to Elizabeth and Jake, in case they run into him."

"I imagine Madame Ophelia keeps her inner circle very small, so they probably will."

"I suppose she doesn't want to have to keep track of a lot of associates," Gideon guessed.

"Or split the money with a lot of other people," Cybil added with a grin. "Will I need to bring Mr. Waterson to consult with you?"

"That is up to him. I can't imagine he'll want an attorney involved in his project, though."

"I'll let you know if he does."

"I hope you do. I'm feeling a bit left out."

Cybil could only laugh.

Jake roused himself from his nap when Harriet shouted from the front office that he had a visitor. Harriet was too professional to do such a thing

253

in front of a mark, so Jake knew who his visitor must be. When he'd rubbed the sleep out of his eyes and shrugged back into his suit jacket, he found his old friend Texas John waiting for him in the front office.

"I see you got my message," Jake said.

"This should be fun, although I never ran a con for charity before," Tex said with a grin.

"Don't worry. You'll still get your share, but I warn you, Lizzie will try to talk you into donating part of it to the innocent victims."

"I'm sure I can resist her efforts," Tex said, making Harriet laugh derisively.

Tex frowned, but Jake distracted him by suggesting they go over the plan once more before they left to meet Waterson at his hotel.

Jake escorted Tex to the hotel, and then they took the elevator up to Waterson's suite. Waterson greeted them enthusiastically and Jake introduced Tex as Roger Coleman. Waterson offered them a drink and the three men sat for a few minutes, making small talk. Waterson asked Tex and Jake how they knew each other.

"Young Miller here is handling my stocks," Tex said, giving Jake a fond look. "I was skeptical at first, because he's so young, but he's done pretty well by me. That's why I agreed to meet with you, even when he told me it wasn't a stock deal. He's never steered me wrong before, and he told me this was something special."

"What else did he tell you?" Waterson asked, glancing at Jake, who kept his face expressionless.

"Not much, except it was a land deal and confidential and you'd explain why."

Waterson nodded. "I'm handling the sale of twenty-five thousand acres of oil-rich land in Texas."

"Oil?" Tex echoed, suitably impressed. "You didn't say anything about oil," he reminded Jake.

"I didn't want you to get too excited and start bragging to your friends," Jake said with a smile.

Tex turned back to Waterson "If it's so valuable, why are the owners selling?"

Waterson exchanged a glance with Jake. "The owners are Germans. They are unable to travel to the United States and they are . . . Well, I don't suppose I need to explain that they are rather short of funds at the moment."

"I don't suppose you do need to explain," Tex said. "The Germans pretty much bankrupted themselves over that ridiculous war."

"Yes, well, in any case, my clients can't travel here to develop the land themselves and they can't sell the land to the big oil companies because they have refused to do business with them, so they have given me the authority to sell it privately."

"They must trust you a lot?" Jake observed, making it a question.

Waterson shifted uneasily in his chair. "Yes, well, they are related to me. To my wife, actually."

Tex nodded knowingly. "I can see why you didn't mention that before." Many people of German descent had experienced prejudice and outright violence during the war.

"But that shouldn't make any difference now. The war is over, and there is no reason you shouldn't benefit from my wife's family's misfortune."

Tex nodded his agreement. "Then let's see this map young Miller told me about."

Waterson was only too happy to pull it from his briefcase and spread it out on the table. Tex had a lot of questions and Waterson patiently explained all the notations on the map. Plainly, a large deposit of oil lay under the land, and adjoining properties were owned by the same oil companies that had reportedly refused to purchase the property.

When he had run out of questions, Tex scratched his head. "What I don't understand is how I got to have first crack at this."

"A series of fortunate events," Waterson said. "I hadn't been able to meet with any eligible buyers, and then I happened to meet your friend Mr. Miller. When I told him my story, he said he thought he had a client who would be interested."

"What do you suppose would be the profit if I

started pumping oil out of this land?" Tex asked as if he couldn't imagine. He probably couldn't.

"Millions, but I must warn you, Mr. Coleman, that not every oil well comes in a gusher. A lot of them never produce at all."

"Yeah, yeah, everybody knows that, but I can see with my own eyes that we're bound to hit if we drill right there." He pointed his well-manicured finger at the black blob representing an oil deposit. "So tell me, Waterson, how much are your clients asking for this property?"

Waterson cleared his throat as if reluctant to say. "Well, as I said, it could be worth millions, so I think ten dollars an acre is a fair price."

"A quarter of a million dollars?" Tex scoffed. "Miller here hasn't made me that rich!"

"You said yourself that you're bound to hit oil on that property," Waterson said.

"And you said not every well comes in a gusher," Tex countered.

Jake settled back to enjoy the show as the two men haggled and argued and haggled some more. Jake admired the way Coleman stuck to his guns. You would have thought it was his own money he was spending. In the end, an apparently unhappy Waterson agreed to three dollars an acre.

After the two men shook on it, Tex said, "I'll need a few days to raise the money."

This was to be expected. Con men even had a name for it. Coleman would go on the send.

Often a mark had to leave town to return home and get the cash. Coleman supposedly lived in the city, though, so he wouldn't have to travel far.

"How much time do you need?" Waterson asked.

Jake jumped in. "Mr. Coleman has all his money in the stock market. It will take me a few days and maybe as long as a week to make sure we choose the right stocks to sell to raise that much cash."

"That's reasonable, I suppose," Waterson said, less than pleased.

"But what guarantee do I have that you won't change your mind and sell to somebody else in the meantime?" Tex said. "Or raise the price on me? I think we need to draw up a contract to protect my interests."

"A contract?" Waterson echoed with a worried frown.

"Yes, a right of first refusal. That way we're both protected. I can't back out and you can't sell to somebody else without giving me a chance to buy the land."

"And what recourse do I have if you do back out?" Waterson asked.

"I have to put down some earnest money, and you'll get to keep it if I don't buy the land, but don't worry. I wouldn't pay a lawyer to draw up this contract if I wasn't sure I wanted this deal. Nothing could stop me now." He pulled out his gold pocket watch. "If you aren't busy now, I can telephone my attorney and he can draw up the papers while we wait."

"I don't know . . ." Waterson hedged.

"It's for your own protection," Jake said. "And it won't cost you a thing."

That seemed to settle it for Waterson, and they went downstairs so Tex could use the public telephone. Jake begged off on the trip to see the attorney, saying he had to get back to his office, and Tex and Waterson set out for the venerable offices of Devoss and Van Aken.

This was shaping up to be an interesting day, Gideon decided when Smith announced that Mr. Waterson and Mr. Coleman were here to see him. He recognized Waterson's name from Cybil's visit, but he had no idea who Coleman might be. The confidential message Mr. Coleman had given when he telephoned to make the appointment was that he had been recommended by Jake Miles. Since Jake was unlikely to be recommending an attorney to his friends for legitimate business, Gideon knew this was part of the Madame Ophelia project. Gideon wasn't sure if he should be flattered or insulted that con men now trusted him to support them in their shenanigans.

Gideon had no problem guessing which man was Waterson. The side-whiskers were a dead giveaway. The other man must be Coleman, and apparently, he was an old friend of Gideon's.

"Bates, good to see you," he said, coming forward to shake his hand. "Thanks for seeing us on such short notice. I know how busy you are."

"Never too busy for you, Mr. Coleman." Gideon could see the glint of appreciation in Coleman's eye before he turned to introduce his companion.

When the men were seated, Gideon said, "Now what can I do for you today?"

"It's relatively simple, I think. As I told your clerk when I telephoned, I'm going to buy some property from Mr. Waterson's clients, and I'd like a right of first refusal drawn up to hold the deal until I can get the cash together."

"You're right. That's relatively simple, but let me ask you a few questions first. This land you're going to buy, you said Mr. Waterson's clients own it."

Waterson frowned. "Well, that's not exactly correct. They transferred it to me to make the process of selling it easier."

"That's . . . unusual," Gideon said tactfully.

"They're family members," Coleman hastily explained, although that didn't really explain much.

"So the deed is in your name?" Gideon asked to clarify.

"Yes."

"Do you have an abstract?"

"Oh yes. I know I can't sell the property without it."

"I'll need to see it and the deed to get the legal description of the property for the contract."

"Of course." Waterson pulled some papers out of his briefcase and passed them across the desk.

"Could you leave these with me while we draw up the papers?" Gideon asked.

Waterson frowned. "I'd rather not."

Gideon nodded, as if this were perfectly reasonable. "I'll have to copy down some information from them, then, for my clerk."

Gideon found the paperwork extremely interesting. "This land is in Texas."

"That's right," Coleman said, rather proud of the fact. "I expect I'll find oil on it, too."

"Finding oil is a very risky business, Mr. Coleman," Gideon felt obligated to say, even though he suspected the oil was a very minor part of this whole thing.

"I know that, but . . . Show him the map, Waterson," Coleman said jovially.

Waterson plainly did not want to show Gideon the map, but he could hardly refuse. He spread it out on Gideon's desk. It was an impressive piece of work. Gideon doubted that finding oil was as simple as locating it on a map, but he pretended to be mollified. "It looks like a prime location. The Texas Company," he mused, reading it on the map. "Is that Texaco?"

"Yes, it is," Waterson said.

Gideon nodded sagely. "Well, then, I suppose you're in a hurry for this contract."

"We were hoping you could have it done today."

"How long would you like the option period to be?"

Coleman shrugged. "Thirty days should be adequate."

"Thirty days?" Waterson protested. "You said a week at most."

"Thirty days is the minimum for a contract like this, but of course you are free to close the sale sooner than that," Gideon explained.

Waterson didn't look happy, but he could see Coleman was set on this, so he agreed.

Gideon told them to come back in a few hours, by which time Smith would have drawn up the document and Gideon would have done his due diligence.

When the two men returned at the end of the workday to sign the papers, Gideon could see they had spent the interim at a saloon. They were quite pleased with themselves.

"I took the liberty of telephoning the local offices of both Standard Oil and the Texas Company to verify that those companies do own the adjoining property," Gideon told them. He wasn't sure this would please Waterson, but he had only been protecting his client.

"You see, Waterson, this is why I like Bates so much. He takes good care of my interests," Coleman said.

"I don't know why you felt that was necessary," Waterson said, a little affronted, "but I'm sure you discovered that they do own the property."

"As a matter of fact, I did." He'd also discovered that they had made no efforts to develop it and seemed ignorant of the vast oil deposits shown on Waterson's map. He didn't think mentioning that would serve any purpose, though. He wouldn't lie, but if no one asked . . .

"Good, good," Waterson said, not asking anything at all.

"We just need your earnest-money payment, Mr. Coleman," Gideon said.

"A thousand, wasn't it?" Coleman asked, reaching for his wallet.

Gideon would not have been surprised to be paid in boodle, which was a wrapped stack of bills with real money on the top and bottom and the rest blank paper, but Coleman gave him ten one-hundred-dollar bills. Then both men signed the contract, although Gideon figured neither was using his legal name, so the whole thing was certainly unenforceable.

"We will hold the contract and the earnest money for thirty days or until you close the sale on the property," Gideon explained. "If Mr. Coleman purchases the property as agreed, he will be refunded the earnest money. If he does not, it will be payable to you, Mr. Waterson."

"Don't worry, Waterson," Coleman said because it appeared he really was worried about something. "I'm going to close this deal as fast as I can."

Waterson gave him a thin smile. "My clients will be very pleased."

CHAPTER ELEVEN

F reddie wants to help," Anna told Elizabeth. She had come by on her way home from class on Monday afternoon to convince Elizabeth to let her new friend participate in the Madame Ophelia con.

"I'm sure she does if you've made it sound as exciting as you think it is," Elizabeth said. "But what could she actually do?"

"You don't know her like I do. She could do anything." Anna looked so determined. She had really developed self-confidence since she had started studying at Hunter College.

They were sitting in the parlor with Mother Bates, who was working on a needlepoint pillow cover. She didn't even look up. "So you think she could do anything? That is an impressive recommendation coming from someone who first helped Elizabeth by committing a murder."

"You see," Anna said with a smug grin. "You probably didn't think I could shoot someone when you first met me, either."

"Of course, I didn't," Elizabeth admitted. "You were like a little mouse, but you grew into a tiger."

"Freddie is already a tiger. You don't know her background. She was raised on a farm, so she's used to hard work and slaughtering animals."

"Oh dear, I don't think we'll need to slaughter anyone, or at least I hope not," Elizabeth teased her.

Anna refused to be discouraged. "What are you going to do for your next prediction?"

"I don't think I really need to do anything much. My last prediction killed a man, after all. How do I top that?"

"And you think Madame Ophelia is going to be terrified on the basis of a horse-race win, a found will, and the death of a man she never even set eyes on?"

Elizabeth frowned. "Anna, you are far too astute. You may also be entirely correct. I probably do need another prediction, just to seal it."

"And it should be of hair-curling importance," Mother Bates said, still engrossed in her needlework.

How did she do that? Elizabeth would either forget the needlework to think or think and end up stabbing herself with the needle.

"Hair curling, I like that," Anna said. "I think Freddie would, too."

"I wish *you* could help, Anna," Elizabeth said wistfully. "I trust you, but Freddie is so innocent. . . ."

"She's very pretty."

Naturally, Anna thought so, but . . .

"Jake thinks so, too," Anna said as if reading her mind.

"Did he say so?"

"Grudgingly, I think," Anna admitted.

"He's jealous."

"Maybe a little."

"She seems very nice. Very sweet," Elizabeth added, reminding her.

"She has brothers. Older brothers. She can stand up for herself. You should hear the way she argues with our professors."

"Arguing with professors can't require that much courage."

"You'd be amazed," Anna said. "And as you suggested, Freddie came up with an idea."

Elizabeth listened to the idea with great interest. Then she considered the matter for a long moment. "I think I need to talk to Jake."

When Gideon arrived home, he could hardly wait for Elizabeth to finish her enthusiastic greeting before telling her he had a lot of news. He let her pour him a small glass of whiskey and then forgot to drink it as he told her and his mother about his visits with Cybil and the two con men, Coleman and Waterson.

"And Waterson is the same man who called on Cybil about that unfortunate girl?" his mother asked to clarify.

"I can't be certain, but she said her Mr. Water-son had rather distinctive side-whiskers, and the one who visited me did, too."

"But how can he be working on both of these projects at the same time?" his mother marveled.

"It's simply a matter of remembering every-one's name, Mother Bates," Elizabeth said. "Con men often have more than one con going at the same time. You also have to be careful managing your schedule, so your marks don't run into each other."

"They should have been careful that their marks don't have the same attorney," Gideon said.

Elizabeth smiled at that. "I assure you that con men seldom use reputable attorneys, and they usually advise their marks not to consult their own attorneys, for fear that they will warn them off."

"Which I certainly did with Mr. Coleman. If there was any oil on that land, Waterson wouldn't be selling it. Even Standard Oil and Texaco aren't interested in it, and they own the land surrounding it."

"How do you know they aren't interested in it, darling?"

"Because I asked them."

For some reason, Elizabeth seemed very sur-prised at this. "How did you ask them?"

"I telephoned their local offices. I wanted to make sure they really owned the adjoining land.

It's what any responsible attorney would do."

"How very diligent of you, darling. I don't suppose your telephone call aroused their interest, did it?"

"I can't imagine that it did."

"But I can. Tell me, did the paperwork show that this Waterson really does own the land himself?"

"It did, and it also showed that he lied about his family members deeding it to him so he could sell it more easily. He apparently bought it two months ago from some Texan."

"I hope you didn't mention that in front of Mr. Coleman."

"I did not. If Coleman had been an ordinary client, I would have, naturally, but I didn't want to spoil whatever was going on by introducing facts."

"That's so smart of you, darling. And did you tell Mr. Waterson that you had contacted Standard Oil and Texaco?"

"Yes, I did."

"Even better. If you will excuse me, I need to telephone the Old Man right away. You just solved a thorny problem."

She was smiling when she returned. Gideon had made a point of not listening to her side of the conversation. Ignorance was bliss when it came to Elizabeth's plans.

"And speaking of thorny problems . . ." he

began as she took her seat beside him again. "Mrs. Darlington came by today to demand that I release the funds she requested. It's been almost three weeks now, and I don't know how much longer I can hold her off."

"Mrs. Darlington?" Elizabeth echoed in confusion.

Gideon slapped his forehead in frustration. "Blast. I forgot I hadn't told you her name."

"Lucretia Darlington?" his mother said. "You are so right not to give her the funds. She is just the sort of person to be taken advantage of."

Gideon groaned.

"It's no matter, darling," Elizabeth assured him. "Your mother and I won't say a word. But you're right. We should deal with her. I don't suppose she mentioned when she would next be attending a séance."

"What does that have to do with anything?" he asked in confusion.

"Because the easiest way to stop her from bothering you is to have the spirits warn her against making this investment."

"Didn't the spirits tell her to make it in the first place?" his mother asked.

"Madame Ophelia told her to," Elizabeth said. "My spirits might have a different opinion."

"Won't that make Madame Ophelia a little angry?" Gideon asked.

"Perhaps, but she also knows the investment is

a con, so my prediction that it is dangerous will be correct," Elizabeth explained. "Even Madame Ophelia won't be able to argue with that."

"And Elizabeth will once again be giving an accurate prediction," his mother pointed out.

"What if she bans you from her séances after that?" Gideon asked.

"She'll be even less likely to after another correct prediction, since it will convince her even more that I really can see the future and she can make a fortune off of me."

"I don't know how she could think that. Doesn't she know I wouldn't allow you to make a spectacle of yourself as a professional fortune-teller?"

"I'm sure she's perfectly willing to destroy our marriage and help me obtain a divorce if necessary," Elizabeth assured him.

His mother smiled sweetly. "But don't worry, Gideon. It won't come to that."

Jake was turning into a regular Gideon Bates, early to bed, early to rise, although he doubted that Gideon stopped off at a pub on his way home from the office every evening. Having to report to an office so early in the morning was deadly dull, so he needed a little something to look forward to. Even still, it was only ten minutes after nine when he arrived at his rooming house that evening.

His landlady emerged from her own room to glare at him. "You have a visitor," she told him with obvious disapproval. "She's been waiting for *hours*."

A woman? "Who is it?"

"She says she's your sister," the landlady said, not believing it for a second.

What would Lizzie have been doing here at this time of night? He hurried into the parlor, which was the room all the boarders used to gather and to entertain visitors of the opposite sex. But the woman waiting there was not Lizzie.

Jake frowned in confusion but decided to play along. His landlady would never permit a visit from an unrelated female, and he didn't want to antagonize her. "Hello, sis."

Freddie grinned slyly. "Where on earth have you been?"

"Out with friends," he said, glancing back to make sure his landlady was witnessing this reunion. "I would've been home early if I'd known you were coming."

"And spoil the surprise? I didn't mind waiting. I brought a book."

She'd brought more than one, actually, probably her schoolbooks. He should pretend to be a bit solicitous of his sister, he figured. "Did you have supper? Can I get you something to drink?"

"My hostess has been taking very good care of

me," she reported, gesturing to a tray bearing the remains of a pot of tea and some cookies.

The landlady made a huffing sound and retired back to her apartment. Jake sighed and moved into the parlor. Freddie sat down on the sofa and he sat beside her. "What are you doing here?"

"Maybe I wanted to see you." She was still grinning like the cat who ate the canary.

"Why would you want to see me?" he asked suspiciously. They were speaking softly, in case the landlady hadn't completely lost interest in them.

She frowned her disappointment. "You underestimate your charms, Jake, if you can't imagine why I'm here."

He knew exactly how charming he was, and he hadn't made any effort at all to charm Frederica Quincy, so he really couldn't imagine why she'd sought him out. "Does Anna know about this?"

"About us, you mean?" she asked coyly. "She may suspect."

Jake didn't understand this at all. He could have sworn that she was in love with Anna. And Anna was clearly in love with her. How could he have been so wrong? And what on earth was he going to do about it? "Look, Miss . . ." He caught himself and glanced over his shoulder to see if his landlady was anywhere in sight. "Look, Freddie, I don't know how you got the idea that I'd be interested in you but—"

"Oh, I think you'll be more than interested in me. I think we'll have a torrid love affair."

Jake ran a weary hand over his face. He should have stayed longer at the pub.

On Tuesday afternoon Waterson stopped at the front desk of his hotel to pick up his key, and the clerk handed him a message along with it. He didn't bother to read it until he got up to his suite and poured himself a stiff drink. This business was getting too complicated. Anytime you got lawyers involved, it was time to pack up and move on. He'd have to point that out next time he spoke to his partner. They'd done well enough in New York. There were plenty of other cities ripe for the picking. No sense in being greedy.

When he was settled comfortably and puffing on a brand-new cigar, he opened the message slip. He'd been expecting to hear from Coleman or maybe even Miller, but this message was from a man he'd never heard of, Thomas Stillwell. It seemed Mr. Stillwell was interested in speaking with him about some property he owned in Texas.

That made Waterson smile. He rarely had marks come forward and volunteer. Of course, he had just signed a contract requiring him to give Coleman right of first refusal, but if he remembered the terms correctly, he could sell to someone else if the new buyer offered a higher price. Waterson wasn't going to deny this

Stillwell the right to buy property, especially if it meant he could get the two potential buyers into a bidding war that would jack up the price. Even if it didn't come to that, he could probably sell the same property twice. Neither man was likely to find out they weren't the only owner once they discovered that the land was worthless.

Waterson checked his watch and realized Stillwell would probably still be in his office, so he went downstairs and telephoned the number Stillwell had left. To Waterson's surprise, the secretary who answered identified the company as Standard Oil. Intrigued now, Waterson was tapping his foot impatiently by the time Stillwell came on the line.

"Mr. Waterson, thank you for answering my message so quickly. I'm quite anxious to speak with you."

"Your message said you are interested in the land I own in Texas."

"Yes, we've been trying to track you down for several weeks without success, so I was delighted to hear from your attorney, Mr. Bates, yesterday and find out you're right here in the city."

"What is it you wanted to speak with me about?" Waterson asked, more than curious now.

"It's, well, not something I'd like to discuss on the telephone. Would it be possible to meet so we can speak privately? I'll gladly come to your hotel. I don't want to inconvenience you."

That was odd, since big oil company executives usually didn't mind inconveniencing anyone. "I guess my attorney told you where you could find me."

"Yes, he was quite helpful once I explained our interest."

"Well, I'd like you to explain your interest to me, too. Are you free this afternoon?"

They arranged to meet in the hotel bar at five o'clock.

Jake was relieved to find Persephone still at the storefront. The afternoon séance had been over for a while, but he'd had to wait until the supposed end of his workday to come looking for her.

She greeted him with a smile. "What brings you here? We've finished for the day, I'm afraid."

"I need to attend another séance."

Her smile widened. "I told you that you would want to keep in contact with your loved ones."

He shrugged. "It's not that so much as . . . Well, my mother seems to be determined to do me a good turn now, even though she never seemed interested in doing that when she was alive, so I figured I should keep the channels open."

"Did the deal you told me about work out?"

"It's going to very soon."

"And I suppose you're hoping for another message like that."

"I sure am. So, can you schedule me for another séance? Where is your book? Let's find a time when I can come."

She shook her head at his eagerness, but she was still smiling. She probably figured she'd just hooked a live one. She got the appointment book, an impressive leather-bound diary, and she didn't object when he peered over her shoulder at the pages as she turned them, looking for a spot where she could write him in.

"Why does Madame Ophelia limit the séances to six attendees?" he asked, noting that pattern.

"She says the spirits get confused if too many people participate," Persephone said absently, still scanning the pages.

"I don't think they'd get confused from just one more person," he argued.

She was unmoved. "I'm afraid we don't have anything for you for at least two weeks."

He frowned. "Even if I sneak away from my office during the day and risk getting fired?"

"Even then. Madame Ophelia is extremely popular."

"Well, put me down for the first opening and let me know if you can fit me in earlier. Somebody might get sick or something."

"Very few people cancel, even if they are sick," Persephone said.

Jake gave her a mock scowl. "Keep me in mind just the same."

"Oh, I will," she promised, crossing her heart and grinning flirtatiously.

"And just to make sure you don't forget me, why don't you let me buy you supper this evening?"

"That would be lovely," she decided.

"When should I call for you?"

They set a time and Jake left, satisfied he had accomplished every task needed to set up the final stage of the con.

Waterson was sitting at the hotel bar when Stillwell walked in. Waterson would have known him as an oil company executive anywhere. He was tall and well-dressed and as arrogant as a king. Waterson had purposely not ordered a drink because he expected Stillwell to order and pay for both of them.

Waterson rose from his barstool. "Mr. Stillwell?"

"Yes, so good to meet you, Waterson. Shall we find a booth so we can talk?" Without waiting for a reply, he signaled the bartender and ordered two whiskeys.

Arrogant.

When they were seated, they made small talk until their drinks arrived. Stillwell paid as expected.

"Now, what was it you wanted to discuss with me, Mr. Stillwell?" Waterson said, pulling out his watch and checking it to imply that he had a later appointment and no time to spare.

Stillwell smiled his arrogant smile. "As I explained on the telephone, we have been trying to locate you, Mr. Waterson. It has come to our attention that you own a piece of property in Texas that borders some land we own."

"By *we,* do you mean Standard Oil?" Waterson asked with interest.

Stillwell glanced around as if checking for cavesdroppers. "That is correct," he said softly. "And since we are planning to develop this property, we were hoping to add your acreage to it."

"When you say *develop,* do you mean, drill for oil?"

Stillwell shifted uneasily in his seat. "You must understand, Mr. Waterson, that the oil business is extremely uncertain. Just because you drill, that doesn't mean you will find oil, and finding oil in one place does not guarantee that you will find more nearby. It's much like gambling, and one can drill in one spot and come up dry while ten feet away is the richest deposit mankind has ever discovered."

"And what is it you expect to find on my property, Mr. Stillwell?" Waterson asked slyly.

"Naturally, we hope to find the rich deposit. That is what we always hope."

"Then what is to stop me from drilling my own wells on my own property?"

Stillwell gave him a condescending smile. "Nothing at all, Mr. Waterson, but be advised that it costs tens of thousands of dollars to drill for oil. First you must test to find the most likely places to drill, then hire the roughnecks and buy the equipment and spend months or perhaps years drilling wells until one finally comes in . . . if it ever does. You might end up a multi-millionaire but you also might end up dead broke."

"Why isn't Standard Oil dead broke, then?"

"Because we already have hundreds of successful oil wells. Because we can afford to spend tens of thousands of dollars on wells that don't come in. Because we already own the equipment, and we have the men to operate it. An individual usually doesn't have those resources."

"So you'd recommend that I sell my land to you," he guessed.

"We are prepared to make you a generous offer. We can't afford to pay you what you might conceivably earn if you struck oil on your property, but we also don't want you to feel cheated if we do strike oil on it."

"How generous an offer?" Waterson asked as if it was of no importance.

"We were thinking of ten dollars an acre."

Waterson managed not to whistle his appreciation because he knew they were negotiating and it was not smart to accept the first offer or even be impressed by it. "That sounds like a nice deal, but I already have a buyer lined up."

"Have you completed the sale?" Stillwell asked with a frown.

"Not yet, but we do have an option contract."

"I see. Well, I suppose we can just wait and deal with the new buyer. How long until you expect to close?"

But Waterson wasn't interested in letting Coleman turn that kind of profit when Waterson could do so himself. "I doubt he'd sell for that price," he lied.

"We are prepared to pay whatever is reasonable to get the property, Mr. Waterson."

Ah, so he was right that the ten dollars was just the opening gambit. "My contract with the buyer allows me to sell to someone else instead if they offer more money than the buyer is willing to pay."

Mr. Stillwell frowned again as he considered this. "That is typical in such contracts, of course, but Standard Oil prefers not to get involved in third-party negotiations."

"I don't see why that would be a problem," Waterson said genially. "My buyer has already indicated he isn't willing to pay that much for the property."

Stillwell gave him a pitying smile. "That is because he doesn't yet know that Standard Oil is also interested."

"Why would that make a difference?" Waterson scoffed.

"Believe me, Mr. Waterson, it makes a tremendous difference. If your buyer learns that someone like Standard Oil is willing to pay more for the property, he will demand that you sell to him at the same price we offer no matter how high it is, and then try to negotiate an even higher price to sell it to us. As I'm sure you can see, that isn't in Standard's best interest. So we will simply withdraw our offer to you and wait for the sale to take place. Then we can do business with the new owner."

"But . . . but that isn't fair," Waterson tried lamely.

"I can see why you would think so, but my job is to protect Standard Oil's interests, not yours."

Waterson's brain was churning. How could he get out of the deal with Coleman? The seventy-five thousand Coleman was going to pay him was nothing compared to the quarter million or more that this fellow would pay, and he wasn't going to let Coleman make that profit if he could help it. A quarter million was enough to set them up for life. No more fake séances and cons. With that and what they'd already made on the séances, they could retire in style.

"What if I can get out of the contract with my buyer?"

Stillwell considered the question for a long

moment. "Do you think you can do that without alerting your buyer to our offer?"

"I'm the only one who knows about it, and I'm not going to tell him."

"What excuse will you use for breaking the contract, then?"

"That's my problem, isn't it? But don't you worry. I'll do it."

"I wish you good luck, Mr. Waterson."

"And if I succeed, will you still be interested in buying the land?"

"We will certainly be willing to negotiate with you. In fact, let me give you my card." He reached into his inside pocket and pulled out a small silver case. Inside were his business cards, engraved on ivory vellum. They practically screamed money. He laid one on the table and slid it over to Waterson. "Feel free to contact me whenever you find yourself unencumbered."

"I certainly will," Waterson said happily.

"But I must ask you to keep Standard Oil's interest in this property confidential. If word gets out, I'm afraid we will have to withdraw our offer completely."

Waterson figured they didn't want to get into a bidding war with Texaco, although it might be highly beneficial to him if the two giant oil companies were bidding against each other. "I understand. You have my word." For what that was worth.

"Thank you, Mr. Waterson. It's a pleasure doing business with a man who understands these things."

"How did you get involved with Madame Ophelia?" Jake asked Persephone while they waited for their dinners to arrive. They had returned to the same restaurant as before—since it was supposed to be Jake's favorite—and the waiter had already filled their wineglasses. Jake again noticed Persephone didn't take more than a sip or two.

"Madame Ophelia was a friend of my mother's," Persephone said without hesitation. When people were lying, they usually hesitated before answering, getting their story together before speaking. But then Persephone might have told this story often enough that she didn't have to think about it anymore.

"And she hired you to work for her?"

"Not exactly. She took me in when my mother died. I was only fifteen, and all alone in the world. She's always treated me as if I were her own child."

"Then I can understand why you're so devoted to her. Was she already doing séances when you went to live with her?"

"She . . . she already knew she had the gift, but she was just learning to use it."

"When did she start the séances?"

"A few years ago."

"That must have been exciting."

"I—"

"There you are," a woman said, startling them both.

They looked up to see Frederica Quincy glaring down at them.

"Freddie," Jake said, jumping to his feet. "What are you doing here?"

She glared at him. "What am I doing here? I'm following you, of course. The question is, what are you doing here with this . . . this *woman?*"

Persephone gasped at the naked hatred in her eyes. "John, who is this?"

"Who am *I?*" Freddie asked, outraged. "Who are *you?*"

"I . . . I . . ." Persephone sputtered.

"Freddie, please," Jake tried in a fierce whisper. "You're making a scene."

"Shut up," Freddie snapped, dismissing him with a wave of her hand. "Who *are* you? What is your name?" she demanded of Persephone.

"P-P-Penny," she stammered.

"Penny?" Freddie echoed. "Is that your name or what you charge?"

"Freddie, stop this," Jake demanded, but the headwaiter had already arrived.

He glowered his disapproval. "I'm sorry, miss, but you have to leave."

"Why do I have to leave? They're the ones in the wrong," Freddie insisted.

"You're disturbing the other customers," the waiter said, taking her gently by the arm.

She shook him off. "Don't touch me. I don't care about the other customers. These two are disturbing *me*. Do you know what he promised me? Do you have any idea? And now he's here with her and I—"

"Don't make me call a policeman, miss," the waiter said sternly.

"Freddie, just go. I'll come to see you later and explain everything. This isn't what it seems. It's just . . . it's business. She's a client of mine."

"A client?" she scoffed. "I thought you must be a client of hers."

Persephone gasped in outrage but no one paid her any mind.

"Come along, miss, before I have to get rough with you," the waiter said even more sternly.

Freddie turned to him and burst into tears. "He promised me."

"Men are cads," the waiter said, taking her arm again. This time she didn't protest and allowed him to escort her out.

For a long moment, no one broke the tense silence. Then the other customers apparently decided the show was over and resumed their private conversations, although the topic now was most certainly Freddie's little display.

"I'm so sorry, Persephone," Jake said, sinking back into his chair.

"Who was that woman?" she asked in a fierce whisper as if afraid of drawing attention again. "Oh dear, now I sound just like her!"

"She's just a girl I know."

Persephone was not placated. "Plainly, she is more than that to you."

Jake tried his most sincere expression. "But it's true. I hardly know her, but for some reason she decided she was in love with me."

"You must have given her some encouragement."

"I was nice to her, but I'm nice to all the girls I meet. She wasn't anything special, or at least I didn't think she was until she decided she loved me. Then she wouldn't leave me alone. I tried telling her that we were just friends, but she wouldn't accept that. She started talking about getting married, so I decided I should just avoid her."

"How did she know you were here, then?"

"I have no idea. She must have followed me, like she said. I certainly didn't tell her where I'd be."

"Are you sure you aren't, uh, involved with that girl? She seems awfully possessive for someone you hardly know."

"I swear, I only met her a few weeks ago. I think she might be . . . crazy," he admitted reluctantly.

Persephone's eyes widened. "If she's crazy, she could be dangerous."

Jake couldn't help but chuckle at such a thought. "I'm sure she's not dangerous, just annoying."

"Are you really going to see her later?"

He shook his head vehemently. "Oh no, I just said that to make her leave. If I did go see her, it would just encourage her, I think. She won't listen to reason anyway. Maybe seeing me with another girl will convince her to leave me alone, though."

Persephone wasn't convinced. "But you told her I was a client and we were meeting for business."

"Did I?" He scratched his head. "I guess maybe I did. I was just trying to calm her down so she wouldn't make a scene, but that probably wasn't the best thing to say."

"It was if it keeps her from being mad at me," Persephone said primly.

"I'm really sorry you got caught up in all this. I wish I could convince you that I was never seriously involved with that girl."

"It doesn't really matter, since you aren't seriously involved with me, either."

Jake tried his charming smile. "Maybe not yet, but I was hoping to be."

Persephone didn't smile back. "Were you? Or are you just trying to get close to me because of Madame Ophelia?"

"If that's what I wanted, I would have taken Madame Ophelia to dinner," he said, affronted.

At least that made her smile. "She wouldn't have gone."

"You underestimate my charms," he said provocatively, aware that he was quoting Freddie. Good thing Persephone didn't know that.

"But you understand that I must be careful where clients are concerned."

"I know. You also can't afford to show favoritism. Does Madame Ophelia even know that you've been seeing me?"

She dropped her gaze to the tablecloth. "Uh, no, I haven't mentioned it to her."

"Would she forbid you to see me?"

"I don't know."

"But why take a chance, eh?"

She smiled at that. "Exactly."

"I'm flattered that you've chosen to break the rules for me, and I just hope you can forgive me for . . ." He gestured helplessly in the direction that Freddie had gone.

"Just don't let her show up at a séance," Persephone said.

Jake smiled with relief. "Absolutely not."

CHAPTER TWELVE

Gideon knew immediately what the problem was when his clerk came into his office the next morning. Smith's sour expression could mean only one thing.

"Has someone shown up without an appointment?" Gideon asked, managing not to grin.

"Mr. Waterson has asked to see you if you have a moment," Smith said stiffly.

Gideon knew a frisson of excitement and then a moment of dismay to think how boring his ordinary life must be if a visit from a con man caused him pleasure. "I'll be happy to see him." It was too true.

Smith showed Waterson in, making his disapproval known by the set of his shoulders, something only Gideon would have noticed. Gideon greeted him, and Waterson declined the offer of refreshment.

When they were both seated, Gideon said, "How may I help you today, Mr. Waterson?"

Waterson shifted uneasily in his chair. "It's about that contract you drew up for me and Coleman."

"I assumed as much. Is there a problem? I'm

afraid it's a little late to make changes, but if you have a concern—"

"Nothing's wrong with the contract, at least not that I know of, but . . . Well, you see my relatives in Germany aren't happy about it."

It was rather soon for word to have reached someone in Germany and for them to have responded with concerns, but Gideon didn't mention that. "What aren't they happy about?"

"They've decided they don't want to sell the property at all."

Gideon frowned. "It's a shame they didn't inform you of this before you signed a legally binding document."

"Yes, well, that's foreigners for you, isn't it? Always changing their minds."

Gideon wasn't aware that foreigners were more likely than anyone else to change their minds, but he knew better than to disagree. "I'm sure if you explain that you are now legally obligated to make the sale to Mr. Coleman, they will understand."

"You don't know my relatives, Mr. Bates. They can be pretty stubborn."

Gideon smiled his sympathy. "The law can be pretty stubborn as well. If you refuse to sell, Mr. Coleman would be within his rights to sue you." If he could find Waterson, which seemed unlikely.

Waterson obviously also knew how unlikely it

was and appeared unmoved. "A lawsuit would be terrible, of course, but I know you lawyers always know a way to make something happen. I was hoping you could figure out how to get Coleman to cancel the sale."

Gideon sat back in his chair, considering the request. No one had warned him this might happen, so he wasn't sure what he was expected to do. On the other hand, if he hadn't been warned, he was probably expected to do what he would normally do in a situation like this. So, he already knew exactly what to do. "You could, of course, simply explain the situation to Mr. Coleman as you have just done to me and ask him to cancel the contract."

For a moment, Waterson looked hopeful but then common sense prevailed. "He's not likely to do that, though, is he?"

Gideon shrugged apologetically. "Although I warned Mr. Coleman that he may well not strike oil on this land, he seems convinced that he will. Since that is the case, he is unlikely to cancel the contract."

"But if I convinced him to, he could, couldn't he?"

"Of course, but how would you convince him?" Gideon asked with a worried frown. "I can't condone anything that might be illegal or even unethical."

"Would buying him out be illegal or unethical?"

Waterson asked, his black mood having lifted considerably.

"Not at all, but I thought—" Gideon caught himself. He certainly didn't want to talk Waterson out of his plan.

"I know what you thought, Mr. Bates," Waterson said confidently. "You thought we were selling the land because my relatives desperately needed the money."

"It isn't my place to speculate about such things, Mr. Waterson."

"But you are entitled to your opinion, and I admit I gave Mr. Coleman that impression. But I assure you, things are not nearly as desperate as all that."

"So you would be in a position to offer Mr. Coleman some financial remuneration for his trouble?"

"That seems like the only thing likely to convince him, doesn't it?" Waterson asked cheerfully.

"I've found that money often has that effect on people."

Waterson was nodding his agreement. "I don't suppose you have any idea how much it would take to convince Coleman."

"I couldn't possibly guess. As I said, Mr. Coleman is hoping to become a millionaire oil man."

Waterson ran a hand over his face. "Maybe I can explain to him that it's not very likely."

"That would certainly help you, but you'll need to take it up with Mr. Coleman."

Waterson studied Gideon for a long moment. "Maybe I could bring him here to talk it over. You can help by reminding him of your warnings."

Gideon wouldn't have missed that opportunity for the world. "And we'd need to draw up the quitclaim if Mr. Coleman does agree to cancel the contract with you, so meeting here does make sense."

"Maybe you could have it ready for him to sign, just in case."

"I'm afraid we'll have to wait until the two of you decide on the terms, but we can have it ready in a day or two."

Waterson frowned, but he said, "That's fine."

"Then I'll get my clerk in here to make the arrangements," Gideon said. At least Smith would be pleased that Waterson was going to make an appointment this time.

Gideon would never have approved of Elizabeth attending a séance alone, but she really had no choice. Jake had managed to look in Madame Ophelia's appointment book and discovered that Mrs. Darlington attended the Wednesday afternoon séances. If she hoped to protect that good lady, she had to go when Mrs. Darlington was there. Gideon was working at his office at that hour and Mother Bates couldn't go because

Mrs. Darlington knew her. She might mention that Gideon was her attorney. Since he was the one blocking the release of her money and he was also already coincidentally representing too many of Madame Ophelia's other clients, it seemed foolish to let Mrs. Darlington see Mother Bates.

For all those reasons, Elizabeth found herself entering Madame Ophelia's storefront all by herself at the appointed time. Persephone was greeting the latest arrivals when Elizabeth walked in.

"Mrs. Gideon, I wasn't expecting you," she said before she caught herself and remembered to smile professionally. "I mean, how lovely to see you. Perhaps you made arrangements with Madame Ophelia and she neglected to mention it."

"I didn't make arrangements with anyone, I'm sorry to say, and I do apologize for showing up unexpectedly, but . . . may I speak with you privately for a moment, Persephone?"

Having no other choice, Persephone drew her to the far side of the room, as far from the others as possible, although Elizabeth felt certain they would be trying desperately to overhear.

"I would never have just turned up here without letting you know, but I . . . I have had this feeling all day that I needed to be present at this séance. I wasn't even certain until I walked in that you have them on Wednesday afternoons, but I just knew I had to come here today."

Persephone's initial surprise evaporated into concern. "Do you think you have a message to deliver?"

"I have no idea. Oh, Persephone, I don't know what to think. What if someone else is going to die?" she added in a tortured whisper.

Persephone's eyes widened. "Is that the message you're getting?"

"No, not really. And it's not like the other time, not as dark and frightening. Just urgent, I guess. That's the only way I can describe it. As if I have an important appointment and I have to keep it, no matter what. Will Madame be too upset that I just showed up unannounced?"

"I'm sure she'll be fine when I explain."

"If she sends me home, I'll understand. I just knew I had to come, and I've done that. Thank you for your help, Persephone."

Persephone nodded and scurried off to the séance room, presumably to consult with Madame.

Elizabeth took the opportunity to study the other people in the room. They were all women of various ages and stations in life. The smallest and oldest one came forward the moment the door closed behind Persephone.

"You're new, aren't you, dear?" she asked.

"I've attended séances before, just never at

this time," Elizabeth said, returning the older woman's smile.

"I'm Mrs. Phineas Darlington," she said. "I always attend at this time." She looked to be about Mother Bates's age. Her face was too plump for age lines, but her eyes and lips were creased from years of use. Her once blond hair was now silvery, but she hadn't lost her sense of style. Her dress was the height of fashion and obviously custom-made.

"Have you been coming to Madame Ophelia for a long time?" Elizabeth said, carefully not introducing herself. Persephone had called her "Mrs. Gideon" when she came in, so she saw no need to clarify that for Mrs. Darlington.

"For several months now. I've spoken to nearly all of my family members who have passed. Who are you trying to contact, my dear?"

"I . . . No one in particular."

"Oh, you must have someone in mind, or it won't work. The spirits won't know who to send to speak with you."

"That makes sense. Perhaps that is why I haven't had much luck so far."

"I'm sure it is. If you aren't getting messages, it is because you aren't asking anyone in particular."

"What kind of messages do you receive?" Elizabeth asked with creditable innocence.

"All sorts," Mrs. Darlington said proudly.

"I'm never sure what to ask, you see."

"It often doesn't matter what you ask. Sometimes you just get advice you didn't know you needed."

"What kind of advice?"

Mrs. Darlington glanced around as if afraid of being overheard, although it was obvious everyone else in the room was listening to every word. "Business advice."

"Why would you need business advice?"

Before Mrs. Darlington could reply, Persephone emerged from the séance room and came straight to Elizabeth. "Madame Ophelia would be pleased to have you attend this afternoon's séance."

"I hope you told her how sorry I am to just barge in like this."

"She understands completely," Persephone assured her. "One cannot deny the spirits when they speak to us."

With that piece of wisdom, she announced that Madame was ready and ushered them into the other room. Mrs. Darlington sat beside Elizabeth even though Persephone indicated she should use another chair. Elizabeth gave her a grateful smile.

When Persephone had finished with the questions and the burning of them and withdrawn, Madame began her ritual humming. As usual, Madame's spirit contacts answered various questions from the other attendees. Finally, Madame's spirit voice said, "Lucretia, have you done what I told you to do?"

"Phineas, is that you?" Mrs. Darlington asked eagerly.

"Of course it is. Answer me. Have you done as I instructed you?"

"I'm trying, but I haven't been able to get the lawyers to release the funds."

"You must try harder, Lucretia. This is for your own good."

"I know. I will do as you instructed me, Phineas. I promise!"

"Aaaaahhhhh!" Elizabeth cried in her spirit voice. "Stop! Don't do it!"

Elizabeth had closed her eyes, but she could feel everyone's startled attention turn to her.

"What is it?" Madame asked in her own voice. "What do you see?"

"This lady," Elizabeth said, moving her head from side to side as if she couldn't control it. "Do not give that man your money. He will steal it all!"

"What?" Mrs. Darlington asked, obviously bewildered. "Are you talking to me?"

"Lucretia," Elizabeth said to confirm it. "That man is a thief. He will take all your money."

"But . . ." Mrs. Darlington said plaintively. "Phineas told me to do it."

"He is mistaken. Do not trust the man from the water."

"From the water?" one of the other women asked, obviously confused.

"I see water," Elizabeth said. "It is dark and dangerous, and your money is sinking, disappearing, lost forever. . . ."

"What does water have to do with it?" another woman asked.

"He's a child of the water," Elizabeth's spirit said. "He will devour you and leave you alone and penniless."

Mrs. Darlington gasped at the horrible prospect and others joined her.

"Who are you?" one of the women asked. "Who is she? How does she know these things?"

"I am nobody," Elizabeth groaned. "I am just a vessel."

"Do you have a message for me?" another woman asked. "I need to know what happened to my son."

But Elizabeth had no idea what had happened to her son, so she groaned again and opened her eyes. She didn't have to pretend to be surprised to find everyone staring at her with mingled horror and fascination. Except for Madame Ophelia, who was apparently quite furious and trying her best to hide it.

"Did it happen again?" Elizabeth asked Madame in dismay.

"You had a message for Mrs. Darlington," she replied without the slightest trace of pleasure.

Elizabeth turned to the lady in question. "I hope it was helpful."

"Don't you remember?"

"I'm sorry. I don't."

Mrs. Darlington did not appear pleased, either. "You told me not to do something that my husband's spirit had told me to do."

"I'm so sorry. I'm afraid *I* didn't tell you anything at all, though. I don't even know what I may have said."

"Oh, I understand. It was the spirits speaking through you, but what am I supposed to think? One spirit tells me one thing and another spirit tells me something else."

Elizabeth knew that nobody liked being told what to do, and the best way to ensure they would balk is to give them an order. If a mark made the decision himself, however, he would go to his grave thinking it was the right choice. "I don't know what to tell you, and I am probably the last person you should ask for advice. You should do what you think is best."

"But I don't know what is best," Mrs. Darlington whined.

Elizabeth laid a hand on Mrs. Darlington's arm. "Perhaps the spirits will tell you which message is the right one."

"Yes," Madame quickly confirmed. "I am sure they will." Madame would probably make sure that they did.

Mrs. Darlington sighed. "This is all so difficult. I don't know why Phineas had to die. It has made my life so complicated."

The other women murmured their sympathy. Madame called for Persephone, who hurried in to escort them out.

Elizabeth didn't rise with the others. She took a moment to rub her temples, as if her head ached. "I'm sorry. I feel a bit dizzy."

"That is to be expected," Madame said, unable to keep all the anger from her voice. She must have been livid that Elizabeth had given Mrs. Darlington second thoughts when she was so ready to turn over a fortune. Still, she apparently couldn't help her interest in Elizabeth's powers. "Tell me, what made you believe you needed to attend today's séance?"

"I can't really explain it. I felt completely normal when I woke up this morning, but sometime after breakfast, I started thinking I had an important appointment. At first I thought perhaps I did and had just forgotten, but I checked my diary and didn't find anything. I tried to brush it off, but the feeling kept getting stronger and then I had a flash of something."

Madame frowned. "A flash?"

"I know it sounds strange, but I don't know how else to describe it. For just an instant, I saw this room and you and . . . and other people, although

I couldn't see anyone clearly. It happened much too quickly."

"You actually had a vision?" Madame demanded, still frowning although her anger had become something else entirely.

"I don't know if I'd call it a vision. It was just the barest glimpse of something. The stranger part was that afterward, I couldn't think of anything except coming here. I didn't want to do it, you understand, and I tried to distract myself and think of something else, but nothing worked. I felt like I would just start screaming if I didn't come here, so I did." She smiled helplessly. "I thought perhaps you could explain it to me."

"And you didn't know Mrs. Darlington before this?" Madame asked suspiciously.

"I don't think so. I don't remember ever meeting her, and she must not have remembered me, either. She introduced herself to me out in the waiting room."

"She may have felt drawn to you," Madame said a little uncertainly.

"So, I did the right thing by coming here?"

"Oh yes, you were right to come to me. The gift can be overwhelming, I know."

"Yes, that is exactly how I felt, *overwhelmed*. Thank you for being so understanding. I'm very fortunate to have you to advise me."

"And you have no memory of what you said to Mrs. Darlington?"

Elizabeth frowned. "No, and obviously, it was a confusing message. I'm so sorry she was upset."

Madame waved away her concerns. "We cannot control the messages, as you know."

"How could we if we don't even know what they are?" Elizabeth agreed, although Madame always knew exactly what they were.

"Yes, well, we should arrange for another séance soon. Your powers are obviously gaining strength, and I don't want them to get out of control. That would be very bad for you."

"Thank you for your concern. I suppose you're right. I've been reluctant to reschedule, but now I see that's foolish. If I don't do it, the spirits will drive me here anyway."

"So it seems," Madame agreed. "Please tell Persephone to arrange a special séance for you to attend."

"Thank you, Madame. I don't know what I would do without your help."

Madame smiled at that, although it was a little rueful. "I am happy to be of assistance."

Elizabeth decided she was recovered enough to make her exit. She found everyone from the séance still in the waiting area and gathered around a handsome young man.

Jake had always been popular with ladies of all ages.

Mrs. Darlington had just asked him, "What do

305

you think I should do?" when he caught sight of Elizabeth.

"Is that the lady who gave you the message?" he asked Mrs. Darlington.

Elizabeth froze, as if uncomfortable with the attention as everyone turned to her.

"Yes," Mrs. Darlington said. "She got a special message just for me."

But Jake was no longer listening. He smiled at her. "You were here the other night, when the accident happened, weren't you?"

"Yes," she admitted with apparent reluctance.

He glanced at Persephone, as if for confirmation, but she refused to meet his gaze. She probably wasn't pleased that he had seen Elizabeth. He turned back to Elizabeth. "Are you the one who predicted the accident? You are, aren't you?"

Elizabeth shivered. "Please . . ."

"What accident?" someone asked.

"A man got run over by a wagon," Jake said, gesturing. "Right out front here. I was on my way to talk to Madame Ophelia, and I saw the whole thing."

Mrs. Darlington was gaping at Elizabeth now. "And you predicted it?"

"I didn't predict it," she insisted.

"Persephone told me you did," Jake insisted. "She said you knew the man was going to die, too."

306

"He *died?*" someone gasped.

"And she knew it was going to happen?" another asked in amazement.

While they were still immobile with shock, Jake stepped forward. "I've been wanting to meet you. I'm John Miller."

Elizabeth automatically offered him her hand. "And I am Mrs.—" She cried out as if his touch had burned her, and jerked her hand loose again. "No!" she gasped, taking a step back and covering her mouth with her other hand.

"What is it? Did I hurt you?" he asked, looking at his hand as if it might have been guilty of something.

But she was shaking her head and still backing away.

"What is it?" Persephone asked, hurrying to her side. "Mrs. Gideon, are you all right?"

She caught Elizabeth's arm and gazed deeply into her eyes.

Elizabeth shivered again and tried to shake off whatever had seized her. "I . . . I'm sorry. I just . . ."

"Are you hurt?" he asked again, frowning in confusion.

"No, I just . . . For a moment, I had this terrible feeling, but it's gone now." She managed a feeble smile. "I didn't mean to frighten you."

But he wasn't smiling back. "Did you have another premonition?"

She tried shaking her head, but no one was convinced.

"You did, didn't you?" one of the other women asked.

"Just a feeling," she hastily explained.

"Was it about me?" Jake asked anxiously. "Was it something about me?"

"I . . . I don't know. It was so fast, I don't know what it was."

"Did you see something?" someone asked.

"What did you see?"

"Was it the spirits or something else?"

"Can you do it again? Can you answer my question?"

"Please," Persephone pleaded as Elizabeth became visibly upset by the barrage of questions. "Stop tormenting her."

"I must go," Elizabeth said, pushing her way through them, but she stopped at the door and turned back and looked straight at Jake. "Be careful," she said urgently, and then fled.

Cybil and Zelda had just arrived home from their teaching duties when someone rang the doorbell. Cybil answered it and was not surprised to find Mr. Waterson on her doorstep.

"I hope this isn't an inconvenient time, Miss Miles," he said.

"Not at all. Please come in, and before you ask, we haven't seen a trace of the girl you were seeking the last time you were here."

"I don't expect you have. She returned to the shelter shortly after we spoke. I think she may have found hunting through garbage pails a bit too disappointing."

"I'm so glad to hear that, Mr. Waterson," Zelda said, having followed Cybil to the door.

"I'm not quite as glad as you are, Miss Goodnight," Waterson said when they had moved to the parlor and taken seats. "You see, Sally was not the innocent child she appeared to be. She turned out to be far more devious than I had any right to suspect."

"I'm sorry to hear that, Mr. Waterson. Has she run away again?" Cybil said.

"Yes, but more important, she ran away with all the money I had collected from my generous donors to finance the purchase of a permanent house of refuge for the girls."

"How awful," Zelda exclaimed. She might actually have believed this tale. Cybil would have a talk with her later.

"Yes, I'm afraid it's my fault for being so trusting."

"I'm surprised you didn't keep the money in the bank," Cybil said, allowing herself to sound reproving.

"I did, of course, but I'd just taken it out to make the purchase, you see. The owner wanted cash. I have a safe, and I thought it would be secure there overnight, but as I said, I underestimated Sally."

"Are you saying the girl broke open a safe?" Cybil asked, not even having to feign her disbelief.

Waterson hung his head in shame, which he had every right to feel. "I hadn't underestimated her that much, I'm glad to say, but she was clever enough to discover where I had written down the combination." When both women gasped their dismay, he added, "I know, I know. It was foolish of me. I deserve everything you are thinking about me, but the real victims here are the poor girls. I was hoping to have a permanent home for them so they would never have to worry about being homeless again, but now . . ."

"Mr. Waterson, I cannot fault you for being foolish," Cybil lied. "We have all made mistakes and trusted the wrong people, so you are no worse than the rest of us."

"You are very kind, Miss Miles."

"But I can't help wondering why you came to tell us in particular your sad tale," she added.

He had the grace to look abashed. "I was afraid that Sally might find her way back here and try to take advantage of you as well. I have been following in her footsteps to warn everyone who encountered her on her last escape. I'm sorry to have bothered you, but I did feel it my duty to warn you."

"That is so thoughtful," Zelda said, plainly impressed. "Just think. I actually invited her into our home that day. Heaven knows what she might have done."

"Indeed," Mr. Waterson agreed.

"But perhaps it was more than just your sense of responsibility that led you to us today," Cybil said, surprising both Zelda and Waterson.

Waterson smiled kindly. "What else could it have been?"

Cybil smiled mysteriously. "Fate."

Waterson glanced speculatively around their cluttered parlor. "Are you thinking of offering your own home as a refuge, Miss Miles?"

Cybil couldn't help but smile. "Not my own house, but perhaps another one. I have recently come into an inheritance that I have been tasked with allocating to some good work. I can't help wondering if your arrival here isn't a sign that your refuge is the good work I should support."

"My goodness, Miss Miles, I can hardly believe it. I would never have suspected . . . I mean, how wonderful for you to have such an opportunity to do some real good in the world."

"I do count myself fortunate, Mr. Waterson. Tell me, how much money will you need to purchase the house you are thinking of?"

Mr. Waterson hemmed and hawed a bit, apparently reluctant to discuss money with a female.

Cybil got the impression he was actually debating with himself how much he could take her for. Finally, he admitted he could purchase the house for around ten thousand dollars, but that it would need a lot of work to make it worthy of its intended purpose.

"Ten thousand?" Zelda marveled. "It must be a rather large house."

"It was once a rich man's mansion, but he fell on hard times."

"And let it fall into ruin, I imagine," Zelda said, plainly trying to imagine it.

"Sadly, yes. But I will be happy to fill it with young women who are determined to make something of themselves."

"What do you suppose they can make of themselves?" Cybil asked with genuine interest.

"I would hope many of them become virtuous wives and mothers. Others might be teachers, as you two ladies are."

Very predictable, but Cybil couldn't argue with his goals.

"I would appreciate any help you can give me toward purchasing the house," he continued. "I don't expect you can fund the entire enterprise—"

"But you can expect exactly that, Mr. Waterson," Cybil said. "I hardly thought I would be able to accomplish such an important purpose with such a small portion of my inheritance."

He wasn't able to hide his surprise. "That's very generous of you, Miss Miles."

"Nonsense. It isn't even my money, not really. I suppose legally it is, but I accepted it on the condition that it would be used for charitable purposes."

"Your good heart does you credit, Miss Miles. I can hardly find the words to thank you."

"No thanks are necessary."

"Might we see the house?" Zelda asked guilelessly. "I know you said it needs some work, but I should so love to see it in its original state, so to speak."

"I'll, uh, have to consult the owner. He really hates being bothered."

"Perhaps if you tell him we will be the ones financing the purchase, he will feel less bothered," Zelda suggested. Cybil was beginning to suspect she was only pretending to believe this story.

Mr. Waterson smiled tolerantly. "I will inquire, but at the very least, I can take you to see the outside of the building. It is in a very quiet part of the city."

"I hope it isn't in a wealthy neighborhood," Zelda said with a worried frown. "People can be so snobbish and judgmental. We wouldn't want the girls to feel the weight of discrimination, would we?"

"I'm sure people will be kind once they understand the purpose of the refuge," Mr. Waterson hastily assured her.

"You may be giving people too much credit," Cybil said, "but I hope you are correct."

"When they see that two such respectable college professors are involved with the project, they are bound to be supportive," he said.

"I would like to think that would help," Cybil said quite fervently.

Mr. Waterson sighed with satisfaction. "I will need to make the purchase as quickly as possible, you understand. As I said, the house will require a lot of work, and the sooner we get started, the sooner we can save these young ladies from the streets."

"I couldn't agree more, Mr. Waterson," Cybil said, "but there is one small difficulty."

He didn't look too concerned. "And what might that be?"

"Well, as I said, I have an inheritance from my uncle, but I haven't actually received it yet."

He still did not look too concerned. "How much longer do you think you will have to wait until you do receive it?"

"My attorney says it shouldn't take long. Perhaps a few days or a week."

Waterson nodded. "I'm sure I can convince the owner to wait that long when I explain the circumstances."

"And in the meantime," Zelda said with enthusiasm, "we can see the house."

"Yes, yes, of course," he hastily agreed, but then he frowned. "Uh, it's none of my business, of course, but you said purchasing the house would use only a portion of your inheritance. I would like to think the total sum is adequate to fund other projects, too."

Well played, Cybil thought. He did need to know how much she was worth to him, after all. "Indeed it is, Mr. Waterson," she said, not giving anything away. A lady would never discuss such things with a stranger.

"Over a hundred thousand dollars," Zelda added with her guileless smile.

Cybil could barely muster a disapproving frown because she was so proud of the way Zelda had ensured Waterson's continued interest in them. She really would have a talk with Zelda later, but only to caution her about being too good at conning people. "I'm sure Mr. Waterson isn't interested in our private business," she told Zelda, who managed to look embarrassed.

"I certainly didn't mean to pry," he assured them. "But how fortunate you are, Miss Miles. Think of how much good you can do with your uncle's fortune."

"Oh, I've thought of little else since I discovered his will, Mr. Waterson. I'm only sorry to cause you a bit of a delay."

"I'm sure everything will work out. Never fear, Miss Miles. Together we will accomplish much good."

"I have no doubt of it, Mr. Waterson."

CHAPTER THIRTEEN

W hen Jake arrived at the brokerage office the next morning, Harriet greeted him with a knowing grin. "You have a visitor."

Since she was the only other person in the reception area, Jake frowned. "You put a visitor in the back office?" Where they could easily see no real work was happening.

"This visitor assured me that would be fine. She knew this was just a setup."

"She?" he echoed in dismay.

"She's not a mark, is she?" Harriet asked, but she wasn't really concerned. "She didn't act like a mark, at least."

Jake didn't bother to answer her. He strode to the door to the back office and threw it open. She was on the sofa at the very back of the room. She'd brought schoolbooks with her again, and she looked up from one when she heard him.

"You're late," Freddie said.

"Yeah, I might get fired."

She laid the book aside and glanced around. "What do you usually do here?"

"Nothing that concerns you."

She smiled at that. "I'm so glad I met you, Jake."

Jake sighed wearily. "Is that some kind of compliment?"

"I suppose it could be. All I know is that my life got a lot more interesting since I met you."

He tried a frown. "This can't go on, you know."

"Can't it?" she asked a little too provocatively. She rose and started walking toward him, smiling mysteriously. "We'll see about that."

While they waited for lunch to be ready, Elizabeth and Mother Bates were discussing whom they should visit that afternoon. Now that congress was convening in a special session to consider the Susan B. Anthony Amendment for Woman Suffrage, groups were meeting all over the city to discuss strategy. Mother Bates wanted to help, and Elizabeth needed to. The Woman Suffrage movement had led her to her new life, after all, and she owed it all her efforts.

They had just decided whom they would go to see when the maid announced a visitor.

"What an odd time to be calling," Mother Bates said, glancing at the clock.

"She probably had to come between séances," Elizabeth said, rising to greet Persephone. "What a lovely surprise."

"I'm sorry to intrude, but . . . Oh, hello, Mrs. Bates," Persephone added to Mother Bates.

"So nice to see you, Persephone."

"We've missed you at the séances," Persephone

said, remembering her duties. "I thought perhaps you would come with Mrs. Gideon."

"I would love to, but my son doesn't approve," Mother Bates said quite truthfully, not that Gideon's disapproval would have stopped her.

"He allows Mrs. Gideon to attend," Persephone pointed out.

"Only because she seems to have the gift," Mother Bates said. "I think he is hoping she will grow bored with it after a while."

Persephone smiled tolerantly. "Mrs. Gideon isn't likely to grow bored, not when her powers only seem to be increasing."

"Is that why you came?" Elizabeth asked with a frown. "To talk about my powers?"

But Persephone seemed to be genuinely concerned about something. "Not exactly. I wanted to speak with you about . . . about what happened yesterday with Mr. Miller."

"Mr. Miller?" Elizabeth asked uneasily.

"Yes, the young man you spoke with after the séance." She glanced at Mother Bates questioningly.

"Oh dear, I'm thinking you would like me to leave so you can speak in private," Mother Bates said, gathering up her needlework.

"I don't want to drive you out of your own parlor," Persephone protested weakly.

"Of course you do, dear, and don't think anything of it. My son would prefer I knew nothing at all about what Elizabeth gets up to at these séances. Please excuse me." This was easy for her to say because she knew Elizabeth would tell her everything they discussed.

When she was gone, Elizabeth closed the parlor door behind her and turned anxiously to Persephone. "I'm sorry about what happened with the young man. I think I may have frightened him."

"Not frightened, exactly. I think he was more intrigued," Persephone said, taking a seat on the sofa at Elizabeth's silent invitation. Elizabeth sat down beside her. "Can you tell me more about what you saw when you touched his hand?"

Elizabeth reached up and rubbed her forehead. "As I said, it was very quick, just a glimpse."

"But you saw enough to frighten you."

Elizabeth smiled wanly. "Everything about this . . . this *ability* frightens me, Persephone. I think I was already in a state after what happened in the séance, and then . . ."

"What exactly did happen in the séance? Madame doesn't discuss those things with me, you understand, but perhaps if I knew . . ."

"I actually don't know myself, but from what the others said, I had a special message for Mrs . . . Mrs. Darlington, I think. Is that her name?"

"It is."

"Yes, a special message for Mrs. Darlington,

presumably from my spirit contact or whoever it is who speaks through me. Madame Ophelia seemed a bit angry about it, and Mrs. Darlington was terribly confused."

"Confused about what?"

"It seems my message contradicted another message she had received from her husband."

Persephone nodded. "I understand he instructed her to invest some money."

"And what did I tell her? Or rather, what did my spirit tell her to do?"

Persephone shrugged. "As I said, Madame doesn't discuss these things with me, but I gather that you told her not to invest."

"I can't imagine why I would do something like that. I don't know anything about investing."

"I don't think it is a matter of knowing anything about it. Rather, the spirits simply advise us to do or not to do something. They are the ones who know."

"And it appears my spirit advised her to do something different from what Madame Ophelia's spirit had advised her to do, but could my spirit have been right and her spirit have been wrong?"

"I think Madame believes that is the case. We have, after all, observed that you are always right, which is why I wanted to know what exactly you saw when you took Mr. Miller's hand."

"You make it sound very romantic," Elizabeth said with a small smile.

"If only it was. You actually did scare me. The look on your face . . ." She shivered slightly.

"I'm so sorry. I wouldn't scare you for the world," she lied. "Or Mr. Miller, either."

"You did tell him to be careful," Persephone reminded her.

Elizabeth winced at the memory. "I'm sure I overreacted. Did he take what I said seriously?"

"I can't speak for him, but I do know he is anxious to speak with you again."

"Oh dear, I was afraid you would say that."

"Don't you want to see him?"

"It's not that. It's just that I don't know what I would say to him."

"Is that really what you are worried about?" Persephone challenged.

"What do you mean?" Elizabeth asked uneasily.

"I mean, you saw something. I know you did, and it frightened you almost as much as seeing the wagon accident frightened you."

"I don't really remember much of what I saw about the wagon accident," Elizabeth said. "It happened during the séance."

"Not all of it did, and you did remember a lot. You said you knew the man would be hit by the wagon and that he would die. You remembered that much, so what did you see that involved Mr. Miller?"

"I . . . Nothing really. I mean, nothing in detail.

I just . . . Persephone, you must promise not to tell him this."

"Why not? If he's in danger—"

"But I don't know that he's really in danger. I just . . . Persephone, all I saw was blood."

"Blood?" Persephone echoed in alarm.

"Yes, but not anything specific. Just blood and just for a second. It could mean anything."

"It could mean he is going to die," Persephone cried, not feigning her distress. Could she really care for Jake?

"Or it could mean he is going to cut himself shaving," Elizabeth insisted reasonably. "I've been thinking about it since yesterday, and I'm not even certain that it's his blood. It could mean anything. Anything at all."

"And you didn't see his death?" Persephone asked, still distressed.

"No, nothing like that! I'm so sorry I upset you."

"But still, you saw something. We need to figure out what it means."

"Is that really up to us?"

"Someone needs to interpret what the spirits tell us."

Elizabeth frowned. "Aren't the spirits usually very clear when they speak? They are during the séances I have attended."

Persephone waved away this logic. "Your visions are different. They aren't . . . clear."

323

"The one about the horse race seemed very clear, or so I was told," Elizabeth said with a smile. "And also the one when the spirits told that lady where to find her uncle's will."

"But then you saw the accident."

Elizabeth frowned. "Yes, that was . . . different."

"Very different," Persephone confirmed. "For one thing, you remembered what you'd seen in the vision, even a lot of what you saw during the séance."

Elizabeth couldn't deny it. That would have been foolish, and it would also have spoiled everything. "I did. I still have nightmares."

"And now you've seen something that concerns Mr. Miller. Don't you think he should be warned?"

"I did tell him to be careful," Elizabeth reminded her defensively.

"What good will that do if he doesn't know what to be careful of?"

Elizabeth shook her head. "I can't warn him when I have no idea what I'd be warning him against."

"Then you should sit down with him and see if you get another message, a clearer one this time."

That did make sense. "You mean, have a séance?"

"Yes, but, uh, you would have to request it." Plainly, Persephone didn't have the authority to offer that, which meant Madame Ophelia hadn't sent her. How interesting.

"Do you think Mr. Miller would participate? I can't promise I'll see anything that has to do with him, after all."

"He is willing to take that chance," Persephone said. Jake had thoroughly charmed Persephone.

"Even after he found out I predicted that poor man's death?"

"Especially then. You would be amazed how desperately people long to know their future."

Elizabeth wouldn't be amazed at all, as a matter of fact, but she didn't say so. "Even if the news is bad?"

"No one ever expects the news to be bad."

"But the blood . . ." Elizabeth gestured helplessly.

"He needs to know so he can protect himself," Persephone said.

Elizabeth sighed in defeat. "In that case, I will do what I can. Let's schedule another séance."

While his wife and mother were plotting suffrage strategy that afternoon, Gideon met with Coleman and Waterson at his office to discuss the deal for the Texas land.

"So you see," Waterson concluded after explaining how his German relatives had ordered him not to sell the land, "I can't very well go against their wishes."

"I think you can," Coleman said. "We signed a legally binding contract, after all."

"And I'm asking you to release me from our agreement, Mr. Coleman," Waterson said, managing to sound pathetic without actually begging.

"I know it must be difficult to communicate with your relatives in Germany," Gideon tried, aware of his role as mediator, "but what do your relatives hope to accomplish by holding on to the land?"

Waterson shrugged. "I suppose they hope to strike oil, just as Mr. Coleman does, but what does it matter? It's their land, so I must respect their decision."

"And yet legally it is actually your land," Coleman pointed out.

"In name only. I don't think you appreciate the trust they put in me when they turned over ownership. They have every right to expect I will act in their interests."

"Isn't it in their interests to sell the land?"

"They don't think so."

Coleman sighed in frustration.

"Mr. Coleman," Gideon said reasonably, "the law is certainly on your side, and you have every right to expect to purchase the land as the two of you agreed, but under the circumstances, I'm sure you can also understand Mr. Waterson's reluctance to betray the trust that was put in him."

"I can *understand,* but I don't have to like it, do I? I know, I know. You're going to tell me there's no guarantee I'll find oil on that land, but what if I did? I'd be a millionaire. You can't expect me to give up that possibility without a fight."

"Would you settle for something less than an actual fight?" Gideon asked.

Coleman frowned. "What do you mean?"

"I'm sure Mr. Waterson doesn't expect you to give up your option on the land without some compensation."

Plainly, Coleman liked this idea. "How much compensation are we talking about?"

"Now, you have to understand that my relatives aren't wealthy," Waterson hastily explained.

"Which is why I thought they wanted to sell the land in the first place," Coleman said.

"They've, uh, well . . . things are not as dire for them as they had first feared. The situation in Germany is bound to improve with the Armistice, and once the peace treaty is signed, I'm sure things will rapidly get back to normal in Europe."

Gideon had his doubts about that, but his job wasn't to discourage the negotiations. "Do your relatives have the means to compensate Mr. Coleman for his trouble?"

"Within reason, of course," Waterson said.

Coleman didn't look as if he would be easily persuaded. "I was going to pay seventy-five thousand for the land, which was a pittance if I

327

struck oil, so that's my price for giving up my rights to it."

Waterson was suitably outraged at such an amount and offered ten thousand in return. Gideon needed all his powers of persuasion, but in the end, the two gentleman agreed that Coleman would sign a quitclaim, nullifying the option agreement they had signed only days ago, in exchange for a payment of thirty thousand dollars.

"I'll want it in cash," Coleman said, letting Waterson know he wasn't above being petty at having his dreams of fabulous oil wealth dashed. "And I'll count it before I sign."

"If you aren't careful, I'll think you don't trust me," Waterson said, but he wasn't nearly as angry as Coleman. In fact, he didn't seem angry at all, even about having to pay Coleman such a handsome fee.

Gideon couldn't figure out why Waterson was so anxious to renege on a deal that would have brought him seventy-five thousand dollars, and he especially couldn't figure out why Waterson would have been willing to pay for the privilege. Of course, Waterson was a con man, so he had probably figured out a way to get out of actually handing over the cash. Using boodle would be the usual technique, but Coleman was a con man, too, so he wasn't going to be fobbed off with packs of plain paper. He'd made that clear by announcing he planned to count the money. Still, Waterson didn't know Coleman was also a con man, so he probably thought he could make some kind of switch. Gideon had seen such switches happen and still wasn't sure exactly how it was accomplished. He knew only that con men always walked away with the money.

But these were two con men conning each other, so anything could happen.

"If you'd like to meet at my hotel suite," Waterson was saying, "Mr. Bates can bring the documents for us to sign and I will have the cash ready for you."

Gideon managed to hide his elation. He would get to see this happen! But he should at least pretend to protest. "Why can't we meet here in my office?"

"I'd rather not be traveling all over the city with that much cash," Waterson said. Which meant he needed to control what happened, which he couldn't do in Gideon's office.

"But you don't mind if I carry cash all over the city," Coleman scoffed.

"If we meet here, we will both be at risk, but if we meet at my hotel, only you will be, and you'll have Mr. Bates with you."

"In that case, I'll bring Mr. Miller, too." Coleman said. "He's my broker, Bates. He brought me this deal in the first place, and he's a strapping

329

young fellow. No one will bother us with him along."

Smith would doubtless add an extra charge to the bill for drawing up the quitclaim to pay for Gideon's time away from the office, so he'd be sure to inform his clerk. "How soon do you want to schedule this meeting?"

They arranged to meet late afternoon on Monday. That would give Waterson time to gather the cash. Gideon doubted he would need that much time. He figured Waterson probably kept his money handy, in case he had to leave town at a moment's notice, but he didn't mention that. Instead, he left it to Smith to collect payment for his services while he tried to decide if he'd ask Elizabeth to tell him what to expect when they did meet. He decided he would ask, but she probably wouldn't tell him. It was always better, as he well knew, if he didn't know what was going to happen.

Cybil and Zelda met Mr. Waterson in the Lenox Hill neighborhood on Saturday morning. It was, as he had described, a quiet area of the city where houses were well-kept and neighbors were respectable.

He was waiting for them on the corner of Third Avenue and Seventieth Street.

"Thank you so much for coming, ladies," he said by way of greeting.

330

"We wouldn't have missed this opportunity," Zelda assured him. "I know it's Cybil's money that will make this possible, but I can't help feeling excited to have a small part in it myself."

"I'm sure your advice will be invaluable as we develop our program," Mr. Waterson assured her.

He escorted them down Seventieth Street, chatting about Lenox Hill as they went. It really was a lovely area. Trees grew out of the patches of ground between the sidewalk and the cobblestone street. Flowers were just starting to poke up in window boxes and inside the wrought iron fences that marked the tiny yards in front of the town houses.

"I must apologize for the condition of the house," Waterson said while they strolled down the street. "As I explained, the original owner died, and the current owner apparently lived abroad and didn't bother to rent the property or even keep it in good repair. The neighbors will be thrilled when they see someone returning the house to its original condition."

Indeed, they saw what he meant long before they reached it. The house was like a scar on an otherwise beautiful face. The windows had been boarded up at some point, and the roof actually had a visible hole in it. The grass in front of the house had grown untended, yellowed and died and grown again to turn the small yard into a thatched mess. The fence had rusted in spots and the gate hung on one hinge.

"Oh dear," Cybil couldn't help saying.

"What a tragedy," Zelda agreed. "It must have been beautiful once."

"It will be again," Waterson said enthusiastically. "All it needs is some tender, loving care."

"And a lot of hard labor," Cybil said. "I know you said it needed work, but I never imagined . . ."

"Can we go inside?" Zelda asked, apparently not discouraged by the wreck of the exterior.

"I'm afraid not. As I said, the owner is rather eccentric. He allowed me in once, but when I didn't follow through with the purchase, he is no longer so obliging."

"Then we must provide the payment," Zelda said, then caught herself. "I mean, Cybil, dear, you really should. I can't imagine a better use for that money your uncle left you. Think of all the girls we could help."

"We?" Waterson echoed with apparent delight. "Does that mean you really are willing to offer your talents as well as financial support?"

"I don't see how we could refuse," Cybil said. "If I support this project financially, I must support it in every way. We could involve some of our students as well. Many of them are studying to become social workers themselves."

"How propitious," Waterson exclaimed.

"Do you have any idea how much it will cost to make the necessary repairs?" Cybil asked.

Waterson sighed. "You must forgive my awkwardness. I'm not accustomed to discussing such things with ladies."

Cybil gave him a forgiving smile. "Nonsense, we are quite used to dealing with such issues, being maiden ladies without a man to look after us."

"I hadn't thought of that, but if you're sure, well, I believe I mentioned the owner is asking ten thousand to purchase the house."

"Which is highway robbery, considering its condition," Zelda said.

"Indeed, but one is paying for the location, you see, and when one's purpose is to reform young ladies, it is important to place them in the proper environment, don't you think?"

Cybil thought there were plenty of environments in the city where a young lady could live respectably that didn't cost ten thousand dollars, but she said, "You are right, I'm sure, Mr. Waterson. And do you think another ten thousand would be sufficient to make the repairs?"

Waterson frowned in dismay. "I was thinking it will probably need twenty, at least. These projects are always more involved than you think they're going to be."

"Of course," Cybil said, wanting to be agreeable although she had to fight to keep her expression neutral. "So you'll need thirty thousand dollars."

"To start," he said quickly. "I will keep you informed about every step in the process."

"And you will let me know if more funds are needed, I assume," she replied graciously.

"I hope that won't be necessary, but one never knows. May I ask if you could have the funds ready for me on Monday?"

"I'm sure that won't be any problem at all. My attorney told me I should have access to my funds any day now."

Mr. Waterson gave her an apologetic smile. "I wonder if you could get the funds in cash. The owner demands cash payment, of course, and it will be easier dealing with the contractors if I have money in hand."

"I don't see any problem with that," Cybil said.

"Your generosity is amazing, Miss Miles."

"It's easy to be generous when it isn't really my money. Perhaps you will tell us more about what you have planned."

"And perhaps you will take us to the house you are currently using so we can meet the girls you have gathered so far," Zelda said. "I should love to talk with them and hear their stories."

But Mr. Waterson was shaking his head sadly. "I'm afraid that won't be possible. You see, after Sally, uh, absconded with all our funds, the other girls realized I had no way to provide for them, so they left as well. I'm afraid my first efforts are a total failure." He somehow contrived to appear completely abashed.

"Only because you had failed to understand young women, Mr. Waterson," Cybil said. "Zelda and I can advise you in your future efforts."

"I would be most grateful to both you ladies."

"It's not your gratitude we want, Mr. Waterson," Cybil said quite honestly.

"Who else will be at this séance besides Jake?" Gideon asked as the cab carried them to Madame Ophelia's storefront that evening.

"I'm not sure," Elizabeth said. "She usually likes to have people I don't know there, so I can't make predictions from what I know about them."

"She doesn't know who you really know, though," Gideon pointed out.

"No, thank heaven. I hope it's not Mrs. Darlington, because she knows you."

"Maybe I shouldn't go inside with you."

"Don't be silly. You'll just be very surprised to see her."

"And she'll be very surprised to see me, too, I'm sure."

"I doubt Madame Ophelia will invite her, though. She'll be afraid I'll advise her against Waterson's investment scheme again."

"I hadn't thought of that. You're probably right. She must have a lot of clients who don't know you, though."

"She probably does, although she won't want to take a chance. I expect I'll see some familiar faces."

"I can always sit in if you need an extra hand," Gideon offered, a little ashamed of how much he wanted to see what went on in that back room.

She laughed at him. "Darling, it's not like a game of cards where we'd need another player."

"Then you don't have to have a certain number of people for it to work?"

She gave him a pitying smile. "You don't really believe it works, do you, darling?"

He winced. "No, of course not," he said, although for a minute there he might have.

She patted his hand reassuringly. "Quite truthfully, I have no idea how she decides how many people are there. I do know that Madame Ophelia usually has six people and sometimes seven, in addition to herself, but I think that's probably just the number that fit comfortably around her table."

"You see, I knew there was a scientific method for determining how many people attended."

She rewarded him with a peck on the cheek. "And don't be alarmed by anything you hear tonight."

"I'll be as alarmed as I please, thank you very much. I'll just refrain from rushing to your rescue."

"That is all I can ask."

It wasn't, of course. She often asked a lot more, so this was relatively easy.

Jake was already there when they arrived. He and Persephone were chatting in the far corner while the others sat quietly in the chairs that lined the walls. Gideon recognized the people from the séance where Elizabeth had foreseen the wagon accident. They were all there except for Cybil. He supposed there was a good reason to exclude her. She was probably being conned by Waterson, and Madame Ophelia didn't want Elizabeth to warn her off the way she had Mrs. Darlington.

Everyone froze when he and Elizabeth walked in, and for a long moment, no one spoke. Then Persephone remembered her manners and came forward. "Mr. and Mrs. Bates, I'm so glad you could come."

Since Elizabeth had requested this sitting, Gideon couldn't help smiling at her enthusiasm.

She didn't seem to notice. "I believe you already met everyone, and you'll remember Mr. Miller from the other night."

"Yes," Elizabeth said with a tentative smile at him.

He nodded but made no move to approach her. He might almost have been afraid of her.

"I'll see if Madame is ready for you," Persephone said, scurrying away.

When she was gone, Tilly said, "Persephone

told us that poor man died, just like you said he would."

"I was very sorry to hear it," Elizabeth said.

"It wasn't that hard to predict," Cindy's father said, not bothering to hide his skepticism. "He was severely injured."

"But she knew the accident was going to happen before it did," his wife reminded him.

"Is that why you invited all of us back?" Tilly asked bitterly. "Is one of us going to die, too?"

Everyone else gasped, although Gideon figured they had all been wondering the same thing.

Elizabeth looked suitably horrified. "I certainly hope not."

"I hope not, too," Tilly's mother said fervently.

"And why is he here?" Tilly asked, gesturing at Jake, who frowned.

"I'm taking someone's place," Jake said.

"Yes, he's taking Miss Miles's place," Cindy's mother said knowingly. "She got what she wanted from the spirits, and now she doesn't need them anymore."

"Is that why she isn't here?" Tilly's mother asked.

"It's obvious, isn't it?" Cindy's mother said. Why was she so angry? Probably because she hadn't gotten what she wanted from the spirits yet.

"Madame Ophelia is ready for you now," Persephone announced from the doorway.

338

Jake was the first one to enter, barging in with ungentlemanly haste, followed by Tilly and her mother and then Cindy's parents. Elizabeth gave Gideon a resigned smile and followed them, leaving him to wait alone.

Elizabeth took the only remaining seat, across from Madame Ophelia. Jake had taken the chair next to Madame where Cybil usually sat.

"Tonight, I would like for you to address your questions to Mrs. Bates," Madame Ophelia said.

No one protested, but Elizabeth could actually feel the wave of shock that washed over the group. All eyes had turned to her, and none of them were friendly. A full minute passed before anyone even reached for a paper and pencil. Jake was the first and then the others followed, although reluctantly. They were all probably afraid of receiving bad news from her, and she found herself wanting to remind them of the good news she'd given Cybil.

But she refrained. No sense setting unrealistic expectations.

The writing of questions seemed to take longer than usual, but finally, Persephone collected them and burned them and left. Since Elizabeth didn't have the headset, she wondered how she was supposed to know what the questions were, but perhaps Madame Ophelia was testing her abilities again. At least she knew what Jake had asked. She had a pretty good idea what the others would ask, too, although she had no answers for them.

Everyone placed their hands on the table and Madame began to hum, even though Elizabeth assumed she wasn't really trying to summon her spirit guide. Elizabeth waited, knowing the tension would be growing with every second. After what seemed too long and really was, Madame called out, "Is someone there? Speak to us, spirits."

"Ahahahahah," Elizabeth said in her spirit voice.

"Who are you, spirit?" Madame demanded. "Speak to us."

"Mother," Elizabeth's spirit said.

Two women gasped.

"Andy?"

"Cindy?"

"Mother," the spirit voice said, "it's Andy."

"Andy, darling," his mother cried. "Tell me what I should do."

"Let me rest."

"What do you mean?"

"Let me rest!" the spirit shouted. "You don't need me. You have Tilly. She can take care of you."

"But, Andy—"

"Tilly knows what you should do, but you won't listen to her. Leave me in peace!"

"Oh, Andy," his mother sobbed.

"Mother, he's right," Tilly said. "Listen to him."

Elizabeth managed not to smile. She'd guessed correctly that Tilly's mother hadn't yet accepted the spirits' admonition to accept her daughter's counsel.

"Is Cindy there?" her mother demanded. "Can you hear me, Cindy darling?"

"Oooooooo," Elizabeth groaned, closing her eyes to sway back and forth.

"Who is it?" Madame asked. "What do you see?"

"Blood," Elizabeth said. "So much blood."

"Whose blood?" Jake asked, sounding as terrified as he should.

"A knife, a knife," she said anxiously. "Watch out! Watch out!"

Then she screamed and slid to the floor in a dead faint.

CHAPTER FOURTEEN

For a long moment, no one moved, and then the door burst open and Gideon was beside her.

"You can't come in here, Mr. Bates," Madame Ophelia was shouting. "It's very dangerous to interrupt when someone is conversing with the spirits."

"What did you do to her?" Gideon demanded. "Darling, can you hear me?"

Elizabeth moaned to let him know she was fine and then almost smiled at the irony. Moaning was usually a sign that someone was not fine. He was turning her over and lifting her to a sitting position. She let her eyes flutter open. No sense subjecting herself to the smelling salts.

"What happened?" Persephone cried from the doorway. "Mr. Bates, I told you that you couldn't come in here until the séance was over."

Gideon ignored her. "Are you all right?"

"I think so, yes. Can you help me up?"

He did so. Someone had righted her chair and he helped her sit down in it. Everyone but Madame Ophelia was standing, staring down at her in horror.

"What did you see?" Tilly asked. "You must tell us."

Elizabeth shivered. "I . . . I don't know."

"Yes, you do," Cindy's father insisted furiously. "I can see it in your face. You remember but you don't want to tell us. Someone else is going to die, aren't they?"

Elizabeth shook her head, but when her gaze touched Jake, she froze, allowing her expression to reveal her fear.

"It's me, isn't it? I knew it," Jake said. "What is it? What did you see?"

She shook her head again, this time desperately.

"It was enough to make you scream," Tilly reminded her testily.

"If you don't want to talk about it," Gideon said, "you don't have to. I can take you home."

"No!" a half dozen voices cried in unison.

"You must tell him what you saw," Persephone said, earning a black look from Madame Ophelia.

"It was the same as before," Elizabeth said to Persephone. "I told you, I just saw blood."

"And a knife," Cindy's father said. "You said you saw a knife."

"Who was holding it?" Jake asked.

"I couldn't see. It was just a knife and the blood. That's all," Elizabeth insisted unsteadily.

"And me," Jake said. "You knew it was me."

But Elizabeth shook her head. "I didn't actually see you, not either time."

344

"But you knew the vision was about me, didn't you? That first time you saw it."

She couldn't deny it.

"Am I going to die? Is that what it means?" Jake demanded. "You've got to tell me!"

"I don't know. I didn't see that part," she said, starting to weep.

"That's enough," Gideon said. "Stop harassing her!"

"Maybe she didn't see it," Cindy's father said grimly, "but you'd better have a care, son."

Jake nodded, obviously more than frightened.

"If I just knew who to watch out for . . ." Jake tried weakly.

But Elizabeth gestured helplessly. "I'd tell you if I knew. But he's right. You should be careful."

"Maybe you already know. Is there someone who wishes you harm?" Tilly asked him.

"No one," Jake insisted, although Elizabeth could have named a few. Persephone might have known at least one as well, if her cough meant anything. Jake apparently didn't notice. "I'm the kind of fellow everyone likes."

"Then maybe it isn't you who . . ." Andy's mother began, and caught herself.

"Yes, maybe it's someone else's blood," Cindy's mother said, picking up the argument.

"And maybe no one is going to die at all," Andy's mother concluded.

No one believed that, though. Elizabeth could

see it on every face, even Madame Ophelia's, although she was trying to remain calm.

"I should really get you home," Gideon said.

"Perhaps you will wait a few minutes," Madame said in the tone that brooked no argument. "I should like to speak to Mrs. Bates in private."

The others started to file out, obviously reluctant but too used to obeying Madame to argue. Jake lingered until last. "What should I do? What if you have another vision and you need to warn me?"

"Do you have a card?" Gideon asked practically.

Jake reached into his pocket and pulled one out. Gideon produced his own and they made the exchange.

"You'll tell me if you see anything else, anything that will help me?" Jake asked almost desperately.

Elizabeth nodded, not quite meeting his eye.

Persephone escorted him out of the room, closing the door behind them, leaving Elizabeth and Gideon alone with Madame Ophelia.

"Mr. Bates?" Madame said by way of dismissal.

"I'm not leaving her in here alone again," he said, matching her iron will with his own.

Madame turned her gimlet gaze to Elizabeth, who said, "I didn't tell Mr. Miller the truth."

"What?" Gideon said as if learning Elizabeth

could lie was a complete surprise to him. He was getting better at this.

"I didn't think you had," Madame said, ignoring Gideon's outburst. "What else did you see?"

"Not much. I don't know who was holding the knife, but he . . . It was definitely his blood."

"Why didn't you tell him?" Gideon demanded.

"And frighten him completely out of his wits?" Elizabeth said, swiping at her tears. "At least now he's warned. That's the most I can do, and he still thinks there's a chance for him. I don't know. Maybe there is. I had to give him that hope."

"She's right," Madame Ophelia said. "And perhaps she is completely misinterpreting the message. We cannot be careless with the communications the spirits give us."

"Then you agree that I did the right thing?" Elizabeth asked, absurdly grateful.

"I do. People think they want to know the future, but no one really wants to know how they will die."

Elizabeth blinked at the wisdom of that remark. "I'm sure that's true."

"And you have no idea who was holding the knife?" Madame asked.

Elizabeth frowned and rubbed her temples as if trying to remember. "I . . . It's just a feeling, but . . . I believe it is someone close to him."

"So he's wrong about everyone liking him," Gideon said.

347

"We all have enemies, Mr. Bates," Madame Ophelia said.

"Enemies who want to murder us?" he asked skeptically.

"Does one ever truly know the heart of our enemies, Mr. Bates?"

"Is it almost finished?" Anna asked Elizabeth in a fervent whisper after church the next morning. She and her mother had wandered over to speak to the Bates family while other parishioners mingled and chatted at various places around the sanctuary.

Elizabeth glanced over to make sure Mrs. Vanderslice was engaged in conversation with Mother Bates. "We're getting close, I promise. I'm sorry it's taken so long, but we had to make sure the tale was convincing."

"I know, and I'm the one who insisted you add an extra act to the play, but that woman is pressuring Mother to bring more of her friends to séances."

"Because she knows she won't get anything more than the séance fees from your mother, so she's trying to attract some wealthier victims."

"I know that, but Mother doesn't or at least she won't admit it if she does. She's determined to get all her friends addicted to visiting the spirits. That woman actually offered her a discounted fee if she brought a friend."

Elizabeth winced. "I can't imagine Madame Ophelia is that desperate for new clients, but maybe she's just trying to fleece as many victims as she can before she has to leave town."

"Do you think she will? Leave town, I mean?" Anna asked.

"People like her can't stay in one place too long. They promise people will earn a fortune on the schemes Madame predicts, so they can't afford to be around when everything goes bust. Imagine if a dozen people all came after her at the same time."

"Oh my, the newspapers would get wind of it for sure."

"If the victims weren't too embarrassed, but someone would probably go to the police, at least. Then it would all come out, and Madame would have to have vanished."

Anna sighed. "I just get so tired of hearing about the messages poor David is sending me."

"What kind of messages?"

"That I should take the séances more seriously and accompany Mother and invite my friends."

Elizabeth smiled. "Maybe Freddie would enjoy one."

Anna scowled. "Freddie is a faithless woman."

"So it appears. Still, she might enjoy a séance."

"She's poor as a church mouse, though, and I can hardly afford Mother's fees, much less mine and Freddie's."

"If everything goes as planned, you should be reimbursed."

"I'll hope for the best. In the meantime, I'll keep Freddie away from séances. I just wish there was something I could do to help."

"You can help us celebrate when everything is over."

"Mother won't be happy, though."

"I wouldn't be so sure. She might be relieved."

"Do you think so?"

"Let's hope. You, at least, will be relieved."

"I will. I'll just be glad when it's all said and done."

Elizabeth smiled. "Be careful what you wish for."

Cybil had arranged to meet Mr. Waterson during her lunch break on Monday. He had actually offered to treat her at a café near the college, but he frowned when she entered the café carrying nothing but her purse.

She took her seat and said, "I can see from your expression that you're wondering where the money is."

He managed a smile. "I didn't think it would all fit into your purse. Did your attorney convince you not to take it in cash?"

"It's not that." Cybil picked up her napkin and nervously began to refold it. "You see—"

But before she could make him see, the

waitress came to take their orders. When she was done, Waterson turned back to Cybil. "You were saying?"

Cybil sighed. "Well, it's so embarrassing, but it looks like I won't be receiving my inheritance as quickly as I had hoped."

Waterson wasn't pleased but he managed a concerned expression. "What do you mean?"

"Well, I think I told you the inheritance was from my uncle. He . . . he also had a son, but his son was somewhat of a disappointment to him."

"A black sheep?" Waterson offered helpfully.

"Exactly, and extremely irresponsible with money. Uncle chose to disinherit him completely and give his entire estate to me. He specifically asked me to use his money for good works."

"That seems perfectly straightforward. I assume he left a will."

"Oh yes, but you see, he had hidden it. It took me several weeks to locate it and I only found it because . . . Well, no matter. I did find it and presented it for probate. I think that is the legal term."

"Yes, it is."

"And everything seemed to be in order until my cousin discovered that he was not to inherit his father's estate, as he had always assumed."

"Your uncle hadn't warned him that he had been disinherited?" Mr. Waterson asked, aghast at such irresponsible behavior.

"I really don't know what Uncle told him. I guess I assumed he had, but Uncle did hate arguments of any kind. Perhaps he simply avoided the subject entirely, knowing I would do what needed to be done. My attorney suggested that perhaps Uncle was worried his son might try to locate the will and destroy it if he knew about it."

"Which would also explain why he hid it."

"Oh yes, I hadn't thought of that, but you're right. At any rate, my attorney informed me this morning that my cousin is contesting the will. He claims I asserted undue influence on my uncle to rob my cousin of his rightful inheritance."

"Oh dear," Waterson said, genuinely distressed.

"Indeed. I didn't influence Uncle at all, I assure you, and I have no idea how my cousin could prove that I did, but my attorney explained that these things must be settled in a court of law, so it will be some time before I have access to my funds. I know this puts you into a rather awkward position in regards to the house, which seems so perfect for your purposes and—"

"Yes, you're right," Waterson interrupted when Cybil threatened to slide into hysterics. "You mustn't upset yourself, though. I'm sure we can work something out." He frowned as he considered. "I don't suppose you have any money of your own? We could use it to get started on the project, and when the court settles your uncle's estate, you can replenish your own funds."

"I . . . I do have a little put by, but not nearly enough to also cover your expenses."

"If you could just provide enough to purchase the house itself . . ."

"I might be able to manage that. Zelda would help, I'm sure, especially when she knows my uncle's money is forthcoming." Cybil thought Waterson should have pointed out that when a will was contested, there was no guarantee as to who would receive the money in the end, but of course he didn't.

"There, you see, things aren't as bad as you feared. I don't like to seem to be rushing you, but the owner is rather anxious to sell, and I wouldn't want him to find another buyer while we're waiting for your settlement."

"I understand completely. I won't be finished with classes today before the banks close, but perhaps I can make the arrangements tomorrow. And I'll need to discuss it with Miss Goodnight, although I'm sure she'll agree. Then she will need to withdraw her funds as well."

Waterson didn't like that one bit, but he smiled politely. "That sounds fine. I'll do my best to convince the owner to wait a few more days."

"I'm so glad we were able to work this out, Mr. Waterson."

"So am I," he said, although he didn't look glad at all, probably because he wouldn't have Cybil's cash to use to pay off Coleman this afternoon.

• • •

Gideon met Jake and Mr. Coleman in the lobby of Waterson's hotel, as they had arranged. Mr. Coleman and Jake greeted him.

"You have all the contracts?" Coleman asked, just as if this were a perfectly normal transaction.

"Yes." Gideon patted his document case. "All ready to be signed. I don't suppose you have any instructions for me."

"None at all," Jake assured him. "Just act as you normally would."

Coleman checked his pocket watch. "I guess we can go on up."

The men went up to Waterson's suite. He opened the door and welcomed them warmly, shaking each man's hand. "I can't tell you how much I appreciate your cooperation in this, Mr. Coleman."

"I'm going to be really bitter if you end up a millionaire, Waterson," Coleman said with just the right amount of irony.

"I'd be a lot happier about this if I thought that was going to happen," Waterson said. "As it is, I'm bitter myself that my relatives have put me in such an awkward position."

"I hope this is their money you're using to pay me off."

Waterson merely smiled grimly. "Can I get you gentleman a drink?"

"Perhaps after I count the money," Coleman said with a grin.

"It's right here on the table."

An ordinary carpetbag sat in solitary splendor on a table that had been placed near a door that probably led to the bedroom of the suite. Gideon couldn't be sure, of course, since the door was firmly shut, but it was in the right location for it, and the parlor of a suite wouldn't need a closet, so it probably wasn't that.

Coleman opened the carpetbag and pulled out fifteen neatly wrapped bundles of cash. They appeared to be twenty-dollar bills. Coleman broke open the first packet and determined there were really one hundred twenty-dollar bills in it. Gideon took a seat on the sofa, figuring they'd be there a while if Coleman intended to count every packet.

He didn't, though. He simply fanned the packets, making sure that every bill was a twenty. Halfway through, he broke open another packet and counted it, too. Satisfied, he merely fanned the rest of them. Then he placed them all back in the bag.

"Thirty thousand, as agreed," Coleman said. "I think we're ready to sign those papers now, Bates."

Gideon took out the papers and Waterson brought over a pen and ink from the desk. Waterson made a little show of moving the bag to make room for the signing ceremony, setting it on the floor in front of the door, where it would be out of the way. The two men signed, and Jake witnessed the signatures.

"This calls for a celebration," Waterson said.

"I don't really feel much like celebrating," Coleman said.

"Why not?" Waterson argued. "You just got paid thirty thousand for doing almost nothing."

"I hadn't thought of it that way," Coleman said.

"No, you were too busy mourning the money you might've made, but I've learned that a man is better off with cash in hand than with pie in the sky. I think we're ready for that drink now."

"And while he's getting it, I'll give you your commission, Miller," Coleman said, snatching up the bag and setting it back on the table again. He reached in and pulled out one packet of bills and then counted out another thousand from the loose bills.

Jake gave a wolf whistle when Coleman handed it to him. "This is the best week I've ever had, Mr. Coleman." He tucked the bills into his coat pocket and patted the bulge lovingly.

Waterson had stopped on his way to the sideboard, where the liquor bottles sat, to frown at the exchange, but before Gideon could figure out why he was so displeased, someone started pounding on the door.

"What on earth?" Coleman muttered, and

Waterson turned to answer it, frowning thunderously. He threw open the door, obviously ready to berate the intruder, but she pushed past him before he could even draw a breath.

"Where is she?" Freddie demanded.

Gideon blinked in surprise. She looked absolutely wild. She wore no hat and her hair was mussed, as if she'd pinned it up in a hurry. She was dressed for the street, but her suit jacket was buttoned crookedly. Everything else paled in comparison to the fire in her eyes, however. She seemed actually deranged.

"Freddie, what—" Jake tried, but she was having none of it.

"Where is she?" she nearly screamed.

Waterson had quickly shut the door, probably not wanting to attract the attention of anyone who might call the house detective or even worse, the law. "Young lady—" he tried, but no one paid him any mind.

"Where is who?" Jake asked stupidly.

Freddie had marched right up to him, and he had put up both hands as if to ward her off. She wasn't making any threatening moves, though. Both of her arms were hanging stiffly at her sides.

"That girl, Penny. I saw her. She came in here."

Who was Penny?

Jake looked around as if he expected to see

another girl. "She's not here. It's just us. This is a business meeting and—"

"Don't lie to me! I saw her. You're keeping her in this hotel, aren't you?"

"No, I'm not keeping her anywhere," Jake insisted.

"You're lying! I saw her! You lied to me!" she screamed, and before anyone could do anything, she raised her arm and plunged a knife right into Jake's chest.

Jake cried out, and Gideon did, too, because of the blood that immediately began to spread, soaking his shirt and his vest.

Someone screamed, someone who wasn't Freddie, and all eyes turned to the other door that was open now. Persephone stood there, her face white with shock.

"She *is* here," Freddie cried in triumph. "I knew it! *You lied to me,*" she repeated, and pulled out the knife and plunged it in again.

"Bates, let's get out of here," Coleman said, snatching up the bag of money. "We don't want to get mixed up in this."

"Wait. What about—" Gideon tried, but Coleman was gone, leaving the door hanging open behind him.

"Penny, come on," Waterson said to Persephone, but she was still in shock, watching Jake sink to his knees as the blood continued to soak his shirt.

Freddie suddenly started to weep. "Oh, my darling, what have I done?" she asked, falling to her knees beside him. At least she'd pulled the knife out again.

Waterson went to the doorway where Persephone stood and pushed her into the other room, slamming the door behind them.

"What have I done?" Freddie continued to wail.

Gideon went to help Jake, not sure exactly what he should do but knowing he had to do something. Then he heard another door slam and voices in the hallway, Persephone and Waterson. They were half running down the hotel corridor, having obviously just fled the suite's bedroom through the hall door. Waterson carried a Gladstone bag in one hand and was propelling a reluctant Persephone with the other. Persephone carried a carpetbag and turned as they passed the open door to see Freddie weeping while trying to hold Jake upright. Persephone stumbled to a halt, but Waterson took a moment to pull the door closed, shutting off her view and probably hoping to conceal the crime until he and Persephone could make their escape.

Jake keeled over onto his side while Freddie continued to moan over him.

There was even more blood than Elizabeth had seen in her vision. Gideon would have to be sure to tell her.

• • •

"You're drinking much more than usual tonight," Mother Bates remarked as Gideon refilled his whiskey glass from the sideboard in the parlor.

"I think I'm entitled," he said grimly. "It's not every day I see a member of my family murdered."

This was true. While he did have to see members of his family murdered, it happened only *occasionally*. Still . . . Elizabeth understood it must have been a shock nonetheless. "Jake gave his life for a good cause."

Before Gideon could respond, the maid tapped on the parlor door and announced a visitor. Mother Bates glanced meaningfully at the clock. It was after eight, far too late for a casual visitor.

"It's that woman with the funny name," Lucy reported.

"Madame Ophelia?" Elizabeth asked in surprise.

"No, ma'am, the young one."

"Persephone," Gideon guessed.

"Yes, sir, that's the one."

One look at Gideon told Elizabeth how reluctant he was to see her. Seeing her would also involve some lying, so it was just as well if he wasn't involved. "Would you show her into the library, Lucy?" When she was gone, she added to Gideon, "I'll talk to her alone."

"What do you think she wants?" Mother Bates asked.

"I'm sure she's just here to ask after Jake's welfare."

"She'll be disappointed, then," Gideon said.

Elizabeth exchanged a knowing look with Mother Bates and went out to find Persephone in the library. The girl was pacing when Elizabeth walked in, and she stopped instantly, turning to face her, but she was indeed disappointed. "I asked to speak to Mr. Bates. Is he here?"

"He is but . . . Oh, Persephone, he told me what happened. It's so horrible."

Her face crumpled in despair. "What happened to Mr. Miller? Is he . . . ? Is he all right?"

Elizabeth let her eyes fill with tears. "I'm afraid he . . . he died. I'm so sorry. I feel like I'm somehow responsible, as if I could have saved him if I'd just known how."

"But I don't understand," Persephone said, holding on to her emotions with difficulty. "Why was Mr. Bates there?"

"He told me one of the men is his client. They were there to sign some legal documents, I believe."

"His client?"

"Yes, and Mr. Miller represented the man in some way, too, I believe."

"He was . . ." She had to pause to swallow her tears. "He was his stockbroker."

"I see, but Mr. Bates didn't know that until the meeting, I gather." He hadn't even guessed

Jake was a stockbroker. "He has no idea who the woman was, though. She ran out when she realized Mr. Miller was . . . was . . ." She couldn't make herself say the word.

"She was in love with him," Persephone said. "He didn't feel the same."

"Men can be so heartless," Elizabeth murmured. "But the real question is, what were *you* doing there, Persephone?"

Persephone feigned surprise. "Me?"

"Yes. Why were you in that man's hotel room?" It did sound rather sordid, as she had intended.

"I was . . . It wasn't what you think. He . . . I was helping."

"Helping with what?"

"I . . . Oh, Mrs. Bates . . ." She couldn't hold back her tears any longer, and Elizabeth went to her, slipping an arm around her shoulders and leading her to one of the chairs by the cold fireplace.

"Sit down, Persephone. I know you had quite a shock today. Can I get you something?"

Persephone shook her head and continued to weep into the handkerchief she had pulled from her pocket. Elizabeth sat down in the other chair and waited patiently until the storm of tears had passed.

When she could speak again, Persephone asked, "Will the police come?"

"I have no idea, and even if they do, they're hardly likely to come for you, are they?"

"I . . . I don't know."

"Who was that man in the hotel room and how were you helping him?"

"Oh, Mrs. Bates, I can't tell you, but it's not what you think. That man, Mr. Waterson, he's my father."

"Your father?" Could this be true? Sadly, it made perfect sense. Hadn't Elizabeth herself grown up with a con man for a father? That would certainly explain Persephone's involvement in all of this, too.

"Yes, I was . . . I was just waiting until he finished his business meeting. He had told me to stay in the other room because it wasn't proper for me to attend the meeting."

A good story, although Elizabeth knew perfectly well how Persephone would have been involved if the con had gone according to plan. "I can't imagine how frightened you must have been, but my husband said that you and, uh, your father left before the, uh, authorities came, so perhaps no one need ever know you were there."

"Do you think so?"

"Well, your father might be contacted, since he was registered at the hotel," Elizabeth said, thinking he certainly would not be contacted if he hadn't used his real name, "but he needn't mention that you were there."

"He wouldn't, I know, but what about Mr. Bates? Will he tell?"

"I don't know if he already told anyone, but I can ask him to pretend he never noticed you."

"That would be very kind of him."

Yes, it would, if the authorities ever really questioned him about it, which they wouldn't. "I know it must have been a shock to witness such an awful thing, and it's terrible for such a young man to die, but you must remember he was practically a stranger to you."

"But he wasn't," Persephone said in despair. "We were . . . we were seeing each other."

"Oh dear."

"Yes. He was such a nice man, a real gentleman."

"But if he was trifling with that other woman . . ."

"He wasn't, though. He hardly knew her. I think she must be, uh, not in her right mind."

"Her actions do seem to indicate that," Elizabeth said. "I only wish I could blame her instead of myself. I haven't been able to think of anything else since I first had the vision of Mr. Miller's death—"

"So you did know he was going to die," Persephone cried, horrified.

Elizabeth slapped her hand over her mouth as if she could hold back the words she'd already spoken.

"Why didn't you tell him? Warn him?" Persephone demanded.

"I did warn him," Elizabeth tried. "I told him to be careful. What more could I have done?"

"You could have told him who to be careful of!"

"But I didn't know. I told you, I only saw the knife, not who was holding it, and when I told Madame Ophelia that I knew he was going to die, she advised me not to tell him. She said people really don't want to know."

Persephone's eyes widened in horror. "She told you not to tell him?"

"She thought it would be a kindness, and I was just relieved because I couldn't bear to hurt him like that."

Persephone shuddered. "I can't believe she'd do that."

"Would it have changed anything, do you think?" Elizabeth asked.

"He would have been on his guard, at least."

"But don't you think he was already? Would knowing for a fact that he was going to die have made his last days more pleasant?"

Persephone covered her face with both hands. "I can't believe this is happening."

"I can't, either." Elizabeth dabbed at her eyes with a handkerchief. "I never asked for this so-called gift, and it has brought me nothing but misery. I wish to heaven I'd never gone to that first séance."

"I wish you hadn't, too. No amount of money is worth a person's life."

"Do you think Mr. Miller and that other man wouldn't have died if I hadn't foreseen it?" Elizabeth asked with a troubled frown.

"I don't know. I guess we never will."

Elizabeth let her contemplate that for a long moment. Then she said, "What did you mean that no amount of money is worth a person's life?"

Persephone looked up in surprise. "Did I say that? Well, it's true, of course."

"Yes, it is, but . . . Did you mean Mr. Miller in particular?"

"No. I mean, I just mean . . ."

Elizabeth widened her eyes in comprehension. "Was this business deal the one the spirits told him about?"

"I don't—"

"It is, isn't it?" Elizabeth said. "He was there, in that hotel room, because the spirits sent him there."

"Uh, that's possible. I don't really know. I don't attend the séances and Madame doesn't tell me what happens—"

"But you knew about Mr. Miller's business deal, didn't you?"

"Only because he told me," Persephone insisted.

"And that business deal involved your *father,* Persephone. That's quite a coincidence."

"I don't know anything about it," she cried. "I should go. I didn't mean to bother you."

She was on her feet, but Elizabeth rose, too. "Madame Ophelia often predicts that her clients are going to meet someone who will help them make a lot of money."

Persephone tried a laugh but it came out like a croak. "Love and money. That's why people consult the spirits."

"But why would one of the clients happen to meet your *father?*" Elizabeth asked, then widened her eyes again. "Or do they *all* happen to meet your father? Do they all give your father money to invest?"

"No, of course not," she tried, near panic now. "I'm sorry I came. I really must go now." She headed for the door.

"If I ask Madame Ophelia, what will she say?" Elizabeth called after her, but she was gone, slamming out the front door as if the hounds of hell were on her heels.

CHAPTER FIFTEEN

Cybil hadn't expected to hear from Mr. Waterson so soon, but she still wasn't surprised to find him on her doorstep on Tuesday morning. "Good morning," she managed. "Did we arrange to meet today and I've forgotten?"

He smiled his usually charming smile, although it looked a bit strained this morning. "We did not, and I hope you will forgive me for calling on you at this early hour, but I wanted to catch you before you left for school."

"You just did. Miss Goodnight and I like to arrive at the college early in case students want to speak with us, but I'm sure I can give you a few minutes if it's urgent."

"I'm afraid it is."

"Then come in, won't you?"

She ushered him into the parlor, which was still a bit disordered after the salon last night. Cybil would be so happy when this was over so Elizabeth and the others could begin attending the salons again. She really missed them.

Zelda came down the stairs and saw him. "Mr. Waterson, what a surprise. I hope nothing is wrong."

He was still on his feet because Cybil hadn't sat down yet. He gave Zelda a rueful grin. "Things did not go as I hoped with the gentleman who is selling the house."

"I can't believe he found another buyer," Zelda said.

"I have come to understand that he is more interested in being a nuisance than in selling the house, but that may just be my interpretation. In any event, he told me if I didn't come up with the funds, in cash, today, he would never sell me the house under any circumstances."

"How dreadful," Zelda said with apparent sympathy.

"And how unreasonable," Cybil added. "Please sit down, Mr. Waterson. I can see you've had a difficult time of it."

"It will be worth every second of aggravation if I can accomplish my goal of opening a refuge for young ladies, but sometimes I do lose heart."

"You poor man," Zelda said, causing Cybil to bite her lip to keep from grinning. "I do so wish we could help."

"I do, too. I know it will be some time before you receive your inheritance, Miss Miles, but you did indicate to me that you and Miss Goodnight would be able to draw on your personal funds in the meantime to finance the purchase of the house. That would at least get us started and we wouldn't lose this golden opportunity to get a home in such a perfect location."

Cybil and Zelda exchanged a troubled glance.

"I did tell you that, Mr. Waterson, and it is true that Zelda and I have sufficient funds to do just that, but when I consulted my attorney about doing so, he strongly advised against it."

Mr. Waterson's smile was really strained now. "I wonder that you felt the need to consult your attorney on this matter."

"I had to, because of the inheritance," Cybil quickly explained. "I wanted to be sure we weren't endangering our future security, you see. We are two maiden ladies without a man to support us. We have lived frugally so that we could save enough to live on when we are too old to teach any longer, and I wanted to consult with my attorney before I turned those funds over to you."

"Yes," Zelda added enthusiastically. "It would never do if we helped you purchase the house and then found ourselves homeless someday because of it."

Mr. Waterson didn't like this one bit, but he was putting a good face on it. "I don't really think—"

"So naturally I consulted my attorney," Cybil continued, ignoring his interruption, "and he informed me that there is no guarantee I will actually receive my uncle's money. The court might very well decide in my cousin's favor, leaving me without a cent."

"And if we had given all of our savings to you to buy the house," Zelda added, "well, I'm sure you can see how unfortunate that would be for us."

"Yes, but—"

"And Mr. Bates absolutely forbade me to touch my savings for such a risky venture," Cybil concluded.

Waterson's strained smile disappeared completely. "Did you say *Bates?*"

"Yes, Mr. Bates. My attorney. He's a young man, but I trust him completely. His firm has represented our family for . . . Oh, I couldn't even say how long." She could, of course, but it hadn't been very long at all.

"Bates," he muttered.

"But perhaps I haven't explained it properly. If you like, you can speak to Mr. Bates yourself. I'm sure he would be more than happy to clarify the situation. Of course, when I do receive my inheritance—"

"If you ever do, dear," Zelda added.

"Yes, *if* I receive my inheritance, I will be more than happy to supply whatever funds you might need. I realize you will have to find a different house by then, but there are many houses in the city and I'm sure you'll be able to find one just as suitable as—"

"I've kept you ladies long enough," Waterson said, rising abruptly. "I'm afraid I must be going."

"Of course," Cybil said as she stood to show him out. "I'm terribly sorry we couldn't help you with your wonderful project, but I have every confidence that we will eventually be able to. I'm sure things will all work out for both of us."

"Yes, well, I'm sure they will, too," Waterson said, hurrying to the door.

"How can I get in touch with you when I do finally receive my inheritance, Mr. Waterson? It occurs to me that I don't know how to reach you."

"Don't worry, Miss Miles. I'll find you."

Cybil smiled as he hurried out the door and down the front steps. She was pretty certain she had seen the last of Mr. Waterson.

Elizabeth didn't have to pretend she was angry when she barged into Madame Ophelia's storefront that morning. This probably wasn't going to work, but it was worth a try. It was always worth a try.

Elizabeth had brought Anna with her because Gideon had insisted she not go alone, although what help Anna might be, Elizabeth had no idea. At least he had accepted her wisdom that he should not go with her. His presence would be too threatening since he represented the law and had presumably already reported Jake's murder to the police, putting both Waterson and Persephone in jeopardy.

Elizabeth and Anna stopped just inside the front door, unsure how to proceed. No one was waiting for the morning séance, which was odd, but Persephone had obviously heard the door and rushed out of that mysterious other room to see who had arrived. She was wearing an apron and had tied a kerchief around her hair as if she were doing housework of some kind.

Or packing.

"Oh," Persephone said in dismay, stopping short when she saw them.

"I demand to speak to Madame Ophelia," Elizabeth said.

"She . . . she isn't here," Persephone said, although Elizabeth noted that her gaze darted briefly to the séance room door.

"But don't you have a séance this morning?" Anna said.

"Uh, yes, usually, but . . . Madame isn't feeling well, and—"

"It's all right," Madame said, appearing in the doorway to the séance room. "Mrs. Bates is naturally concerned after what happened to Mr. Miller." She wore her séance robes but not the turban. Plainly, she hadn't intended to do a séance this morning.

"I'm concerned about many things, Madame Ophelia. You told Mr. Miller he would make a lot of money on some sort of business deal, and it turns out Persephone's father was involved in that deal, and now Mr. Miller is dead."

"Please, *I* did not tell Mr. Miller anything," Madame said quite reasonably. "The spirits told him. I am only a vessel."

"A vessel that gives false information. How many other people have you sent to that man?"

"I do not send anyone. I only—"

"Yes, I know," Elizabeth interrupted, outraged. "You are only a vessel, but I notice you never predict anything of importance. You didn't foresee Mr. Miller's death, for example."

"I will not compare powers with you, Mrs. Bates," she said haughtily. "It is not a contest."

"Not a contest?" Elizabeth said, lunging toward where Madame still stood in the doorway, but she stopped short, as if she'd hit a wall and cried out in anguish, clapping a hand over her heart.

"Elizabeth!" Anna shouted, hurrying to her side to keep her from collapsing when she staggered back.

"What is it?" Persephone demanded, rushing over to grab Elizabeth's other arm.

But Elizabeth could only stare at Madame Ophelia in horror, and mutter, "No, no, not again."

"Not again what?" Persephone asked in alarm. "Do you see something? Something about Madame Ophelia?"

Elizabeth shook her head, but they could all see

that she was lying. She couldn't take her horrified gaze off the medium, who was staring back at her with her own growing horror.

"What do you see?" Madame demanded. "Tell me. You must tell me."

Elizabeth shook her head again, frantically this time. "I can't! You said people don't want to know."

Persephone and Madame both gasped, and Anna said, "What is it? What's happening?"

"We must go," Elizabeth said. "I can't . . . I can't do this again."

"But you must," Madame insisted, frantic herself now. "You must tell me what you see."

"It's all . . . blurry . . ." Elizabeth stammered. "Please, I can't!"

"We'll do a séance, then," Madame declared, her terror-filled eyes at odds with her determination. "That will help you see."

"But I don't want to see!" Elizabeth begged, turning to Anna for help.

"What is it you don't want to see?" Anna asked, glancing at Madame Ophelia and then at Persephone with a silent plea.

"She sees someone's death," Persephone said. "It's true, isn't it?"

Elizabeth made a mewling sound and began to weep.

"How can she see something like that?" Anna asked. "We aren't even having a séance."

"She has the gift," Madame said grimly.

"Gift? What gift?" Anna demanded. "Elizabeth, what's going on? Do you want me to take you home?"

"I don't want to do this," Elizabeth said weakly.

"But you must," Persephone said. "You can't just leave us not knowing what you've seen."

"But I haven't seen anything yet, not really. I don't even want to!" Elizabeth said, tears running down her face.

"Then we will help you," Madame said. "Bring her into the séance room."

"But she doesn't want to," Anna protested.

"No, I don't," Elizabeth confirmed.

"You can't leave us in ignorance," Madame said. "You can't leave us unprotected."

"I wasn't able to protect Mr. Miller," Elizabeth said.

"Because you didn't tell him the truth," Madame replied.

"But you told me not to!"

"I was wrong. You have this gift for a reason. You must use it."

Elizabeth sighed her defeat. "All right, but don't blame me if I frighten you."

"You have already frightened us," Persephone said, glancing anxiously at Madame Ophelia.

"I didn't mean to," Elizabeth said sadly.

"Come along," Madame Ophelia said. "Let us not waste any more time."

Anna kept a tight grip on Elizabeth's arm as they moved into the séance room. Madame's usual ornate chair was gone, probably packed up to be moved on to their next stop, but the other chairs were still tucked neatly beneath the table.

"Persephone, close the door. Sit down, everyone. We'll summon the spirits."

"You want me to sit in?" Anna asked uncertainly.

"Yes, please stay," Elizabeth begged. "I don't know what might happen and I'll feel safer if you're with me."

Anna was apparently terrified now, but she took a seat beside Elizabeth. Persephone adjusted the lighting and removed the extra chairs so just four were left. The others sat down and she took the empty one, although it was obvious from her stiffness that she hated doing so. There was no need for the ritual writing of questions since Madame would not be answering any today. She didn't even have her headset on.

"Close your eyes and focus," Madame said. "Help Mrs. Bates summon her spirit guide."

They all laid their hands on the table and Madame began to hum. After a few moments, Elizabeth joined her. Everything seemed peaceful for several minutes and then Elizabeth jerked in her chair.

"What is it?" Anna asked in a terrified whisper.

"Shhhh," Madame said. "Spirit, can you hear us?"

"Yes," Elizabeth answered in her spirit voice. "I hear you. Shame on you! Shame!"

Persephone gasped, but Madame remained calm. "Who are you?"

"I see you," Elizabeth's spirit said. "I know what you have done. You have lied and cheated the innocent."

"Who is she talking about?" Anna asked, her whisper a little louder this time.

"Maaddddaaammm," the spirit said, drawing out the syllables ominously, "you have sinned."

"What do you see for me, spirit?" Madame asked, her usual confidence missing from her voice.

The spirit cackled in a laugh that startled the others at the table. "You do not even deny it. You are evil, and your sins will find you out."

"How? What do you see?"

"I see blood. I see blood."

"Whose blood?" Persephone asked sharply.

"Madame's blood streaming down," the spirit reported gleefully. "She will pay the price."

"How? Who causes this blood?" Persephone demanded.

"Persephone, stop," Madame said sharply. "Who is it? Who will hurt me?"

"I seeeeee . . . I seeeeee . . . someone's hand. Someone close to you."

"Close to her?" Persephone echoed in horror.

"Someone she hurt," the spirit said. "I see money. Lots of money. She stole it."

"No!" Persephone cried, but Madame shushed her instantly.

"Who is it? Whose money is it?" Madame asked unsteadily.

"Don't you know?" Anna asked in dismay. "How many people did you steal money from?"

No one paid any attention to her question.

"Revenge," the spirit purred ominously. "Revenge the money with blood."

"Can I stop them?" Madame asked. "How can I stop them?"

"Stop them?" the spirit echoed eerily. "Stop them, stop them. This is a mystery. How can you stop them?"

"*Can* she stop them?" Persephone demanded. "Is it possible?"

"Possible. Possible," the spirit chanted. "Cannot change the past. Can change the future."

"How?" Madame asked anxiously. "How can I change the future?"

Elizabeth began to rock back and forth. "Change the future. Change the future. Do what is right to change the future."

"What is right?" Persephone echoed in confusion.

"Don't you even know what that is?" Anna

380

asked venomously. "Even I can figure it out. *Give the money back.*"

"Give the money back?" Persephone echoed incredulously.

Plainly, Madame didn't like that idea, either. "Who is it? Who is the danger to me?"

"Danger, danger," the spirit chanted. "Cannot see. Cannot see. Anger. Hatred. Cheated, cheated."

"You must see something," Madame insisted.

"I see blood. Running down your face. Blood and death and blood and death and blood and death and—" Elizabeth screamed and collapsed, nearly knocking Anna out of her chair.

"Elizabeth!" Anna screamed, jumping up and falling to her knees beside her. "What happened? Can you hear me?"

Elizabeth moaned.

"Her hands are like ice," Anna said, chaffing Elizabeth's wrists. "What happened to her?"

"It's nothing," Madame said, rising from her chair. "It will pass."

"What do you mean, it will pass?" Anna asked in outrage. "She's unconscious."

"She always faints when the spirits speak through her. Persephone," she added, motioning her out with a wave of her hand. Persephone scurried out obediently.

"Elizabeth, can you hear me?" Anna tried again.

This time her eyes fluttered a bit. "Anna?"

"Yes, dear, it's me. I'm right here. Are you all right?"

Persephone reappeared with a container of smelling salts. She tried to wave it under Elizabeth's nose, but Anna pushed it away. "She's awake now, can't you see?"

"Did I faint again?" Elizabeth asked.

"I'm afraid so. Did you hurt yourself?"

"I never do, but . . . Can you help me up?"

Anna and Persephone assisted her, and between the two of them, they got her into a chair.

Then she looked around at the three faces staring down at her. "Did you learn anything? Who is going to, uh, hurt you, Madame Ophelia?"

"Someone close to her," Anna said.

Elizabeth's gaze shifted instantly to Persephone, who shook her head emphatically. "No, it's someone she cheat—" She caught herself just in time, but she still earned a scowl from Madame.

But Elizabeth knew what she meant. "It's someone you stole money from, then. I don't think anyone can blame them, though."

"But murder is still wrong," Anna said. "We have to stop them if we can, if only to save them from becoming a killer." Madame scowled at her, but she just scowled back.

"If you could tell us who it is . . ." Persephone said.

"Didn't I give you any idea at all?"

"Just that Madame Ophelia cheated them," Anna said caustically. "But apparently, she cheated so many people, she has no idea who it might be."

"No one forced them," Madame said with as much dignity as she could muster. "Their own greed made them invest."

Elizabeth and Anna just stared at her, speechless.

"But we're leaving town," Persephone said, apparently oblivious to the undercurrents. "Surely, that will save you."

Elizabeth shivered. "If you are willing to take that chance, good luck to you."

Anna glared at Madame. "I'd follow you to the ends of the earth if you cheated me."

"Anna," Elizabeth chided her, taking her hand, "we've done all we can here. I think it's time we went home."

After leaving Cybil Miles, Waterson returned to his new hotel, which was far less luxurious than his old one. No sense wasting money on a fancy suite, though. They'd all be leaving town as soon as he closed the deal with the Standard Oil people. He couldn't believe how easy it was to make money legitimately. Maybe the time had come to pack it in and go straight. At this rate, he'd make a killing if he did.

He used the public telephone in the lobby of his hotel to contact Thomas Stillwell. As the operator made the connection, Waterson fingered the rich paper of Stillwell's business card, thinking he'd get some like this printed for himself. They sure did make an impression.

A secretary answered and informed him Mr. Stillwell was in a meeting and couldn't speak with him, but she was happy to make an appointment. Waterson checked his watch and asked if Stillwell could see him in an hour. The secretary allowed that he could and set the appointment. That gave him just enough time to hire a wagon and arrange to pick it up after his meeting with Stillwell. The women should have everything at the storefront packed by then and they could drop the big stuff off at the express office and catch the next train out of the city.

He wouldn't breathe easy until they were well away from New York. At least they'd made enough money here to set them up even without the thirty thousand they'd lost, and they were about to do even better.

"You can't leave," Madame Ophelia said.

Elizabeth and Anna looked up in surprise.

"Are you going to kidnap us?" Anna asked scornfully.

"You can't leave until you tell me how I can save myself."

"How can I do that?" Elizabeth asked.

"I think you're forgetting, she already told you how to do it," Anna said.

"I did?" Elizabeth asked. "What did I say?"

"You said she had cheated the person who wants to kill her, so it's obvious that the way to stop them from killing her is to give that person their money back."

"But you didn't say who the person is," Persephone added plaintively. "Surely, you know."

"I . . ." Elizabeth looked around at the circle of faces still staring down at her. "Are there really so many that you can't figure it out?"

Madame glared back and Persephone sighed in frustration. "Not *many*, but more than one," Persephone admitted.

"Didn't I give you any hint at all?" Elizabeth asked.

Anna patted her shoulder. "I don't think so, dear. You were rather vague, except when describing the blood running down Madame Ophelia's face."

Madame winced at that.

"Maybe if you concentrate, you'll remember something," Persephone said. "You did remember a lot of what happened with the wagon accident and Mr. Miller."

"What wagon accident?" Anna asked. "Don't tell me more than one person has died."

"Two died," Elizabeth admitted in a very small voice.

"*Two?*" Anna echoed, horrified.

Elizabeth winced but turned to Madame Ophelia. "Are you suggesting another séance, because I don't think I can endure that again."

"Let's try just sitting quietly," Persephone said. "Perhaps that will be enough."

"Or I'll take you home and we forget all about them," Anna said.

Madame chose not to hear Anna's suggestion. "Yes, sit back down at the table. We will try to focus and help Mrs. Bates to see more clearly."

"Elizabeth?" Anna asked.

"Yes, that . . . that sounds fine. But if I faint again—"

"Then we're leaving for sure," Anna said.

They moved their chairs back into the correct positions. Madame Ophelia's chair had actually been knocked over, Elizabeth noted, and when she laid her hands on the table, she saw that Madame's were shaking just a bit.

Elizabeth closed her eyes and drew a deep breath, letting it out slowly as she tried to relax. "May I touch your hand, Madame Ophelia?" she asked after a moment.

"Of course." Madame slid her hand underneath Elizabeth's.

"Oh," she cried.

"What is it?" Persephone asked anxiously.

"I . . . I just felt that overwhelming sense of dread that . . . that I felt before." Elizabeth wrapped her fingers around Madame's hand, which, she noticed, was rather cold. Anna had been lying when she said Elizabeth's were cold, but Madame's really were.

"Concentrate," Madame whispered, tightening her grip on Elizabeth's hand.

"I . . . oh . . . oh no . . ."

"What do you see?" Madame asked, her voice a mere shadow of her usual commanding tone.

"I see anger and someone is shouting. Cheat. Stolen. Ruined." She shook her head against the vision.

"Who is it? Who's shouting?" Persephone demanded.

"Can't see, can't see. Something heavy. Something heavy and pain . . . Ahhhh!" Elizabeth jerked back in her chair, but Madame didn't let go of her hand.

"What happened?" Anna asked desperately.

"Pain, so much pain," Elizabeth cried, writhing. "And blood, more blood, and shouting and screaming and then . . ." She sagged in her chair, panting from the effort.

"Then what?" Persephone nearly shouted. "What did you see?"

Elizabeth opened her eyes and gave Madame a despairing look. "I saw only darkness."

Madame made a small sound in her throat, and all the color seemed to have drained from her face.

"I didn't want to tell you," Elizabeth said. "You were right. People don't really want to know, do they?"

"You also said that we can't change the past but we can change the future," Madame reminded her.

"When did I say that?" Elizabeth asked.

"When you were in a trance or whatever it was, during the séance," Anna explained helpfully. "But is that true? Can you change what happens in your visions or whatever they are?"

"I don't know. I've never tried." She gasped. "I should have tried with Mr. Miller, though, shouldn't I? He might still be alive."

"And you have to try now," Persephone said. "How can we stop this person from . . . from . . . ?" Her voice broke as tears flooded her eyes. Plainly, she was fonder of Madame Ophelia than she had seemed to be.

"These people you've, uh, cheated," Elizabeth said, pretending to be embarrassed to mention it, "do any of them seem violent?"

"Of course not."

"Would a woman be violent?" Persephone asked.

"If someone stole all her money, she very well might," Anna said.

"Then it could be anyone. But surely the ones who have been cheated have already confronted you about it," Elizabeth said. "You'd know who was most angry."

But neither Madame Ophelia nor Persephone would quite meet her eye.

"You mean, they haven't confronted you about it?" Anna asked in amazement.

"They . . . they don't know yet," Persephone said.

"They don't know they gave this man their money?" Elizabeth scoffed.

"They don't know that . . . that they'll never see it again," Persephone said, earning a scowl from Madame.

"When will they find out?"

Persephone opened her mouth to speak but Madame beat her to it. "Not until after we have left the city."

"Is that what you're planning to do, leave the city?" Anna asked.

"What do you think they were doing when we arrived?" Elizabeth asked. "They're packing."

"Yes, we . . . After Mr. Miller's unfortunate accident, we decided that was the best course of action to take," Madame said.

"Mr. Miller's death was hardly an accident, but I can certainly understand your desire to get away from the city," Elizabeth said. "If you really think that will help you escape your . . ."

Elizabeth dropped her gaze and quickly released Madame's hand, which she was still holding.

"Escape her what?" Persephone asked. "What were you going to say?"

"Her *fate*," Elizabeth said ominously. "Anna, we should go."

She started to stand, but Madame cried, "No! You can't leave. I can't spend the rest of my life looking over my shoulder and wondering who is going to try to murder me."

"From what Elizabeth saw, they did more than try," Anna said helpfully.

"But what can you do if you don't know who it is?" Persephone wailed.

Color flooded Madame's pale face. "I will do what Miss Vanderslice suggested. I will give back the money."

All three of the other women gaped at Madame Ophelia for a full minute in stunned silence.

Finally, Persephone found her voice. "Give it back?"

"Yes. Today your father is going to collect far more than we have in our safe, so we won't even miss it."

"But won't the person he's stealing it from also want revenge?" Anna asked logically.

Madame Ophelia glared at Anna. "He is not stealing it. He is conducting a legitimate business deal, so no one will be seeking revenge for that." She rose, once again the Madame Ophelia who commanded her séances with authority.

Persephone was shaking her head. "But . . . but . . ."

"Don't quibble. We have to take care of this before he gets here."

"But he'll be furious," Persephone said.

"And I'll be alive," Madame Ophelia said, ending the argument. "Come along."

Persephone followed her obediently out to the waiting room.

Elizabeth and Anna exchanged a startled look before getting up and following them. It had worked! Elizabeth couldn't believe it and Anna seemed pretty amazed as well.

Madame and Persephone had gone into the mysterious other room and a quick glance showed that whatever equipment had been in there was now stowed in a couple of wooden crates. A small safe stood at the far end of the room, and Persephone was on her knees, turning the dial.

"Put the money in here," Madame said, picking up a carpetbag and dumping its contents unceremoniously onto the floor. It was packets of blank paper, banded the way a bank would band currency.

"What's that?" Elizabeth asked, recognizing the most basic type of boodle, which would just be used to approximate the weight of actual cash when the bag was switched.

"Nothing," Madame said, sliding the bag across the floor to Persephone. She began transferring bundles of cash from the safe to the bag.

"Papa will be so angry," Persephone muttered.

"I'll handle him," Madame said.

"I suppose we should go, then," Elizabeth said.

"Not yet," Madame declared. "You must take the money."

Elizabeth didn't even bother to hide her astonishment. "What do you mean?"

"I mean, you have to return it. We won't have time to do it before we leave."

"But I don't know who you took it from."

"I will give you a list."

Before Elizabeth could even think, Madame had snatched a ledger from the top of the safe and torn out a page. "It isn't all there. Robert lost some of it in a deal yesterday, but you can divide up the loss among them."

"You trust me to do this for you?" Elizabeth asked, getting a little misty at the very thought.

"I think you know what will happen if you fail, and my blood will be on your hands. Do you want to carry that burden?" Plainly, she thought more highly of Elizabeth's character than she had any right to.

"Of course, she doesn't," Anna said. "We'll figure it out and return the money to its rightful owners." She snatched the ledger page out of Elizabeth's hand and scanned it. "Oh my, no wonder you were frightened."

Persephone had finished her task and she closed and buckled the carpetbag. Madame snatched it up before Persephone had even risen to her feet.

"Here," Madame said, thrusting the bag at Elizabeth. "Take this and return the money as quickly as you can."

Elizabeth took the bag and nodded. "I will, I promise. And I wish you luck. I hope with all my heart that this will change my vision."

"Just go," Madame said, "before I change my mind."

Elizabeth and Anna had started for the front door when it burst open and a man stepped in. Everyone froze for a long moment before the man said in a very unfriendly tone, "What is going on here?"

CHAPTER SIXTEEN

Elizabeth knew better than to answer that question, so she just stood perfectly still and glanced at Madame Ophelia for guidance. Madame came rushing forward. "I didn't expect you so soon."

"Who are they?" he demanded, indicating Elizabeth and Anna with a wave of his hand.

"They're my clients, Mrs. Bates and Miss Vanderslice," Madame hastily explained. "They were just leaving."

"Mrs. Bates, eh?" Plainly, he knew the name and wasn't pleased to hear it. His gaze dropped to the carpetbag Elizabeth was carrying. "What's she got?"

"She was helping us gather our things," Madame said a little too defensively.

"Papa," Persephone said, emerging from the other room and instantly identifying him as Waterson for Elizabeth. "Did you bring the wagon?"

"It's right outside," he said, still gazing suspiciously at the carpetbag. "What's in there?"

"Just some things we didn't need," Madame said. "Mrs. Bates is going to dispose of them for us."

She sounded so anxious, no one would have believed her. "I'll save her the trouble, then," Waterson said, snatching the bag out of Elizabeth's hands.

"Robert, wait," Madame tried, but Waterson was already unlatching the bag.

One glance inside was all he needed. "Are you out of your mind?"

"I had to do it. Someone is going to kill me if I don't give it back."

"Give it back?" he echoed in horrified astonishment. "What is wrong with you?"

"I told you, I'm going to die if I don't give it back," Madame explained desperately.

"Who says?"

"She told me," Madame said, gesturing at Elizabeth, who was trying to decide what the best course of action would be. If they ran, they'd never get the money, although staying did not seem very promising, either.

Waterson looked Elizabeth over disdainfully. "*She* told you? You really must be losing your mind. Did you forget that all this séance stuff is phony?"

"*My* séance stuff is phony, but not hers. Everything she predicts comes true, and she told me I'll die if I don't return all this money. She's going to give it back to the people we took it from."

"It's Bates," Waterson said furiously, turning

on Elizabeth. "I should have known. He's behind all of this."

"I don't know what you mean," Elizabeth lied, although she managed to look legitimately frightened.

"He's trying to ruin everything," Waterson growled, turning back to Madame. "You're not giving her this money."

"But I'm going to die if I don't!" Madame wailed. "And what difference does it make? You've got all that oil money. We won't even miss this!"

"We'll miss it," he said tightly.

"How greedy can you be?" Madame cried. "The money, that's all you care about! You don't care about us! You don't care that someone is going to bash my brains in and—"

He slapped her hard, the sound like the crack of a whip.

Elizabeth and Anna both gasped in horror. Waterson turned on them. "Get out of here. Get out and tell Bates he's not getting his hands on this, too."

"I—" Elizabeth began, unwilling to hear her husband insulted like that, but Anna grabbed her arm.

"We need to go," Anna whispered fiercely.

Persephone rushed over. "Yes, you should go."

She herded them out onto the street, nervously

397

glancing over her shoulder several times. Elizabeth kept glancing back, too. She wanted to see if Madame Ophelia was all right and if Waterson would pursue them. Madame still stood as if frozen in place, her hand pressed against her burning cheek and her gaze fixed on Waterson, who stared back at her. Elizabeth couldn't see his face, but she decided she didn't want to know what emotion it expressed.

A wagon was parked outside the storefront, ready to receive the crates Persephone had packed. They stopped on the sidewalk beside it.

"I'm sorry," Elizabeth said quite honestly. She was very sorry indeed to leave all that money behind, but she couldn't figure out a way to get it from Waterson without a fight, which seemed likely since he obviously wouldn't hesitate to strike a female.

"It's all right," Persephone said. "And don't worry. He won't really hurt her."

Elizabeth could have pointed out that he already had, but she bit back the words. "Where are you going when you leave here?"

"I don't know yet. He'll decide. We'll stop at the express office and ship the crates, then catch a train somewhere, I guess."

"From Penn Station?" It was the only logical place if they wanted to leave New York behind.

"Yes."

The storefront door opened, and Waterson came

out carrying one of the wooden crates. He wasn't pleased to find them still there.

"Good-bye, Persephone. I wish you luck," Elizabeth said with what she hoped sounded like sincerity. "Come along, Anna."

Anna needed no further encouragement.

When they were far enough away that they couldn't be overheard, Anna whispered, "We were so close!"

"We aren't finished yet."

Anna's eyes widened in surprise. "Are you going to follow them?"

"Eventually. First, I need to find a telephone."

The cavernous main waiting hall of Penn Station was bustling with travelers coming and going from the many trains that arrived here from distant cities or began their journeys here to those cities. Half of the people were either coming or going, and the rest were standing in small groups or alone while they waited for their trains to be called. A few lucky folks had claimed a seat on the cluster of benches at one end of the massive room.

Elizabeth and Anna had found a spot near one of the staircases down which visitors came to enter the hall, so they would see their quarries arrive. From here they could see all the stairways. They had been waiting about twenty minutes when they saw Madame, Waterson and

Persephone arrive. They each carried a Gladstone bag and Waterson also carried the carpetbag containing the cash.

Anna and Elizabeth turned their backs, but it didn't matter. The trio wasn't looking for them or anyone else. Why should they worry about being followed? They were making their escape before their victims were any the wiser.

The trio stopped for a moment to discuss something. Elizabeth couldn't help noticing Madame's reddened cheek and the meek way she hung her head when Waterson spoke to her. Madame had certainly done evil things, but no one deserved to be treated like that. She watched as they moved off together to the ticket windows.

"Should we follow them?" Anna asked eagerly.

"Not until they have their tickets. No sense risking being seen, and there's no telling which direction they'll go to catch their train."

So Elizabeth and Anna waited.

The lines were long, but eventually, the trio of con artists had their tickets to wherever they intended to go next. Waterson checked the board for the track number, and they walked slowly over to the stairs that would take them to the correct part of the train concourse below when the time came. Plainly, the train hadn't been called yet, and from the way Waterson checked his watch, they were in no hurry. Good. This could work.

They had found a spot to wait and set down their luggage, even the bag of money, although Waterson kept it close. Elizabeth and Anna began to stroll slowly over to where they stood. Elizabeth shifted the bag she carried to her other hand.

They were about twenty feet away when a ghostly voice wailed out, "Persephone. Persephone."

Persephone whirled around to see Jake standing in the middle of Penn Station, his shirt bloodied, his face chalk white. He raised an unsteady arm and pointed at her accusingly.

"Persephone," he wailed again as the crowd around him fell back in horror. "Don't leave me."

When she finally found him in the crowd, Persephone screamed, and she wasn't the only one. The onlookers fled from him, everyone running into everyone else in their haste to escape the terrifying specter who had come to haunt his lady friend.

Persephone ran, too, joining the hysterical crowd streaming toward the doors, pushing and jostling and tripping and screaming. Madame Ophelia went after her, and after a moment of uncertainty, his gaze darting between the specter and his fleeing females, Waterson snatched up the bag of money and followed them.

Elizabeth and Anna nearly got run down in the melee, but they finally managed to find a safe spot against the wall, while the last of the travelers made their escape. By then Jake had buttoned up his suit jacket to conceal the bloody shirt and fled to the men's retiring room.

"Come on," Elizabeth said when the crowd had thinned enough. "The Old Man said he'd have a motor waiting for us."

They crossed the main floor as quickly as they could with Elizabeth hindered by the heavy bag, and took the exit that led to the carriageway. The Old Man did indeed have a motorcar waiting. He wasn't driving it himself, of course, but he was lounging in the back because this was probably the most fun he'd have all day.

He allowed the driver to get out and open the door for them, but Elizabeth heaved the heavy carpetbag into the backseat without his help.

"How much do you think is in it?" the Old Man asked with way too much interest.

"You know what they say," Elizabeth replied with a smile, "the first count is always the best." She turned to Anna, who had climbed in behind her. "That's an old saying. It means the total gets smaller each time it passes through a con man's hands."

"Where's Jake?" the Old Man asked.

"Probably washing his face. We should wait for him. I don't want to take a chance that any of them see him on the street."

"Yes," Anna said gleefully. "I imagine they're

going to be a little leery of going back into the station for a while."

"Did you have any trouble?" the Old Man asked.

"Not a bit. It was lucky Jake had kept the carpetbag from Waterson's hotel room. When everybody started screaming it was a simple matter of making the switch. Waterson didn't see a thing."

"Even I didn't see a thing," Anna marveled. "I was too busy looking at the ghost."

"I'm glad to know we haven't completely corrupted you, Miss Vanderslice," the Old Man said with his charming smile.

The driver had climbed back into the front seat, and now the other door opened and Jake slid in beside him. "Did you get it, Lizzie?" he asked over his shoulder.

"We certainly did," Elizabeth said.

"And I have the list of people to give it back to," Anna said.

"I hope I'm at the top of that list," Jake said as the motorcar pulled away from the curb.

"I can't believe you did this without telling me," Gideon said that evening. Everyone involved in the con had gathered at their house to celebrate and trade stories and, most of all, to find out how much money was in the carpetbag. Mother Bates was having a wonderful time playing hostess.

"I couldn't tell you about it, darling, because I didn't know it was going to happen until it did," Elizabeth excused herself.

"So, tell us about Jake's murder," Anna said.

"I already told you," Freddie said with mock outrage.

"Yes, but I want to hear Jake and Gideon's versions."

Freddie harrumphed, but she was grinning too much for anyone to take her seriously.

"Freddie was magnificent," Gideon said. "Even I almost believed she'd stabbed Jake. I only wish I'd known it was a trick knife."

"Where on earth did you get a knife like that?" Cybil asked.

"It's a theater prop," Jake said. "The blade retracts on a spring. I've got a bunch of them in different sizes."

"The blood looked so real, though, I was afraid at first that I'd really stabbed him," Freddie admitted.

"I had to ruin two shirts with it, too. If I'd known Lizzie was going to turn me into a ghost, I would've kept the first shirt instead of throwing it away."

"Where did the blood come from?" Zelda asked.

"It's called a cackle bladder," Freddie explained importantly. "It's a rubber bladder full of chicken blood, isn't it?" She glanced at Jake for confirmation.

"Yes. I had it tucked inside my shirt."

"When I punched Jake with the knife, the blood squirted out and soaked his shirt. I wasn't pretending when I started crying, either. Seeing that blood really scared me. We didn't use it when we practiced."

"Yes, why ruin a perfectly good shirt with practice," Elizabeth remarked.

"You certainly did a good job of looking like an enraged abandoned woman, Freddie," Gideon said.

"Thank you," Freddie said modestly. "You should have seen me in that restaurant when I scared Persephone. I was afraid they were going to throw me bodily out into the street."

"I'd already warned the waiter," Jake said. "He wouldn't have gotten too rough with you."

"Aren't you going to tell Freddie how well she did?" Anna chided him.

Jake grinned unrepentantly. "I didn't think she needed to be any more conceited."

"Next time use a real knife on him," Elizabeth advised Freddie, making everyone laugh.

"I still don't understand the business with the bag of money," Mrs. Bates said.

Elizabeth looked at Jake, but he indicated she could do the honors. "Well, I wasn't in the hotel suite, but we know that Waterson intended to switch the bag with the cash in it for another one exactly like it that just had blank paper in it."

"Boodle," Gideon said wisely.

Elizabeth gave him an adoring smile. "That's right, boodle. Sometimes they wrap up bundles of blank paper with a real twenty on the top and bottom so a casual glance will make people think it's all real money. Waterson didn't have to be that fancy, though, since no one was going to open the bag again, so he'd stuffed the other bag with just blank paper so the weight felt right."

"How do you know it was all blank?" Jake asked with a frown.

"Oh, I know that," Anna said with great delight. "Because Madame Ophelia dumped it out when she told Persephone to put the money from the safe into it."

"That's right, which was also how I knew it was the bag they had used at the hotel," Elizabeth said.

"So it was identical to the one that had the real cash in it," Gideon added.

"It had to be," Elizabeth explained, "because Waterson was supposed to set it down in front of the door to the suite's bedroom, and when everyone was distracted by whatever Waterson was going to do, Persephone would open the door and switch the bags."

"But Coleman moved the bag before Persephone could make the switch," Jake said. "When she opened the door, she saw Freddie stabbing me, and then Coleman ran out with the real money so she never had a chance to make the switch."

"But didn't you switch the bags again?" Mother Bates asked, still looking confused.

"Yes, strangely enough," Elizabeth said.

"One thing I'm dying to know: Did you know Madame Ophelia would really give you all the money to return?" Anna asked.

"Truthfully, I thought we'd only get the thirty thousand from the land deal, or at least the half of it that Mr. Coleman would give us after taking his share. I didn't imagine she'd give the rest of the money to me, but I was hoping she'd decide to give it back herself. I'd done everything I could to frighten her, and I think your contempt went a long way toward convincing her that she should, too."

Freddie reached over and patted Anna on the shoulder. Anna smiled. "We almost got away with it, too, but then Waterson barged in and ruined everything."

"Yes, thank heaven Texas John had left the other carpetbag behind."

"And thank somebody that I was still hiding out at Dan the Dude's place when you telephoned," Jake said.

"And how lucky you had some more chicken blood handy," Anna said.

"I may have had the carpetbag, but I didn't have any chicken blood," Jake lamented. "I had to use red wine. It's just not the right color."

"It worked though," Elizabeth said, "and that powder on your face was positively terrifying."

Jake tried to look modest. "I could've done better, but you didn't give me much time."

"Poor Persephone. I'm afraid she'll never be the same," Anna said.

"But you still haven't explained how you switched the bags," Mother Bates said again.

"Oh, that part was easy. When Jake went into his ghost act, Persephone wasn't the only one he scared. Lots of people started screaming and running and I just walked up and switched the bags while Waterson was staring at the ghost. Then he picked up the other bag and ran out with it."

"He shouldn't be too upset, though," Anna said. "Madame Ophelia said he was making a legitimate business deal this morning that would earn him a lot more than was in that bag."

Jake and Elizabeth looked at each other and burst out laughing.

"What else did you do?" Gideon asked, trying to sound disapproving.

He didn't fool Elizabeth, though. "Didn't you wonder why Waterson changed his mind about selling the land, darling?"

"I did wonder why he was willing to pay Coleman to get out of the deal he'd gone to so much trouble to set up," Gideon admitted. "But you always tell me I'm better off not knowing these things."

"Since it's over, I don't think it will hurt to tell you now," Elizabeth said.

"And we really have you to thank, Gideon," Jake said. "You were the one who made sure Waterson legally owned the land and you were the one who telephoned Standard Oil to check that they owned the land next to it."

"I also contacted the Texas Company, but what does that have to do with anything?"

"Well," Jake said, leaning back in his chair so he looked even more smug than usual, "it seems that a Mr. Stillwell from Standard Oil contacted Waterson and informed him they wanted to buy the land and had been trying to get in touch with him about it."

"And that's the legitimate business deal he was going to make today?" Gideon asked in surprise. "It hardly seems fair after what those people did and tried to do that they should still benefit."

"Don't worry. The deal didn't actually go through," Jake said.

"Why not?" Gideon asked, still confused.

"Not for lack of trying," Jake said. "Waterson did telephone this morning to make an appointment with Mr. Stillwell to close the deal. Harriet told me."

"Who's Harriet?" Zelda asked.

"She's Jake's secretary," Freddie said wisely.

"How do you know that?" Anna asked.

"I met her when I went to Jake's office to practice murdering him."

"Does Jake have an office?" Anna asked, because that was the most surprising part of Freddie's statement.

"Not a real one," Jake said. "But Harriet answers all the telephones for these fake numbers, and when Waterson called, she made him an appointment to meet with Mr. Stillwell at Standard Oil."

Zelda was very confused now. "Why would he call Jake's secretary to make an appointment at Standard Oil?"

"Because there is no Mr. Stillwell working at Standard Oil, and when Waterson got to the Standard Oil office building, nobody there knew anything about him or his land or his appointment," Jake said happily. "They also weren't interested in buying his land at any price, much less for the quarter of a million dollars Stillwell had promised him."

Everyone took a moment to contemplate this terrible disappointment.

"Wait. How do you know all that?" Gideon asked.

"I'm only imagining what happened, but you can bet the people at Standard Oil gave him the brush-off."

"I guess that's why Madame Ophelia wasn't too

very upset about giving up all her ill-gotten gains, though," Anna said. "She expected Waterson to show up with a fortune."

"And that explains why he was so unsympathetic to Madame Ophelia giving all the rest of their money to Elizabeth," Anna said.

"And although it's a mere pittance compared to what Standard Oil was supposedly offering," Cybil said, "he was also expecting Zelda and me to give him thirty thousand dollars."

"Why on earth would you give him thirty thousand dollars?" Mother Bates asked.

"To fund a refuge for homeless girls," Zelda said. "And you must admit, it's a very good idea."

"Although Mr. Waterson hardly seems the type to be interested in something like that," Elizabeth said.

"So how much was in the bag, Lizzie?" Jake asked.

"Not nearly as much as Waterson thought he was getting from Standard Oil, but a little over a hundred thousand dollars."

Everyone was quite impressed.

"Does that include the thirty thousand Coleman got from Waterson?" Gideon asked.

"No, but Texas John gets a little over half of that for being the inside man," Elizabeth said.

"Texas John?" Zelda echoed. "Is he with Standard Oil?"

411

"No, dear, that's the real name of the man who took the money in the hotel room," Cybil explained.

"*Texas John* is someone's *real* name?" Zelda asked in amazement. It took a few minutes to explain that con men sometimes adopted colorful nicknames.

"Coleman is donating part of his cut for the greater good, and Stillwell is going to settle for a couple thousand," Jake reported, "since his part of the con didn't actually net any money and it only took him about an hour to do."

"I'm in the wrong business," Gideon muttered, making Elizabeth smile.

"But we'll still have a lot left to return to the people Madame Ophelia cheated," Anna said.

"You're forgetting about me," Jake said. "I should get a cut of the entire thing."

"I'm not sure how you figure that," Elizabeth said. "You can claim a share of the thirty thousand from the hotel room take, but—"

"And where would you be if I hadn't spent all that time courting Persephone and then scaring her to death with my ghost?"

"He's right," Anna said solemnly. "His ghost definitely earned a share."

Everyone laughed at that, even Jake.

"But if you take half the score, we won't have much left to return to the victims," Elizabeth pointed out.

"Charity begins at home," Jake said. "And those people wouldn't have gotten anything at all back if it wasn't for me dying."

"Oh, oh," Elizabeth cried dramatically, clutching her head.

Mother Bates and Zelda were the only ones she fooled, and they came rushing to her side.

"What is it? What's wrong?" Mother Bates asked.

"Are you all right? What's happening?" Zelda asked.

"I see Jake," Elizabeth said, closing her eyes and pressing her fingers to her temples. "And I see blood. So much blood. And . . . and Jake's heart. He . . . he . . . he needs to grow a *heart!*"

Everyone thought that was hilarious except Jake, who finally said, after the laughter died away, "I didn't say I'd take my whole share."

"And once again," Anna said, "Elizabeth's prediction comes true."

"Do you have any more predictions to make?" Gideon asked her when everyone had gone home, and they were finally alone in their bedroom.

She pressed her fingers to her head again. "Yes, as a matter of fact. I predict that your mother and I are going to Washington City next week to demonstrate for the Woman Suffrage Amendment. Congress should be voting on it soon."

"Didn't you get in a lot of trouble the last time

413

you were in Washington City?" he asked her with mock solemnity.

"A little bit, but I ended up meeting the most wonderful man and that made it all worthwhile."

He couldn't help smiling at that, but he said, "Just don't get arrested this time."

"Oh my, that's advice you could give me almost every day," she informed him.

"Remind me to do just that."

"I'm sure I won't have to. This is most certainly the last con I will ever need to run. From now on I'm going to be a perfectly respectable society matron who only has to lie when another woman asks me if I like her hat."

"Oh, darling," Gideon said, taking her in his arms, "I'm afraid that's the biggest lie you've told yet."

AUTHOR'S NOTE

I hope you enjoyed reading about Elizabeth's exploits as much as I enjoyed writing about them. I researched mediums and séances several years ago for one of my Gaslight Mysteries, and when I learned that the loss of so many young people from World War I and the Spanish Flu Epidemic of 1918–19 had created a renewed interest in contacting the dead, I knew I had to use a medium in this story.

As you have undoubtedly guessed, I'm not convinced that we can contact the spirits of the dead. I used to have a book called *How to Earn $1,000 a Week Doing Séances*, in which the author describes how to do the trick with burning the written questions. The author also describes other ways to trick people into thinking you are psychic. The business with the telephone headset came from an actual con described by the famous con man the Yellow Kid in his autobiography. He also tells about running the fake-oil-land sale, although I added the twist to the end of it. You can't make this stuff up!

The Fox Sisters were quite successful as psychics for many years, conducting séances in the mid-1800s. They did all sorts of fancy things like raising tables and receiving messages from spirits knocking, sounds they made by rapping on the table leg with their toe joints! None of my research led me to believe any of this is real, but I did learn that some particularly insightful mediums really do believe they can predict the future.

Please let me know if you enjoyed this book. You can sign up on my website to receive notices when my new books are released, so you don't have to miss a single one! You can contact me at Victoriathompson.com or follow me on Facebook at Victoria.Thompson.Author or on Twitter @gaslightvt.

Center Point Large Print
600 Brooks Road / PO Box 1
Thorndike, ME 04986-0001 USA

(207) 568-3717

US & Canada:
1 800 929-9108
www.centerpointlargeprint.com